SAVING REN

BARRETTI SECURITY SERIES #3

SLOANE KENNEDY

CONTENTS

Published in the United States by Sloane Kennedy
All rights reserved. This book or any portion thereof may not be reproduced or used in any manner whatsoever without the express written permission of the publisher except for the use of brief quotations in a book review.

Cover Images: © FXQuadro, Improvisor, bloodua

Cover Design: Jay Aheer, Simply Defined Art

ISBN-13:
978-1517621810

ISBN-10:
151762181X

SAVING REN

Sloane Kennedy

TRADEMARK ACKNOWLEDGEMENTS

The author acknowledges the trademarked status and trademark owners of the following trademarks mentioned in this work of fiction:

Pontiac

Ford Motor Company

SERIES READING ORDER

All of my series cross over with one another so I've provided a couple of recommended reading orders for you. If you want to start with the Protectors books, use the first list. If you want to follow the books according to timing, use the second list. Note that you can skip any of the books (including M/F) as each was written to be a standalone story.

Note that some books may not be readily available on all retail sites

Recommended Reading Order (Use this list if you want to start with 'The Protectors" series)
1. Absolution (m/m/m) (The Protectors, #1)
2. Salvation (m/m) (The Protectors, #2)
3. Retribution (m/m) (The Protectors, #3)
4. Gabriel's Rule (m/f) (The Escort Series, #1)
5. Shane's Fall (m/f) (The Escort Series, #2)
6. Logan's Need (m/m) (The Escort Series, #3)
7. Finding Home (m/m/m) (Finding Series, #1)
8. Finding Trust (m/m) (Finding Series, #2)

9. Loving Vin (m/f) (Barretti Security Series, #1)
10. Redeeming Rafe (m/m) (Barretti Security Series, #2)
11. Saving Ren (m/m/m) (Barretti Security Series, #3)
12. Freeing Zane (m/m) (Barretti Security Series, #4)
13. Finding Peace (m/m) (Finding Series, #3)
14. Finding Forgiveness (m/m) (Finding Series, #4)
15. Forsaken (m/m) (The Protectors, #4)
16. Vengeance (m/m/m) (The Protectors, #5)
17. A Protectors Family Christmas (The Protectors, #5.5)
18. Atonement (m/m) (The Protectors, #6)
19. Revelation (m/m) (The Protectors, #7)
20. Redemption (m/m) (The Protectors, #8)
21. Finding Hope (m/m/m) (Finding Series, #5)
22. Defiance (m/m) (The Protectors #9)

Recommended Reading Order (Use this list if you want to follow according to timing)
1. Gabriel's Rule (m/f) (The Escort Series, #1)
2. Shane's Fall (m/f) (The Escort Series, #2)
3. Logan's Need (m/m) (The Escort Series, #3)
4. Finding Home (m/m/m) (Finding Series, #1)
5. Finding Trust (m/m) (Finding Series, #2)
6. Loving Vin (m/f) (Barretti Security Series, #1)
7. Redeeming Rafe (m/m) (Barretti Security Series, #2)
8. Saving Ren (m/m/m) (Barretti Security Series, #3)
9. Freeing Zane (m/m) (Barretti Security Series, #4)
10. Finding Peace (m/m) (Finding Series, #3)
11. Finding Forgiveness (m/m) (Finding Series, #4)
12. Absolution (m/m/m) (The Protectors, #1)
13. Salvation (m/m) (The Protectors, #2)
14. Retribution (m/m) (The Protectors, #3)
15. Forsaken (m/m) (The Protectors, #4)
16. Vengeance (m/m/m) (The Protectors, #5)
17. A Protectors Family Christmas (The Protectors, #5.5)

SERIES CROSSOVER CHART

Protectors/Barrettis/Finding Crossover Chart

The Protectors

Mace (P1)	Ronan (P2)	Hawke (P3)	Mav (P4)
(Cole)	(Seth)	(Tate)	(Eli)
(Jonas)		A: Matty	
			Memphis (P5)
Dante (P6)			(Tristan)
(Magnus)			(Brennan)
	Vincent (P9)		
Cain (P7)	(Nathan)		
(Ethan)			
Phoenix (P8)	Jace (P11)		
(Levi)	(Caleb)		
Gage (P10)			
(Nash)	Vaughn (P12)		
(Everett)	(Aleks)		
	(coming in 2019)		

The Barrettis

Dom (E3)	Ren(B3)	Rafe (B2)	Vin (B1) MF
(Logan)	(Declan)	(Cade)	(Mia)
A: Eli	(Jagger)	A: Beck	5 biological
A: Tristan	B: Sierra	A: Toby	children
B: Tanner	B: Jordan	A: Rebecca	
		Zane (B4)	
		(Connor)	
		Brennan (brother)	
		Hannah (sister)	
		B: Leo	

Finding Series

Callan (F1)	Dane (F2)	Gray (F2)	Roman (F4)	Quinn (F5)
(Rhys)	(Jax)	(Luke)	(Hunter)	(Beck)
(Finn)				(Brody)

Escort Series

Gabe (E1) MF	Shane (E1) MF
(Riley)	(Savannah)

Recommended reading order can be found at beginning of my books. Or check out the bundles called A Family Chosen

Sibling	(Spouse/Partner)	MF = Male/Female book
Friend	A: Adopted Child	
Crossover Relationship	B: Biological Child	
() behind name is Series and book # (i.e. B 1 is book 1 in Barretti)		

PROLOGUE

*D*eclan Hale searched out the doorknob to the interview room with one hand while he flipped open the file he'd been holding with the other. It was well past quitting time but his fuckwad of a Captain had jammed the folder into his hand just as he'd been shutting down his computer and told him to deal with the suspect in Interview 3 before he left. Bastard didn't give a shit that he'd been on for more than twenty hours straight or that he'd been too busy to even take a piss in the last six hours.

"Mr. Varos?" Declan said as he scanned the information on the intake form. No response. Declan glanced up from the file and paused at the sight that greeted him.

The man was huge which was saying something since Declan himself was 6'2 and heavily built. This guy looked like he belonged in the wrestling ring, not handcuffed to the steel table that was bolted to the floor. Of course, the shaved head, heavily tattooed arms and leather wrist cuffs didn't make him look like an angel and the ragged scar running across his right cheek was proof that he probably wouldn't be nominated for sainthood anytime soon. And between the last name, the slight olive tint to his complexion and the heavily muscled body, Declan was guessing the guy had an interesting group of people running through his family tree.

Unsurprised by his new customer's lack of response, Declan closed the door behind him and dropped down into the metal chair across from him. There was a slight jangling of chains which told Declan that Varos was cuffed at the feet as well as the hands. He supposed the man's intimidating bulk and dark expression had had the arresting officer pulling out all the stops to ensure he walked out of the interview room in one piece.

"I'm Detective Hale," Declan muttered as he studied the form in front of him and paused at the first name that jumped out at him.

"Jagger?" Declan said with a dry chuckle. "Your folks big Stones fans?"

Still no response. Declan left the file open as he leaned back in his chair and studied the intense man sitting across from him. He was caught off guard by the stirring of lust that suddenly went through him as he took in the firm, full lips and wide jaw. Silver-gray eyes stared back at him and the contempt he saw there unnerved him. Which was saying a lot since he could count on one hand how many suspects had ever actually made him physically uncomfortable. Sure, there'd been plenty of sick fucks that had brought out a visceral reaction that he'd had to work hard to control, but that had to do with the twisted, obscene crimes they committed. His reaction to this man was something else entirely and he didn't like it one bit.

"I understand you had an altercation with a Mr. Jason Sutter-" Declan said as he glanced at the file.

Jagger remained silent, his hands folded together in front of him.

"Mr. Sutter is insisting that charges be pressed against you and your friend-"

"Leave Connor out of this."

The deep, rumbling voice sent a shiver running down Declan's spine and he looked up once more. "That's not likely to happen Mr. Varos, since Mr. Talbot appears to be the reason for the incident that occurred."

Declan paused for a moment and noticed the slight flaring of

Jagger's nostrils at the mention of his friend's name. Perhaps more than just a friend.

"Although 'incident' probably isn't the most appropriate term since Mr. Sutter is currently being prepped for surgery. The doctors say he'll be lucky to regain full use of his hand after it somehow got slammed in a car door. Twice."

Jagger slowly leaned forward. "Fucker touches Connor again, it'll be more than just his hand that needs attention." The deadly tone should have had warning bells going off in Declan's head, not sparks of electricity shooting through his dick.

"Are you saying Mr. Sutter was assaulting Mr. Talbot?"

"You catch on quick, Detective," Jagger drawled. "They teach you to ask such insightful questions in detective school?"

Declan ignored the jab. He was too hungry and too tired to deal with this shit. The guy wanted to be a disrespectful son of a bitch, so be it. A night in lock up might improve his disposition. Declan began to close the file but stopped when another name jumped out at him. *Shit.*

"You work for Barretti Security Group?" Declan asked. "You're one of Dom's men?"

The use of one of the cofounders of BSG's first name had Jagger stiffening, but he finally nodded.

"You're new," Declan declared. A statement, not a question, since he knew most of Dom's security personnel and he sure as hell would have remembered a man like Jagger.

"I joined the firm a couple of weeks ago. Vin brought me on board after I got back to the States."

Declan froze as his mind connected the dots. *Ren.*

"You were on the team that brought Ren Barretti home?"

If Declan hadn't been so distracted by his own discovery of just who this man was, he would have enjoyed watching the confusion that overtook Jagger. He suspected the guy didn't enjoy not being in the know. But Declan was too preoccupied with a vision of the younger Barretti brother to pay much attention to Jagger at the moment. Ren Barretti had been in this same interview room three days earlier, though he hadn't been the same man Declan remembered.

"How do you know the Barrettis?" he heard Jagger ask, his husky voice thick with curiosity.

"Dom was my brother-in-law," Declan answered, only half-aware of the other man now as all his thoughts drifted to the same place they'd been in the three days since Ren Barretti had re-entered his life and changed it yet again.

~

*J*agger Varos wasn't someone that surprised easily but the enigmatic Detective Hale had managed to do just that. At thirty-four and with more than a dozen years of working around the worst kind of men humanity had to offer, Jagger considered himself to be pretty good at reading people and figuring out their weaknesses. He had, after all, learned early on in life that the true nature of a person rarely matched the packaging they cloaked themselves in. Vin Barretti and his brother Dom had been among the rare exceptions so when they'd offered him a job that meant setting down roots in the city he'd spent most of his life trying to escape from, the choice had been easier to make than he thought. For all the reasons he'd come to hate Seattle, he'd finally found some that might make it worth staying.

So to learn that the gruff looking cop was actually related to one of his new bosses was a surprise. Since Vin had never married, that left Dom's deceased wife as the link between the two men.

"Sylvie was your sister?"

The raw pain in Declan's eyes was so gaping and obvious that Jagger nearly reached out to try to offer comfort to the other man before he realized what he was doing. Not to mention the cuffs which he was suddenly grateful for since they prevented his hands from moving more than an inch or two from the huge bolt they were fastened to on the tabletop.

Declan managed a nod and his gaze dropped to the paper in front of him. But the agony in the bright blue eyes was shuttered by the time he looked back up at Jagger.

Jagger guessed the detective to be in his late thirties and he looked exactly like every other cop Jagger had dealt with since the first time he'd been hassled for being in a place that he wasn't deemed good enough to be in. He'd been only fifteen when he walked into a fancy department store with a wad of cash that had represented every penny he'd managed to scrape together from his job stocking shelves at the corner grocery near his and his mom's apartment. It had been the first time he'd been able to afford an actual present for his mother for Mother's Day and he'd settled on a bracelet.

He'd been lurking around the jewelry counter for almost thirty minutes trying to pick out the perfect one when a hand had clamped down on his shoulder and he'd been shoved down on the glass counter. A heavy voice had started accusing him of theft and hand-cuffs had snapped around his wrists before he'd even managed to get a word out. And as the cop hauled him out of the store, not one of the clerks or patrons who'd seen him just minding his own business had spoken up for him. The police officer had lambasted him as a thug and when his mother had shown up at the police station two hours later, that same cop had held up a bag with three watches in it – watches he'd never seen but had supposedly stolen from the store. Three fucking watches and one dirty cop and his whole life had changed.

Jagger forced his attention back to the man in front of him who seemed to be lost in thought. The guy wasn't classically handsome but there was a certain ruggedness about him that had Jagger's dick standing up and taking notice. He didn't usually go for men that were his near equal in size and strength but there was something strangely appealing about the man. His dirty blonde hair was short and neatly groomed and the suit he was wearing was somewhere right between cheap and expensive. Thick fingers brushed over a slight five o'clock shadow as he rubbed his jaw absentmindedly and Jagger had to stifle a groan at the thought of the rough stubble scraping over his skin as those wide lips wrapped around his cock.

"Sorry for your loss," Jagger managed to get out as he tried to get his libido under control. "I never met her but Vin told stories about her…"

Declan waved him off with a brief motion of his hand.

"Tell me about your encounter with Mr. Sutter this evening, Mr. Varos," Declan suddenly said, his demeanor all business again. Jagger went instantly on alert as the cop was back and he cursed himself for being foolish enough to forget first and foremost who the man across from him really was.

~

The mention of Sylvie's name had managed to push thoughts of Ren to the back of his mind for the moment but hearing the pity in Jagger's voice was a stark reminder that the man on the other side of the table wasn't his friend. He may work for Dom and Vin, but Declan had a job to do. But whatever progress had been made in the few moments since Declan had mentioned Dom and Vin were gone and Jagger fell mute once more.

"Look Mr. Varos, personally I don't give a fuck if you spend tonight in lock up or not but I really don't need Dom and Vin crawling up my ass right now. Not to mention they've been through enough shit this past week so let's get on with this," Declan snapped. "Tell me what happened tonight."

A look of anger passed over Jagger's features and Declan suspected if the cuffs were gone, the man might have physically come after him. He was so keyed up that the idea held a certain, sick appeal and he bit out, "You know what, fuck it," as he pulled the keys to the cuffs from his pocket and reached for Jagger's hands.

He ignored the surge of energy that slammed into him at the brief contact with the man's heated skin as he removed the cuffs. He dropped the key in front of Jagger so he could undo the cuffs around his ankles because there was no way in hell he could trust himself to drop to his knees anywhere near the other man.

Declan leaned back in his chair and crossed his arms and waited.

Jagger eyed him for a long moment before he finally leaned down to remove the cuffs and then unceremoniously tossed the key back to him.

"Jason Sutter has been stalking Connor for months," Jagger finally said.

"They were in a relationship?" Declan asked.

Jagger nodded, his sharp eyes never leaving Declan. "Connor broke it off a while ago but Sutter wasn't taking no for an answer. Tonight I made sure he got the message once and for all."

"So you and Mr. Talbot are-"

"No," Jagger interjected. "Not all fags want to fuck each other," Jagger snapped.

The crude remark gave Declan new insight into the man sitting across from him but he kept his mouth shut.

"Connor and I served together. We're friends."

Declan nodded. "What happened?"

"Connor was coming to pick me up so we could go get a couple of drinks. Sutter followed him to my place. He got rough with Connor so I got rough with him." Declan was unsurprised at the lack of apology in the man's tone.

"You can't hold Connor on anything – he didn't touch Sutter. Bastard's lucky Connor was there to pull me off," Jagger added.

"My colleague is interviewing Mr. Talbot as we speak. Charges won't be determined until witness statements have been collected as well," Declan added.

"You're the one who let Ren leave, aren't you?" Jagger suddenly asked, his eyes dark with anger. Declan ignored the question and grabbed the pad of paper that had been stuffed into the file folder and slid it across the table to Jagger and then snagged a pen out of his shirt pocket.

"Write down your statement, then sign and date it," Declan said as he tossed the pen to Jagger. "I'll be back in a bit."

As Declan stood, the pad and pen were shoved back across the table. Any patience Declan had left disappeared and he leaned across the table and stuck his face in Jagger's. "Write down your fucking statement here or in a jail cell. Doesn't matter to me either way," he snarled as he reared back and thrust the pad forward once more and turned to go.

"I can't you asshole. I'm dyslexic."

∼

*D*eclan closed the interview room door behind him. He hadn't said anything to Jagger after he'd written the statement that Jagger recited to him. He'd simply waited for the big man to scratch out his signature on the bottom of the page and then snatched the pad of paper off the table and left the room, not bothering to re-cuff Jagger even though he was technically still a suspect. As much as the guy rubbed him the wrong way, Declan's gut was telling him that Jagger's story was on the up and up and wasn't a threat to him or any other officer in the precinct.

"You get his statement, Hale?"

Disgust went through him at the sound of his Captain's voice bellowing across the room. The man was an absolute dirt bag and it always took every ounce of Declan's iron-like self-control not to beat the shit out of him. He was a blatant racist and homophobe which was saying a lot considering the department itself had never been the most politically correct group of people. Sure, there were a few good apples in the bunch but the majority were more likely to side with Captain Frank Mitchell if push came to shove. The man had been in charge for more than a dozen years and he'd maintained his reign by kissing the right asses and getting rid of anyone foolish enough to question him. Luckily, Declan had managed to make some powerful allies himself and Mitchell hadn't succeeded in ousting him, though it wasn't for lack of trying.

Declan didn't answer as Mitchell strode towards him; he just held the pad of paper up briefly.

"Let me know when he's booked," Mitchell said.

"We're still waiting for Jennings to get back with witness statements and Dwyer is finishing up with his friend," Declan said as he glanced at the interview room next to the one he'd just exited.

"Fucker can sit in lock-up while you get the paperwork started," Mitchell snapped.

Declan leaned back against the door. "You seem pretty certain what the outcome's going to be," he said casually, though he was feeling anything but casual at the moment.

"Guy's a loser who went after a well-respected citizen-"

"Varos' record shows nothing since he was a kid. And Jason Sutter's hardly an angel," Declan observed. "I checked his record before I went in there," he said as he motioned over his shoulder. "Sutter was stopped twice for suspicion of driving under the influence in the last year alone. Looks like his father's got some pretty good lawyers-"

Mitchell's long, bony finger was thrust in his face. "Lionel Sutter has served this city for more than twenty years-"

Declan laughed. He knew Lionel Sutter and the circle he ran in much better than Mitchell ever would. "Lionel Sutter is a pretentious piece of shit who's been buying every position he's ever had since his father left him all his money after he dropped dead while fucking a hooker in the front seat of his Town Car," Declan quipped.

Mitchell's face turned a mottled shade of red, but before he could lay into Declan like he clearly wanted, the door to the next interview room over opened and Adam Dwyer stepped out.

"Well?" Mitchell shouted.

Dwyer hesitated for a moment at the tension he was witnessing. Declan couldn't blame him – the young cop had been on the force less than a year after transferring from Spokane. He seemed like a good enough guy but it was looking more and more like the officer wasn't going to have the balls needed to stand up to Mitchell.

"Jennings called in with the witness statements. They match Talbot's story," Dwyer said as he held up the statement that he'd collected from Jagger's friend. "He's banged up pretty bad."

Declan snatched the statement from Dwyer before Mitchell could get his hands on it. He scanned it and then handed it to Mitchell.

"Talbot and Varos' statements line up," he said. "Varos was defending Talbot."

Something was off in the level of anger radiating off of Mitchell as he studied both statements. A snort left his thin lips and he shoved the documents against Dwyer's chest and stomped off without another word.

"Uh, what happens now?"

Declan watched Mitchell storm back into his office and slam the door. "Release them both. Find out if Talbot wants to press charges against Sutter," Declan said.

Dwyer glanced nervously over Declan's shoulder at the interview room Jagger was waiting in. "Where are you going?" he asked, his voice higher than normal. Declan was guessing the man had gotten a good look at Jagger and his imposing size as he was being escorted to the interview room and was less than eager to confront the man directly, even if it was with good news.

"I'm going to take a piss," Declan muttered. The last thing he was interested in was setting eyes on Jagger Varos again.

CHAPTER 1

"Any word on Ren?" Jagger asked as he extended his hand to shake Vin's.

"No," Vin responded as he motioned for Jagger to take a seat on the other side of the desk from him. Jagger dropped down into the chair as he studied the other man. He respected the hell out of Vin Barretti and had gotten to know him well in the past year as they scoured the unforgiving terrain of the Middle East in their search for Ren. The oldest of the four Barretti brothers had started to look worn down in recent months as each fruitless search for Ren ended the same way. The dark-haired co-founder of Barretti Security Group had never given up hope though, and he and his brother Dom had spent endless amounts of money and time to try to bring their younger brother home.

But Vin's relief at finding his brother alive had been short-lived upon their arrival home a couple of weeks ago because three days after he'd gotten Ren settled in his house, Ren had attacked Vin's girlfriend, Mia. Jagger didn't know all the details but apparently a gun had been involved. It hadn't surprised Jagger to find out had Ren had gone off the deep end because he'd noticed something off in the young man from the moment they'd left the military hospital in Landstuhl, Germany.

Ren had been withdrawn as expected but there'd been a wariness in his eyes too. A haunted look that had held Jagger's attention from the moment they took off until the moment they landed in Seattle. Vin's efforts to draw his brother out during the flight had been ignored and the way Ren had held onto the armrests of his seat had had Jagger suspecting he was barely hanging on to his control. Every noise, every conversation had seemed to pain Ren in some way and Jagger had found himself wanting to soothe his fingers over the tightly drawn skin that stretched across sharp cheekbones.

"How's Mia?" he asked.

"She's okay," Vin answered. "Still blaming herself for Ren disappearing."

While Ren had left Mia unharmed before disappearing from Vin's house in the dead of night, his mistrust of his brother's lover hadn't dissipated and he'd ended up following Mia over the next couple of weeks in the hopes of finding some proof against her to show she was unworthy of the oldest Barretti. In a surprise twist of fate, it was Ren who saved Mia from a stalker tied to her past. He'd shot the man before he'd been able to put a bullet through Mia's chest like he'd planned. Ren had been taken into custody as part of the investigation into the shooting and when he'd finally been released, he'd taken off again, leaving only a note behind telling his brothers not to look for him.

"Anyone's to blame, it's that fucker at the precinct," Jagger muttered. He knew his description of Declan Hale was harsh but the humiliation of having to blurt out his shameful secret still stung. And to have to sit there and recite his statement to the high and mighty Detective had burned his insides like acid.

"Declan's hands were tied," Vin said, his eyes pinning Jagger where he sat. "That man has been good to this family."

Jagger shifted in his chair. It was a well-deserved rebuke but it still smarted.

"I hear you two had a run-in yesterday," Vin said.

Fuck. He'd actually started warming up to this job too. "Thanks for the opportunity," he muttered as he stood to go.

"Sit your ass back down, Jagger," Vin drawled as if unsurprised by Jagger's automatic assumption that he was being let go. "Declan told me what happened. I wanted to make sure you were okay."

That caught Jagger off guard and he slowly sank back down. The only ones who'd ever given a shit about him were Connor and his mother. "I'm fine," he said softly.

"How's your friend?" Vin asked. "Connor, right?"

Jagger nodded. "He's okay," he said warily.

"Good," Vin said with a nod. "We've terminated our contract with Sutter's firm-"

"What?" Jagger interrupted, not sure he'd heard right.

"Lionel Sutter's investment firm was a client. We were doing some analysis on their network security," Vin explained.

"Are you saying…" Jagger couldn't even get his thought out at first. "Are you saying you ended the relationship because of what happened to Connor?"

"Barretti Security doesn't do business with pricks who pay to keep their piece of shit kids out of trouble. Declan clued us in on that little fucker's antics and Lionel's use of his political connections to get him off each time. Hopefully your message got through last night but if it didn't, we can provide your friend with round the clock security until our legal team can hurt Jason Sutter and his father where it counts most – their reputations," Vin declared.

Jagger couldn't say if he was more surprised by the offer or how riled up Vin had gotten on behalf of a man he didn't even know.

"Uh, I'll let him know," Jagger said.

"Good," Vin said as he settled back into his chair. It was then that Jagger noticed how tightly drawn Vin seemed. He looked tired and pale like he hadn't slept and while Jagger could attribute that to what had been going on with Ren, the agonized look in his eyes was new.

"Something going on?" Jagger asked softly. He held back his surprise at what appeared to be a sheen of tears forming in Vin's eyes.

The other man took a moment to get himself under control before he spoke.

"Cade found the hacker," Vin said quietly. "It's Rafe."

What the fuck? Shock went through Jagger's system as he tried to piece together what Vin was telling him. Rafe was the youngest of the Barretti brothers, though Jagger knew the man had to be in his late twenties by now. He'd been removed from Vin and Dom's custody when he was just eight years old after his biological father showed up to claim him. At eighteen and fifteen respectively, Vin and Dom hadn't had the funds or the resources necessary to keep their little brother, but they hadn't stopped searching for him in the nearly twenty years since he'd been taken away.

"Are you sure?" Jagger asked.

Vin nodded. The hack into BSG's servers had started weeks earlier when information about Mia's past was taken. Vin and Dom had only recently discovered that more hacks had occurred, though everything that had been taken had been related to Vin and Dom's personal lives instead of their business. Which made perfect sense now if the suspect really was Rafe Barretti.

"I'm sorry, Vin," Jagger said. God, this family couldn't catch a break. If Rafe was stealing sensitive information, it could only be for one reason – to hurt his brothers.

"I may need to pull you in at some point," Vin said. "So far he's just going after information but if it turns into something more…"

"Of course," Jagger responded. "Is there anything I can do?"

Vin shook his head. "We're in a holding pattern until Rafe makes his next move. Dom's hopeful that he'll come around…" Vin said.

"But you're not so sure," Jagger observed. Vin didn't answer him and he didn't need to. He could tell that Vin was near his breaking point so he quietly stood. "Whatever you guys need, Vin," Jagger said softly. Vin managed a nod and Jagger quickly left the office. He shook his head as he headed towards his car. For once, his life actually seemed like a cakewalk compared to what the Barretti brothers had been forced to endure.

~

"*H*ow's it going?" Jagger asked as he headed behind the bar and searched out a beer.

"Quiet, thankfully," Connor replied as he continued cleaning the glasses in front of him. Jagger popped the top off the beer and took a long swallow as his eyes skated over his friend. At 29 years old, Connor Talbot had seen more in his short life than he should have. And he'd paid more too. From the moment they'd met in Iraq, Jagger had felt drawn to the younger man, though not for the reasons he would have suspected.

Connor was a truly beautiful man with his coffee colored hair and warm, brown eyes. He was just under 6' and had a lean, swimmer's build that should have had Jagger trying to get in his pants from day one since the man was exactly his type. But something about the kind-hearted, fun-loving guy who was always smiling had Jagger wanting more than a quick fuck. Being around Connor was easy and relaxing – the guy just made you feel good. Even with all the shit he'd been through, Connor never lost his sense of humor or his positive outlook on life. But the bruises on his face and swollen lip were a stark reminder that not everyone appreciated Connor for the gentle soul he was.

"You'll break the glass if you keep doing that," Connor said quietly as he motioned to the hand Jagger had clenched around the glass bottle. He set it down on the counter just to be on the safe side and reached up to tilt Connor's face to the side. Even in the dim lighting he could see the angry purple and blue colors mixing together over the swollen skin.

"You putting ice on this?" he asked gently as he released him.

Connor produced an icepack from the small sink. "Yes, Dad," he said with a smirk. Jagger smiled and grabbed his beer.

"You call that cop today to tell him you changed your mind about pressing charges?" Jagger asked.

Connor's lowered gaze answered his question.

"Damn it, Connor, that fucker needs to be punished," Jagger

bit out.

"I think you took care of that last night," Connor murmured. "Besides, I can take care of myself," he insisted. Jagger knew they were bordering in sensitive territory so he let it go for now.

"You off soon?" Jagger asked as he saw Connor shift his weight, a sure sign that the man was in pain.

Connor nodded. "Mags is closing up," he said.

Mags was short for Maggie. She was the only woman Jagger had ever met that nearly matched him in height, width and temperament. But around Connor, all her rough edges disappeared and she became a mother hen. She'd sooner throw every single one of the patrons out of the bar before she let go of Connor because he had one of his "moments" while on the job.

"What did you say?" Connor suddenly asked, his brow narrowed in confusion as he glanced at Jagger. But it was like Connor was staring right through him and his eyes began to dart around the room as if trying to figure out where he was.

"Connor," Jagger whispered as he brushed his hand over Connor's uninjured cheek and forced him to focus on him. "Connor, look at me," he said softly and he gently rubbed his thumb along Connor's skin. It took only seconds for Connor to come back to himself.

"Shit, sorry," Connor murmured as he pulled free of Jagger's hold.

Before Jagger could respond, someone shouted "Bartender, another!" from the other end of the bar. The voice was heavily slurred.

"Another satisfied customer?" Jagger asked with a grin as he glanced up at the drunken figure huddled over an empty glass.

"He was satisfied three shots ago," Connor mused.

"You know him?"

Connor shook his head. "Not a regular. I offered to call him a cab. I told him that was his last one," he said as he nodded at the man. When he started heading towards the guy, Jagger grabbed his arm.

"Finish up, I'll take care of it."

Connor looked like he was about to argue so Jagger quickly moved past him and headed towards the opposite end of the long bar. There were only a couple of other customers in the place which wasn't a surprise since Mags' bar was a hole-in the wall establishment that was surrounded by nothing but warehouses and industrial shops. He'd never understand what had possessed her to open up shop in such a dead neighborhood when the tourist-filled waterfront was just a few streets over.

"Come on, buddy, time to call it a night," Jagger said as he got closer. His pace slowed as something familiar about the man's size and frame had his gut churning…and his dick reacting.

"Fuck off, give me another," the man mumbled as he pushed his empty glass forward.

"You have got to be fucking kidding me," Jagger sighed as he came to a stop in front of none other than Declan Hale.

~

"*Y*ou know him?" Connor asked as he came to a stop next to Jagger.

"Unfortunately," Jagger responded as he reached out and grabbed the glass that Declan had started rolling under his palm. Declan looked up at him with bloodshot, bleary eyes. "He's the cop who interviewed me yesterday," Jagger murmured as he handed the glass to Connor.

Connor must have heard something in his voice because he said, "I'll call him a cab, Jagger. Don't worry about it."

Jagger studied Declan whose eyes had drifted shut when he rested his cheek against his hand. The man was a far cry from twenty-four hours ago. His clothes were wrinkled and looked suspiciously like what he'd been wearing the day before and his hair was sticking up all over the place like he'd been endlessly running his fingers through it.

"No," Jagger said softly. "I'll make sure he gets home."

Jagger could feel Connor's curious gaze on him so he quickly went around the bar.

"He pay his tab?" Jagger asked.

"He gave me a hundred bucks up front and told me to keep 'em coming till it ran out."

Shit, that was a lot of booze. Declan Hale had clearly set out to get plastered which meant he was either a raging alcoholic or something else was going on. Since he hadn't smelled even a whiff on the man yesterday, his gut was telling him the detective had been looking to drown his sorrows, not feed an addiction.

"Consider the rest a tip," Jagger said as he wrapped his hand around Declan's upper arm. "Come on, Detective. Let's take a ride."

"Want a drink," Declan muttered stubbornly but Jagger ignored him and easily dragged him off the barstool. Unfortunately, Declan's balance was off and he stumbled into Jagger, his wide chest brushing over Jagger's in the process. The contact had Jagger cursing under his breath as his whole body lit up with desire and his first thought was that someone as big and strong as Declan would be able to withstand even the roughest fuck.

Jagger forced away the sudden image of Declan on his hands and knees and reached his arm around his waist to hold him upright. He doubted that someone as straight laced as Declan Hale would appreciate the direction his thoughts had taken. Jagger had an excellent gaydar and it wasn't even pinging in the slightest as Declan leaned heavily against him.

"Text me when you get home," Jagger called over his shoulder to Connor as he walked him towards the door. It swung open as he neared it.

"Sweetie, I told you your looks were gonna go someday, but even you can still do better than this," Mags said with a hearty laugh as she held the door open for him and eyed Declan up and down. "He's pretty though," she said in appreciation. "Thought you liked 'em a little scrawnier."

"Funny," Jagger muttered as he passed the large woman. Her burnt orange hair was in its usual braid and the tight top she was wearing showed her ample cleavage and thick waistline. No one would ever call Mags beautiful, or even pretty for that matter, but between her blunt personality and no-nonsense demeanor, she'd had her fair share of interest from the opposite sex. Little did they know that Mags only had eyes for the pretty little wife she kept stashed at home.

"How is he?" Mags asked as she glanced into the dark bar. Jagger didn't need to ask who she was talking about.

"I think his leg's bothering him," Jagger said. "He needs to get off his feet."

That was enough to get Mags moving. Jagger wasn't even an afterthought as she hurried inside and he almost felt a little bit guilty for setting Connor in her sights. But he knew Connor would never admit to any discomfort and Mags was the only person he wouldn't argue with.

"Gonna be sick," he heard Declan mutter and Jagger managed to maneuver him away from the main part of the sidewalk and against the brick wall before he puked. When he was finally done, Declan swiped a sleeve over his mouth. "Tired," he said softly. It didn't make sense to Jagger but Declan's words actually sounded more sad than drunk.

"I know," Jagger answered as he maneuvered Declan to his car. He had no idea if Declan had driven here but he supposed it was good that Declan had picked Mags' bar because Connor was practically a Nazi when it came to making sure patrons didn't get behind the wheel if it seemed like they'd indulged even just a little too much. Even the unruliest of bar goers didn't stand a chance when Connor offered the limited options of either a call to the local cab company or the police department.

Jagger got Declan settled into the front seat of his SUV and searched his pockets.

"Did you drive here, Detective?"

Declan's gaze settled on him and a soft, almost serene smile split his lips. "Jagger," he said and the sound of that husky voice skimmed over Jagger's senses like the gentlest of caresses. "Funny name," Declan said with a snort.

If the guy wasn't so fucking hot when he got all soft and bleary, Jagger might have punched him. Even worse though, if he hadn't just thrown up what seemed like a gallon's worth of booze, Jagger would have done something far more stupid like run his tongue along the firm, glistening lips until they opened for him.

19

After several seconds, Jagger found what he was looking for in Declan's jacket pocket. A quick look at his wallet gave Jagger the address he needed and he painstakingly punched the blessedly simple address into his phone's GPS app. There were a set of keys too and he compared the make on the key fob that was attached to the small, silver keyring to the cars parked along the street in front of the bar. There was no match but he supposed the man could have parked around the corner.

Declan had nodded off by the time Jagger got him buckled in and it took him only fifteen minutes to reach the city's south side. The apartment building was extremely ordinary looking and less than what he would have expected for someone on a Detective's salary to be living in. It wasn't actually run-down or in a poor neighborhood – there was just nothing homey about it. No pretty landscaping, no nice balconies and patios. Just a faded brick building with a dozen or so units that all looked exactly the same.

Jagger got out of the car and pulled Declan's keys from his pocket. He found the key fob and pressed the lock button on it and was relieved when a plain, navy blue sedan at the end of the block lit up. So the man *had* had enough common sense not to drive. But it was also more proof that Declan's plan had been to get shitfaced.

Jagger went around to the passenger side of his car and shook Declan awake. He grumbled a bit but didn't fight Jagger as he hauled him to his feet and searched out the apartment number he was looking for. He had to use his body to prop Declan up against the side of the door as he unlocked it and he bit back a groan when Declan's hand grazed his waist as he tried to maintain his balance. God, he'd deserve a fucking medal after this was over.

It took several long, torturous seconds to get Declan into the apartment and the door locked behind them. His body felt like it was on fire from all the places Declan had been pressed up against him and he wondered if he'd done something wrong in a previous life to deserve the hell of lusting after a straight man. A straight, jackass of a man who was also a cop.

"Where's your bedroom, Detective?" Jagger asked as he flipped on the lights. The place was clean but sparse. There weren't any pictures on the walls and the furniture looked comfortable but basic. Nothing about the apartment gave him any hint into Declan's life other than to say it was perfectly ordinary.

"Back there," Declan said as he waved his arm half-heartedly towards the back hallway. The man's bedroom wasn't any better than the rest of the place and Jagger couldn't help but wonder if he bought all his stuff from the same, low budget big box store. It wasn't like Jagger was a connoisseur of fine living, but even he'd managed to pick out a few furnishings and decorative items that made his townhouse feel like it was his. And he'd only been living in the place for two weeks.

A sigh of relief went through Jagger as he deposited Declan's weight onto the bed. He ignored the strange, empty feeling that overcame him at no longer having the other man's body heat seeping through his own clothes and leaned down to pull Declan's shoes off. He managed to get Declan's jacket off too but that was as far as he was willing to go because putting his hands on Declan seemed like a bad idea. Touching his skin seemed like an even worse one.

Declan's eyes drifted shut as he shifted his body in an effort to get more comfortable and Jagger took a moment to study the relaxed features of his face. When he forced himself to turn to go, he was surprised to feel a hand close over his. He glanced back at Declan and saw that his eyes were half-open though he was still clearly out of it.

"Tell Dom I'm sorry," he whispered. "I didn't know how else to keep him safe."

Declan's voice was so quiet that Jagger had to drop down next to the bed to hear him. "Who?"

Declan murmured a response but his words were unintelligible.

"Who did you have to keep safe, Declan?" Jagger asked. Nothing could have prepared Jagger for the one word that left Declan's mouth on his next shallow exhale of breath.

"Ren."

CHAPTER 2

The familiar mix of shame and desire coursed through Declan as he opened the motel room door. It had been nearly a month since the last time he'd needed this and he'd spent the entire day wishing that need away. But no amount of arrest reports or suspect interrogations had taken the edge off and he'd already been dialing the familiar number before he'd even exited the station.

His eyes instantly searched out the chair in the opposite corner of the room and he sighed in relief when his vision adjusted to the darkness and he was able to pick out the shadowy figure he'd been looking for. As the door closed, he engaged the deadbolt and then reached up to flip the security latch. The man didn't speak or move as Declan removed his firearm and placed it on the nightstand next to the bed and there was no discernable reaction as he began to unbutton his shirt. It was exactly as it always was and the routine eased his nerves somewhat while his body hummed with excitement.

Instead of letting his shirt fall to the ground, Declan draped it over the end of the bed. His fingers went to his pants and it took only seconds to work them free and drop them to his ankles. His underwear followed though it took some maneuvering since his cock was like a steel pipe. But he didn't kick the pants free – he simply leaned over and placed his hands on the mattress and waited. It wasn't long before the figure rose and slowly walked around the bed, his long fingers reaching for the button on his slacks. He'd already removed his jacket, though he'd left his shirt on – Declan couldn't remember a time that he'd actually taken it off and the fact that he didn't was irrelevant. His chest wasn't what Declan needed.

Once the man was out of his line of sight, Declan focused on the opposite wall. He hated the picture that hung there – he suspected it was supposed to be a painting of some perfect little seaside community with happy couples and families walking along the waterfront as boats bobbed in the calm waters of the harbor. The sunset was a sickening shade of rusty orange and washed out yellow and the blue sky couldn't be bothered with even a single cloud. Completely ridiculous perfection.

The sound of a zipper being dragged down had Declan's dick growing thicker and the sound of foil tearing had him sinking his teeth into his lower lip. He shouldn't have waited so long to make the call. He shouldn't have hoped that he could find some other way to ease the ache in his gut.

"How do you want it?"

"Hard," Declan said in the moment before a finger pressed between his cheeks and cool lube chilled his heated skin. "Fast," he added though it wasn't something he needed to say. His partner always knew that fast accompanied hard. He could count on one hand the few times he'd wanted it any differently.

There was no warning as the man's dick slipped between the globes of his ass and began breaching him. Declan bit back a hiss of discomfort as the crown sank into him and he bore down against the unyielding pressure. Pain went through him like a knife as the man shoved into the root but he gave Declan no time to adjust before pulling out and slamming in again. Declan forced his eyes open to search out the one part of the fucking painting he liked as his body tried to adjust to the ruthless invasion.

There was barely enough natural light seeping through the crack in the curtains for Declan to make out the young man at the far edge of the painting. His expression was blurry but it didn't matter because he did what he always did and imagined laughing blue eyes, a wide smile and dark hair that was just a little too long on top.

The knot inside Declan's belly began to unfurl as the pain in his ass started to recede and pleasure simmered along his nerve endings. Broad hands closed over his hips and dragged him back to meet every thrust and Declan wondered if the man's stormy gray eyes were clouded over with lust. The only problem with his train of thought was that he knew for a fact that the man behind him had green eyes, not gray ones.

"Harder," Declan snapped as an image he didn't want began to filter through his mind. He tried to focus on the painting once more but the image of the young man wouldn't stick. The only blue eyes he saw were the ones that looked up at him from the bed in a haze of pleasure as the warm body beneath his drew Declan in while another, heavier body forced Declan farther down. The hips snapping against Declan's were accompanied by one heavily tattooed arm wrapping around his waist and the other coming down to rest on the bed next to them. *Them.*

Declan shouted as his orgasm washed through him and he couldn't stop the moans that escaped his lips every time the cock buried deep inside of him pulsed and throbbed. His own release dripped down his hand as he continued to stroke himself to match the aftershocks winding through him. The fingers digging into his hips eased and Declan closed his eyes as the still semi-hard shaft pulled free of his ass. Before the man had even stepped away from him, Declan felt the familiar cold seep through his body once more and as he watched the man head towards the bathroom, Declan closed his eyes in despair. He managed to lower himself so that he was sitting on the bed but not even his sore ass could ease the burning pain that was spreading throughout his entire body.

"Here."

A washcloth was pressed into his hand. Declan wiped himself clean and dropped the washcloth on top of the thin bedspread before he stood to drag up his pants.

"You okay?"

The silky smooth voice sounded harsh to Declan's ears and he wondered why. Maybe it was because they never spoke afterwards. Then again, they rarely spoke before or during either.

"Isn't this against the rules?" Declan said quietly as he reached for his shirt. The man was somewhere behind him now, probably getting his own clothes back in order.

"You said someone else's name this time," the man replied, ignoring Declan's question.

Declan was so thrown off by the comment that he actually turned around. His eyes had adjusted enough to the dim interior of the room that he could see the man tucking his shirt into his slacks.

"What?" Declan whispered in horror.

"Jagger," the guy said. "All the other times it was Ren, but today it was Jagger."

Jesus.

Declan sank back down on the bed. He knew the guy wasn't offended that he'd said someone else's name since neither of them were here for any other reason than sex, but he hadn't even been aware he was doing it at all. Using Ren's image was bad enough but to be calling out for him? And now Jagger? What the fuck was wrong with him?

"Zane..." Declan said.

"It's like everything else, Declan. What happens in this room, stays in this room," Zane said.

Declan didn't look up when he felt Zane stop next to him. Between Zane's revelation and his almost gentle tone, Declan was feeling raw and exposed.

"You were close today, Declan."

Declan looked up at the tall man who stood less than three feet from him. It was still too dark to make out his face but Declan already knew what he'd see if the lights were on. Black hair, mossy green eyes, wide, strong jaw.

"Close to what?" Declan asked.

"Close to the point where what I can give you isn't enough

anymore. I'm not into hurting the guys I'm with so if that's what you want..." Zane said. He didn't finish the statement as he dragged on his jacket and left the room.

Declan closed his eyes as nausea rolled through him. How the hell could he explain that it hadn't been about pain? At least not in the beginning when he and Zane had agreed upon this arrangement. But the other man was right – Declan was relying more and more on the pain to wipe away the reality that what they were doing wasn't enough. Nothing Zane did would take away the aching, empty need that Declan was drowning in.

But maybe Zane was right and it was time to rethink the relation-ship, though the use of that word to describe what they had between them was a stretch. Even fuck buddies didn't work since they rarely saw each other outside of this room. They were simply two guys who used each other to get off and the reasons they did so were their own. But apparently even Zane was starting to see through him. If Declan didn't get his shit together soon, the world he'd spent his entire life building would come crashing down around him and people would realize he was a complete and utter fraud.

Feeling the need to get out of the suddenly too small room, Declan quickly buttoned up his shirt and reached for his gun. He was just tucking it into the holster when the alarm on his phone sounded. He froze for a second as the ringtone registered and then he snatched the phone out of his pocket. His heart leapt into his throat as the notif-ication flashed across his screen and then he was rushing out of the room.

$\sim$

*D*eclan was so distracted that he didn't even register the sound of the passenger door on his car being opened and by the time he had his gun drawn and aimed, a powerful hand closed around his wrist.

"Put it away, Detective," Jagger muttered. "Unless you want me to pull out my gun and we can compare whose is bigger," he said dryly.

"Jesus Christ, Varos," Declan snapped as he yanked his arm free. His adrenaline surged through his blood as he eased his finger off the trigger. "Are you fucking insane?" he bit out. His words barely cleared his mouth before Jagger's huge hand wrapped around his throat and dragged him forward so only inches separated their mouths.

"You have one minute to explain who is in that God damn cabin, Detective," Jagger snarled as he glanced through the windshield at the log cabin that sat in the clearing more than 500 yards away. The fact that a jet black vintage GTO sat parked in front of the sparsely lit structure had Declan guessing Jagger already had his answer. Add in that Jagger didn't seem to be concerned about the gun still in Declan's hand and Declan was certain Jagger already knew what was going on.

He managed to wrench free of the hold Jagger had on him and snapped, "Why waste time telling you something you already know?"

"Then tell me something I don't," Jagger responded. "Like why I shouldn't call Vin and Dom right now and tell them how a guy they think of as family fucking stabbed them in the back."

Declan shoved out of the car but left the door open so the noise of it being closed wouldn't be heard through the open glade. Even though it was dark, Declan knew this place by heart and the surrounding mountains would act as an echo chamber for any and all sounds. And the last thing he wanted was for the occupant of the cabin to hear them.

Jagger got out too and Declan wasn't surprised to see him mimic Declan's move not to shut the car door. He strode around the car and got into Declan's face once more and Declan wasn't sure if it was out of anger or so their voices wouldn't carry.

"How did you find me?" Declan asked. The road winding up the mountain wasn't exactly teeming with traffic and he sure as hell would have noticed headlights behind him.

"Tracking device. I put it on your car after you said something about keeping Ren safe."

Declan was so surprised that he couldn't even find the words to respond.

"Short memory, Detective?" Jagger asked. When Declan didn't

27

answer, Jagger nodded knowingly. "Didn't you wonder how you got home last night?"

Declan stiffened. His last memory had been staring at the row of bottles behind the bar in the little dive he'd found on the outskirts of downtown. He'd picked it because the chances of running into any people he knew were pretty slim considering how off the beaten path the establishment was and the cab ride home wouldn't break the bank. But apparently there hadn't even been a cab ride home like he'd thought after he'd woken up the next morning with one hell of a hangover.

"You drove me home?"

Jagger nodded.

"You go to that bar?" Declan grated out.

"Connor works there," Jagger said.

A faint memory of the hot bartender flitted through his mind. He hadn't seen Connor Talbot the day he'd interrogated Jagger so he hadn't recognized him when he'd slid him a crisp hundred-dollar bill.

"For a guy who's supposedly smart enough to make detective, you sure do stupid shit. Getting shitfaced, hook-ups in flea-bag motels."

Terror went through Declan at Jagger's statement about the motel.

"Don't worry, I don't give a shit whose wife you're fucking," Jagger snapped.

Wife? Had Jagger not seen Zane leaving the room?

"What I do give a fuck about is how you know where Ren Barretti is," Jagger ground out.

The relief that Jagger hadn't discovered his secret was nearly palpable but the use of Ren's name brought Declan back to the present.

"It's my cabin," Declan said. "I gave Ren the key and the security code after the shooting," Declan finally admitted and wasn't surprised when Jagger grabbed him by the throat once more.

∽

*J*agger was so enraged that it was everything he could do not to wrap both his hands around Declan's thick neck and squeeze. To think Vin and Dom Barretti had been torturing themselves for days wondering where their brother had disappeared to and this asshole had known all along – had lied to their faces.

"Explain," he growled.

"After the D.A. signed off on the shooting as being justified, Ren wanted to leave. I tried to convince him to go back to his brothers but he wouldn't even consider it. I knew it wasn't safe for him out there on his own so I offered him use of the cabin. He said he'd think about it, but only if I promised not to come here...not to check on him. I agreed and gave him all the cash I had on me."

The answer surprised Jagger. "So you've been coming here to check on him anyway?" he asked as he forced himself to release Declan. The feel of the man's pulse beneath his fingers was too distracting. Declan's hand reached up to rub at his throat and the move made Jagger's cock jerk in his pants.

"No. I have an app on my phone that notifies me if anyone disables the security system. It wasn't disabled until this afternoon. I have no idea where he's been since the shooting."

Jagger cursed the fact that it was too dark to see Declan's face. The man had even been smart enough to disable the dome light in his car, presumably so that Ren wouldn't see the vehicle where it was parked in a grove of trees at the base of the driveway.

"Why not tell Dom and Vin?"

Declan snorted. "Do you really believe that if they know where he is, they'd be able to stay away?"

"He's messed up Declan. He needs help." Jesus, why the hell did using the man's name sound so right on his tongue?

"You think I don't fucking know that?" Declan said. "But I also know that short of institutionalizing him, Dom and Vin wouldn't have been able to keep him from taking off if that was what he wanted to do."

Jagger sighed. "So what exactly was your plan?"

Before Declan could answer, a gunshot rang out and both he and Declan instantly ducked behind the car. But Jagger instinctively knew the muffled sound hadn't come from outside and he was running towards the cabin a second after a horrified Declan uttered Ren's name.

~

*J*agger didn't bother slowing as he rammed into the cabin door and it was only his forward momentum that had him dropping his upper body enough so that the bullet that whizzed by him slammed into the doorframe instead of his head. His relief was short-lived though, as he saw a gun aimed directly at him and his eyes connected with Ren's deadened gaze just as he began to pull back on the trigger.

"Ren, don't!" Declan shouted as his large frame filled the doorway and the gun shifted off of Jagger and onto Declan. Jagger instantly tried to step between the two men but Declan's hand closed over his arm to keep him from moving.

"Ren, it's me," Declan said softly.

Ren's icy blue eyes shifted back and forth between Jagger and Declan several times before he finally settled them on Declan and his finger eased off the trigger.

"Declan?" he finally asked, his voice sounding softer than Jagger would have expected. It was then that Jagger noticed the change in the younger man's sunken eyes. They'd gone from cold and empty to heavy with confusion. It was as if he'd been jarred awake from a deep sleep and didn't know where he was or how he'd gotten there.

"Yeah, Ren, it's Declan," Declan said as he slowly moved so that he was standing in front of Jagger.

"Did you see them out there?" Ren asked hopefully. "Did I get one of them?"

"There's no one out there," Declan said gently.

Ren's arm shook in agitation and he suddenly jerked the gun up and down. "Don't lie to me! I heard them!"

"Who?"

"Them!" Ren shouted. "They're coming for me! They're going to try and stick me back in that...that hole!"

"Ren, listen to me," Declan said. "No one will ever hurt you again, do you understand me?"

Ren shook his head vigorously. "You can't stop them, Declan," he whispered. "No one can stop them."

Jagger watched in horror as Ren took several steps backwards until his back hit the wall and then he slid down to the floor, his knees bent up, the gun resting in his lap. It was Ren's fixation on the gun that had Jagger taking a step forward.

"Ren, do you remember Jagger?" Declan asked and Ren's watery gaze lifted to connect first with Declan, then Jagger. Ren shook his head.

"Jagger got you out of that place."

Jagger stayed put as Declan moved closer. He managed to lower himself in front of Ren so they were nearly eye level but the gun's position was still precarious and Jagger didn't miss the way Ren had his finger resting on the trigger.

"I don't remember," Ren said quietly.

"Jagger," Declan called over his shoulder though his eyes never left Ren's. "How many of the guys that were holding Ren did you leave alive?"

"None," Jagger answered.

"Are you going to let anyone take him?" Declan asked.

"No fucking way," Jagger said firmly, hoping like hell Ren could see he was telling the truth. When Ren's eyes shifted to his for a moment, he thought he saw a brief flicker of hope.

"No one ever touches you again, Ren," Declan vowed. "They won't get past me. They won't get past Jagger. And you and I both know they sure as hell won't get past your brothers," Declan added and Jagger could almost hear the smile in his voice.

Ren's free hand shook as he came up to wipe at his face. "I don't want to see them," he whispered.

"You don't have to. They don't know you're here."

Jagger was surprised when Ren glanced up at him as if seeking confirmation...or reassurance. Jagger nodded. "You decide if and when you're ready," he said. He knew in that instant that it was a promise he wouldn't go back on, even if it cost him the newfound relationship with Dom and Vin.

Ren nodded and when Declan finally reached to take the gun from his hand, Ren released it. Tension drained out of Jagger's body and when Declan extended the gun behind his back, Jagger quickly stepped forward and took it.

~

*D*eclan felt a ripple of comfort go through him when Jagger's fingers brushed his as he took the gun. The past two minutes had been some of the worst in his life and had started when that single gunshot rang through the night. As he and Jagger had run towards the cabin, images of Ren lying lifeless on the floor in a pool of blood had flashed through his mind. The sound of wood cracking as Jagger had broken the door down had been punctuated by another gunshot and the relief at seeing Ren alive and well had lasted only a split second as Declan's mind registered that Jagger stood no chance of escaping the line of fire a second time.

The recognition in Ren's eyes and voice as he'd whispered Declan's name had given Declan hope but then there had been that heart wrenching moment where Ren's eyes had glazed over with despair and hopelessness and Declan's heart had nearly stopped when Ren's battered gaze had fallen on the gun he'd been cradling in his lap.

"Have you eaten anything today?" Declan asked as he reached out and closed his hand around Ren's thin arm. This was the closest he'd been to the younger man and his condition was even more shocking than Declan had first realized. Ren was only an inch or two shorter than Declan but he was so skinny and pale that he seemed tiny compared to Declan and could easily pass for a corpse. His eyes looked large in their sunken sockets and his skin was drawn tight over sharp cheekbones. His once thick black hair was gone and the closely cropped shadow of growth that replaced it couldn't hide several scars on his head. More scars mottled his face and a surge of rage went through Declan at the thought of the men who'd put them there.

"No," Ren said and it took Declan a moment to remember he'd asked Ren about food.

"Jagger, can you check the pantry? There should be some soup in there," Declan said as he helped Ren to his feet. Ren had become quiet and withdrawn but he didn't fight Declan as he led him to the small kitchen table. Jagger was already heating up the soup in the microwave by the time Declan got Ren settled and Declan moved quickly to the refrigerator and found the can of soda he was looking for. He prayed that the jolt of sugar would help ease some of the shock that Ren was experiencing.

"Here," Declan said as he wrapped Ren's hands around the can. Ren seemed surprised to see the soda resting between his fingers but he obediently drank some down. He flinched when Jagger appeared next to him and eased the bowl of soup in front of him. He stared tiredly at it for a moment but finally picked up the spoon next to it and began slowly eating. Jagger ended up reheating the food twice before Ren managed to finish it all and when he did finally put the spoon down, his eyes were heavy with exhaustion.

Declan led Ren to the smaller of the two bedrooms in the cabin. It had been the one Declan had used as a child when he joined his grandfather on his fishing trips. While not nearly as large as the master bedroom, the room was the perfect one to stick Ren into since it had only one small window that would be a challenge to climb out of. There was no way Declan was risking another disappearing act like the one Ren had pulled at Vin's house the night he'd gone after Mia.

God, what a clusterfuck, Declan thought as he flipped on the lights. Declan's intent had been to help Ren but all he'd done was make things worse. And if Ren's aim hadn't been off by the smallest of fractions, Jagger would be dead.

Declan guided Ren to the bed. As much as he knew Ren needed a shower, the man clearly needed sleep more. As he pulled back the covers, Ren stood next to him, his arms wrapped around his waist as if trying to soothe himself. Declan maneuvered him into a sitting positon on the bed and got Ren's shoes off before helping him under the covers. His heart ached as Ren's eyes slid closed and it was all he could do not to run his fingers through the little bit of hair on Ren's head.

The man before him was nothing like the old Ren Barretti but Declan still wanted him. He'd met Ren for the first time at Dom and Sylvie's wedding and though Ren hadn't known it, his presence had changed something for Declan. The beautiful, happy go lucky 19-year-old with the perpetual smile on his face and laughing blue eyes had confirmed for Declan that his future wouldn't consist of the wife and kids he'd been expected to have. After years of denying what his body wanted, it had taken only one look at Ren for Declan to know he would always crave the presence of another man instead of a woman.

But the worst part was that his gut had told him even then that it would be this one man that he wanted above all others and he'd been right. Declan had spoken less than a dozen words to Ren that night but he'd lost his heart to him almost instantly. It didn't matter that Ren was straight, that he was younger or that they were practically related by law. And it didn't matter that he hadn't seen Ren again for several years after that. His heart hadn't given a shit that a future with Ren was impossible. It hadn't cared that being in love with someone so completely unattainable would torture Declan in the years that followed.

What had mattered was that when Ren had been led in handcuffs through the precinct doors just a few short days ago, it was his heart that had decided he needed to save Ren and his mind had been in overdrive ever since trying to make that happen. But all he'd ended up doing was making things worse.

~

$\mathcal{J}$agger watched Declan re-enter the kitchen from the back hallway that led to the bedrooms. The man looked as worn out as Ren had and Jagger guessed Declan was now the one crashing as his own adrenaline rush began to fade. Declan paused when he saw him sitting at the table but his eyes quickly fell on the gun Jagger had placed in the center. Ren's gun.

"Serial number's filed off," Jagger said.

Declan slid into the chair across from him and reached for the illegal gun that Ren had bought off the streets. Jagger wasn't surprised when Declan made sure the gun was empty. He examined it briefly and then put it back down before running his fingers through his hair in agitation.

"I gave him the money to buy food," Declan muttered. "I didn't even consider this," he said as he stared at the gun. "I'm such a fool…"

"He would have found a way to get the gun whether you gave him money or not," Jagger said. "It was obviously the only thing that made him feel even somewhat safe."

Declan stood up and went to the refrigerator and yanked open the door. Jagger knew what he'd see – absolutely nothing. Declan slammed the door shut and leaned back against it. "We need to call his brothers," he finally said.

"And break the promise we made him?" Jagger said. "No. One hundred fucking percent no."

"You saw him, Jagger," Declan snapped. He came back to the table and picked up the gun. "He looked at this like it was his only way out. If we hadn't gotten here in time…"

"The first shot he fired went through the wall near the back door."

After a brief glance over his shoulder at the door in question, Declan lowered the gun once more. "We can't risk leaving him alone. He needs professional help. If it means having him committed-" Declan said softly.

Jagger rose and slammed his hands down on the table. "He doesn't belong in a place like that!" Anger went through Jagger at even the thought of Ren being pumped full of drugs and being left in a corner somewhere to rot like a piece of garbage. He'd seen firsthand what passed for mental health care in the military system and there was no way in hell he would let Ren suffer through that after having survived so much.

"Jagger," Declan began to say but Jagger cut him off.

"You want out, Declan? Go!"

"I want him safe, damn it!" Declan snapped though he kept his voice low. "I want to not have to tell his brothers they need to come down to the morgue to ID his body because he put a bullet in his brain. Or that he's going to spend the rest of his life in a jail cell because he shot someone he thought was a threat!"

Jagger straightened. "Finally Detective, something we agree on."

Declan fell silent at that and Jagger felt a strange urge to reach out and wipe the tension from his brow. Which made no fucking sense because he couldn't stand the guy.

"What's your plan?" Declan finally asked.

"We get him through the next few weeks. Make him feel safe enough so that he can focus on other things like seeing a professional and reaching out to his brothers. One of us is with him 24/7 for as long as it takes."

"And if he doesn't go for it?" Declan asked.

"That's one choice he doesn't get to make."

CHAPTER 3

"Ren, you have to do it."

"No."

"Don't tell my parents...don't tell them I was scared, okay?"

"Brandon, please, I can't."

"It hurts so bad Ren. Please, you have to make it stop..."

"No!"

"Damn it Ren, wake up!"

Ren jolted awake as hard fingers dug into his shoulder. The ground beneath him was surprisingly smooth as he scrambled away from his attacker. Even the usually rough earth at his back felt wrong. There were no sharp edges digging into his skin or large rocks that forced his body to curve at unnatural angles. And the dust that perpetually coated his tongue and throat was gone too. And the light? Why was it so fucking light?

A shot of victory went through him as his fist connected with flesh and bone and the sound of a muffled grunt had him swinging out his leg in an effort to bring his captor all the way to the ground where he could strike a lethal blow. But there was no contact as his target anticipated the move and within seconds Ren was flat on his back, a heavy body holding him down.

"Ren, it's me, Jagger!"

Ren fought like a man possessed but his body was too weak and it only took a minute before he was too winded to do anything other than twist and turn his body in a futile effort to knock his opponent free. His eyes slowly began to focus as the sensitivity lessened and he stilled when he realized he was looking at an intricate tattoo on a heavily muscled arm. He followed it up to where it disappeared beneath a black T-shirt.

"If you promise not to take another swing at me, I'll let you go," he heard a rumbly voice say. His gaze lifted until it met a pair of gray eyes that reminded him of the storm clouds he and his little brother used to watch from the window of the bedroom they'd shared as kids. Rafe had always been frightened because he knew the clouds would inevitably be followed by thunder and lightning but Ren had loved them because there was nothing more exciting than the rush of the entire house shaking as a blast of thunder swept over it.

"You're Declan's friend," Ren finally said as the events from the previous night began to play through his head. There was a certain amount of time that remained lost to him but he did remember this man. "You gave me soup."

Jagger's smile was wide and softened his otherwise hard features. His bald head, scarred face and huge body made him look like a biker on steroids but the chuckle that rumbled through his chest as he released Ren was strangely comforting.

"Yeah, well, it was either that or a can of fruit cocktail. I hate that shit," he added as he climbed to his feet and reached his hand down. Ren took it but quickly released it as soon as he was upright. Jagger's hand was warm…too warm.

"I used to do that," he heard Jagger say and he glanced up from the hand he'd been staring at and saw that Jagger was looking at the bed sheet Ren had placed on the floor in the corner of the room. "Took me almost six months to get used to a mattress after I got out." He looked down at the shoes Ren had put back on last night after he'd woken up. "Did that too…never would've guessed I'd need to teach myself how to sleep without shoes on."

"You served?" Ren asked.

Jagger nodded. "173rd Airborne Brigade," he said.

"Paratrooper?" Ren asked in surprise.

"Yeah. Always dreamed of flying fighter jets but that wasn't in the cards so jumping out of a plane seemed like the next best thing," Jagger responded. Something flickered in Jagger's eyes but it disappeared just as quickly.

"What time is it?" Ren asked as his stomach rolled with hunger. It had been a while since he actually felt hungry and the sensation was foreign. His system had gotten so used to surviving on so little that the prospect of food actually nauseated him even as his body yearned for it.

"Just after nine."

A glance at the single small window in the room told Ren it was morning instead of evening so that meant he'd actually slept through the night. He couldn't even recall the last time that had happened. "Where's my gun?" he asked as the familiar tingle began to make his skin itch. He didn't wait for Jagger to answer as he went to the nightstand and began rifling through it.

"It's not there," Jagger said from behind him.

"Where is it? I need it," Ren said quickly as he hurried to the dresser.

"It's gone. You're safe now – you don't need it." The pity in Jagger's voice grated on his nerves.

"What do you mean it's gone?" Ren snapped as he whirled on Jagger. But Jagger didn't answer him and Ren tore out of the room and rushed to the kitchen and began searching all the drawers and cabinets.

"Ren, I swear to you, you're safe."

"Don't you get it? I'll never be safe!" Ren shouted. "They said they'd come after me! They're going to find me...my brothers!"

"It was part of the act, Ren. They were trying to get in your head."

Ren shook his head. Believing that was too big of a risk. "I want my fucking gun!" he yelled. But Jagger just looked at him sadly.

"Fuck!" Ren screamed and he yanked the drawer he was in the

process of opening off its rollers and threw it to the floor. He scanned the contents before doing the same to the next drawer. His breath was coming in heavy pants as he kneeled down and searched through the mess.

"The knives are gone too," Jagger said softly.

Ren rose and viciously kicked at the debris. He *had* been searching for a knife. Even the dullest butcher knife could still be deadly if wielded correctly and he would have been able to take at least two or three guys out before they got their hands on him again. He pushed past Jagger and headed for the front door.

"Your car's been disabled."

What the fuck? Ren froze in the process of reaching for the door-knob. "No," he heard himself whisper. Denial went through him at the realization that if what Jagger said was true, he was stuck here with no way out...no way to defend himself. He hurried out the door and rushed to his car. The GTO was exactly where he'd left it. He had no idea where the keys were but he could hotwire it if worst came to worst. He lifted the hood of the car and felt the panic rush through him as he searched the engine he'd painstakingly restored himself. Sure enough, the ignition and fuel pump fuses were missing. He desperately looked around and his eyes lit up at the sight of the car sitting behind his.

"It's disabled too and Declan took the fuses with him," Jagger said from somewhere behind him.

At that point Ren lost it and he flew at the other man. But as before, Jagger anticipated his moves and quickly overpowered him.

"If you've got enough energy to keep taking swings at me, you've got enough energy to take a little walk. You can see for yourself that it's just us out here," Jagger said.

Strong fingers closed around his arm and started dragging him towards the woods that surrounded the cabin.

∼

*J*agger felt a surge of pity go through him as Ren's eyes darted all around them. The man had only fought him for a few moments when Jagger had forced him onto a narrow hiking trail north of the cabin. Between the heavy plant growth that covered the path and the moderate incline, Ren was breathing hard within minutes. The additional anxiety of expecting someone to jump them at any moment had Ren's hands clenched in perpetual fists and he flinched every time he or Jagger stepped on a branch. With each minute that passed and Ren's anxiety failed to ease, doubt coursed through Jagger. What if he'd misjudged what he and Declan could do for this man?

The idea of condemning Ren to a future in a mental health facility that would dope him with drugs to keep him out of trouble went against everything Jagger believed in; he'd seen far too many good men get lost in the system that was supposedly designed to care for their specific needs. But could he and Declan really help ease Ren's pain long enough that the young man could decide for himself to seek treatment? Last night he'd been so sure they could but seeing Ren's despair as he'd realized he had no weapon or means of escape had ripped something open inside of Jagger.

"How about we take a break?" Jagger said softly when he saw the sweat forming on Ren's flushed skin.

Ren didn't answer him and he wasn't sure if it was because he hadn't heard him or he'd chosen to ignore him. It didn't really matter since Ren made the decision to stop less than ten minutes later. He sank down onto a fallen log, his breath coming in shallow pants as he ran his palms back and forth over his thighs. Jagger carefully lowered himself down next to Ren and considered it a small victory when the other man didn't move away from him.

"Why are you doing this?" Ren asked though his eyes continued to scan the area surrounding them.

Jagger remained silent as he considered his words carefully. "Believe it or not, I know a little bit of what you're going through," he finally said. When Ren remained silent, Jagger continued. "I tried to keep count of the number of men I killed when I was first deployed. Tried to remember their faces too. I guess I wanted to make sure I never got too comfortable doing it."

"Did you?" Ren asked.

"Get comfortable?"

"Keep count?" Ren clarified.

"I lost track after a while. I still see some of the faces though. Especially the innocents."

Ren shifted slightly and Jagger had to force himself to ignore the feel of Ren's thigh brushing against his.

"First guy I killed was using a little boy as a shield," Ren said quietly. "My aim was good but the guy jerked as he fell and his gun went off. Kid was gone before I could even get to him."

As disheartening as their conversation was, Jagger was glad to see that Ren's eyes had dropped to study his hands instead of the woods around them.

"I don't think anyone ever gets comfortable with it," Ren said. "Whether you kill one or a hundred."

Jagger was surprised when Ren looked up at him. "Why are you doing this?" he asked again. The bright blue eyes that were shrouded with pain had Jagger reaching out to stroke his fingers over Ren's face. Luckily he caught himself at the last moment and ran his fingers over his own head instead.

"Because I want you to be able to go home someday."

Ren nodded. "I understand," he whispered. Jagger didn't like the tone he'd used to say it though. He sounded almost...disappointed. But that didn't make any sense.

"What is it that you understand exactly?" Jagger asked.

Ren's eyes stared straight ahead. "My brothers hired you to find me over there," he said. "You're just doing your job."

This time Jagger did reach for Ren and the feel of the man's early morning stubble felt amazing against Jagger's fingers as he closed them around Ren's chin and forced Ren to look at him.

"My 'job' ended the second you stepped onto American soil. I'm here because I know what a good man you are," Jagger said. "Vin has

42

been telling stories about you since the day he asked me to join the team to bring you home. You may not know me from Adam but I sure as hell feel like I know you. I want you to have a shot at a life…a real life. I don't care if it's the one you had before all this shit went down or a new one you create for yourself. As long as it's your choice."

Ren's gaze softened and Jagger wondered what it would feel like to lift his thumb just enough so that he could drag it over the full, soft lips. Jesus, what the fuck was wrong with him? Not only was this guy straight, he was incredibly vulnerable and only a complete scumbag would be lusting after him right now.

Jagger forced himself to release his hold on Ren and dropped his hand. "You ready to head back?" he asked.

Ren considered it for a moment and no one was more surprised than Jagger when he said, "Let's go a little bit farther."

~

*W*hy the hell wouldn't his skin quit tingling? Ren's hand traveled to his chin and smoothed over where Jagger had touched him, half expecting to find some evidence there that would explain the sensation that he'd felt when those thick fingers had held his face. And Jagger's words…he sure as hell didn't mince them because Ren had believed everything he'd said. The brief – and strange – disappointment that had come over Ren when he'd realized he was just a job to Jagger had disappeared when the bigger man had looked down at him with open honesty and explained what he wanted for Ren. Ren knew that the future Jagger envisioned for him wasn't a realistic one, but God it had felt good to have someone want that for him.

"Declan's back," he heard Jagger say and Ren nearly stumbled to a halt when he realized that not only had they completed a half circle and started heading back to the cabin, but that he hadn't once searched the woods around him for shadows or focused on every snapping twig. Not since Jagger had touched him…

~

*D*eclan was in the process of grabbing a couple of shopping bags from the trunk of his car when his eyes fell on Jagger and Ren as they exited the woods. His eyes instantly scanned Ren for any sign of distress and although he looked tense and uncomfortable, it was a thousand times better than how he'd looked last night. And Jagger...well, Jagger looked like he always did – big, overbearing, arrogant...and fucking hot. Declan cursed as the dreaded image of the two men surrounding him filtered once more through his mind like it had when Zane had been fucking him. Jesus, had that only been yesterday?

"Hey," Jagger said as he came over to the car and automatically began pulling bags from it. They'd come to a truce of sorts last night since they'd agreed that calling Ren's brothers wasn't an option at the moment and that together they might be able to get Ren to a place where he felt secure enough to make some reasonable decisions. But they'd both been too drained to work out the details and this morning they'd agreed that it would make sense for Declan to be the one to get some food and supplies since he knew the area and for Jagger to stay behind. In truth, Declan had felt uncomfortable at leaving Ren with a virtual stranger but it wasn't like he'd had a lot of choice in the matter. It had been Jagger's idea to disable the vehicles and remove any potential weapons from the cabin – an insight that Declan hadn't even considered beyond getting rid of the gun.

"How'd it go?" Declan asked as his eyes settled on Ren who was staring at his GTO.

"A little rough," Jagger said quietly. "I'll explain later."

Declan was wondering what 'a little rough' meant but he had his answer a minute later when he followed Ren and Jagger into the cabin. The kitchen was in a shambles and the way Ren had been staring at his car suddenly made sense.

"I'm going to go take a shower," Ren said quietly.

"Here, I got you some fresh clothes," Declan said as he handed Ren a couple of bags. "They might be a little big," he said.

Ren's eyes connected with his as he took the bags and that familiar ache settled in Declan's gut.

"Thanks," Ren mumbled as he turned and disappeared into his room.

"Still think this was the best way to go?" Declan muttered as he stepped over the mess and opened the refrigerator.

"What I think is that you started all this," Jagger snapped.

"Right," Declan said. "And you get to be the big hero and save the day."

"Your words," Jagger quipped.

"God, you're a piece of work," Declan said as he began jamming the items from the grocery bag into the refrigerator.

"At least my plan didn't involve arming a guy with severe PTSD and setting him loose on innocent people. For a cop-"

"What the fuck is your problem with cops?" Declan shouted as he slammed the refrigerator door closed. "Or are you just too stupid to come up with any other digs?"

Jagger's eyes hardened but Declan was surprised when he turned and left the cabin instead of railing back at him. And then he remembered Jagger's admission about being dyslexic on the day he'd interrogated him.

"Fuck," he muttered and he quickly hurried after the other man. He didn't have to go far because Jagger had stopped on the small porch.

"Jagger," he began but all the wind got knocked out of him when Jagger grabbed him and slammed him up against one of the porch columns.

"Does it make you feel like a big man to look down on me, Detective?" Jagger snarled. Jagger's fingers bit into his upper arms and Declan didn't miss the sight of the blood on Jagger's knuckles. A quick glance at the opposite column showed a smear of blood where Jagger had likely slammed his fist against the unforgiving wood.

"No-" Declan tried to say but Jagger cut him off.

"Go on, give me your worst, asshole. I've heard them all!" When Declan remained quiet, Jagger seemed to become more enraged. "No?

Nothing? How about retard or idiot or shit for brains? Oh wait, that's not the only part of me you have a problem with, is it?" Jagger bit out. "You think I'm a thug too. A criminal. A loser."

Sadness went through Declan as Jagger continued to spit out slur after slur. He wished he could ask who'd flung such merciless, hateful words at this man at some point in his life but Jagger was too angry for Declan to even get a word in. His face was practically in Declan's and venom dripped from his voice as he continued his tirade. But his next words had Declan's blood running cold because they were all too familiar and the pain he felt in Jagger was his own.

"Pansy-ass queer, fagg-"

All thought and reason left Declan's head as his need to undo the harm he'd unwittingly caused took over and he slashed his mouth over Jagger's just in time to prevent that ugly last word from fully leaving his lips.

∿

*J*agger's rant died the second Declan's mouth closed over his and it took him several long moments to even process what was happening. His reaction to Declan calling him stupid had been unexpected and over the top, even for him, and he'd escaped outside to try to understand why a word that he'd heard so often in his life and that shouldn't have had an impact on him anymore, had instead left him reeling with pain. He'd spent most of his life learning to be immune to the cruel taunts about his intelligence so Declan's attack shouldn't have even registered. But it had, and the feeling of weakness that had come with it had brought Jagger's infamous temper to the surface and he'd lashed out at the porch column. But the biting pain in his hand had done nothing to ease the humiliation that was coursing through him and when Declan had followed him outside, Jagger's only thought was that he needed to go on the offensive. He needed to show Declan that he had no power over him.

But that argument was shot to hell and all his anger disappeared as

Declan's tongue slipped between his lips and stroked over every surface of his mouth. The kiss was rough and desperate and fucking perfect and Jagger couldn't hold back the moan that escaped him as Declan's tongue licked his. At some point he must have released Declan's arms because he found himself being turned around so that it was his back pressed up against the column. The hard cock brushing against his caused a burning deep in his abdomen as lust consumed him and he reached his hands down to grab Declan's ass so that he could grind their hips together.

Fingers wrapped around the back of his neck to hold him still while he was tortured with kiss after kiss, each one deeper and needier than the last. But just as quickly as it had begun, it was over and Declan was pushing away from him, a look of horror passing through his gaze as his eyes met Jagger's. It was definitely a 'What the fuck have I done' look and Jagger didn't try to stop him when he quickly turned and went back into the cabin. God knew he needed a few minutes to figure out what the hell had just happened himself.

~

*N*o, No, No, No.

What the hell had he just done? Disbelief went through Declan as he reached out an arm to support himself against the kitchen counter. Had he really just fucking outed himself to a man he couldn't stand...who couldn't stand him?

Before he could stop himself, Declan ran his tongue along his lips and he shuddered at how sensitive they were. Jagger had tasted so much sweeter than he ever would have expected. And for someone so hard and unbending, Jagger had opened to him so beautifully...so willingly. The heat of his skin had burned Declan wherever he touched it and that slick tongue had returned every one of Declan's seeking strokes. And their cocks...they'd found each other long before Jagger's powerful hands had closed over Declan's ass.

"Fuck," Declan whispered and when he heard the front door open, a tremor of fear went through him. He couldn't deal with this right now. He quickly reached down and began cleaning up the mess on the floor.

"Declan…" he heard Jagger say softly.

"Want to give me a hand here?" Declan snapped. He hoped to God that his tone made it clear he wasn't interested in discussion.

Jagger didn't answer but Declan's traitorous body could sense the bigger man just behind him. It would be so easy to turn around and pick up where they'd left off. Declan jammed one of the drawers back into place.

"Did you tell Ren what the plan was?" Declan asked.

"No, he didn't," Declan heard Ren say and he glanced up to see him standing in the doorway. His short hair was still slightly damp and the new jeans and T-shirt he was wearing hung loosely on his gaunt body. Declan had guessed correctly that the clothes would be too big but he'd deliberately chosen a larger size in the hopes that Ren would put enough weight on in the next few weeks to fill them out normally. Declan glanced at Jagger who was uncharacteristically silent.

"Why don't we go sit down?" Declan suggested as he motioned to the living room.

Ren remained silent but he moved to the other room and Declan forced himself to ignore the heat of Jagger's body as he brushed past him. His eyes found Ren standing near the fireplace, his arms hanging at his sides. But his hands were clenched and his features were drawn tight. It wasn't a good sign.

Declan dropped down on the small couch and he didn't miss the fact that Jagger placed himself by the front door. He was glad to see that Jagger had managed to get the door back on its hinges at least, even though there were several cracks running down the middle where the old wood had buckled under the pressure of Jagger's weight.

"What do you remember about last night?" Declan asked Ren.

Ren seemed surprised by the question and it took him several seconds to answer.

"I…I remember you guys showing up."

"Do you remember what happened before we got here?"

This time Ren needed much longer to consider it. "I remember getting here and I was glad when the code for the alarm worked. I was tired so I sat down for a while," Ren said as he glanced down at the spot on the floor in the corner of the room. "Then you were there and you made me something to eat."

Declan bent his head and ran his hand over the back of his neck. A quick glance at Jagger showed the other man wasn't eager for what would come next.

"What?" Ren asked in confusion as he glanced between the two men.

"We were outside when we heard your gun go off," Jagger said softly and Ren's eyes shifted to follow Jagger's gaze to the back door. He stiffened when he saw the bullet hole there.

"Jagger came through the door first," Declan said gently as Ren's eyes moved to him. If your aim had been a quarter of an inch to the right, he wouldn't be here."

Ren's eyes widened as Declan's meaning sank in and he glanced at Jagger. But when Declan spoke again, Ren returned his attention to him.

"You were about to pull the trigger again when I came in. You wouldn't have missed a second time," Declan added with emphasis. Ren shook his head in denial but when neither Jagger nor Declan said anything, the truth hit him. And it was quickly followed by anger.

"I told you to stay away, Declan!" Ren shouted. "We had a deal!"

"Our deal didn't include you going out and buying a gun!" Declan returned. "Do you even get what could have happened?"

"I knew I couldn't trust you," Ren suddenly said. The words stung but Declan didn't get a chance to respond.

"Hey!" Jagger yelled. "Where the hell do you think you'd be right now without him?" he said angrily as he pointed at Declan. "Because I can tell you and none of the scenarios end with you being a free man."

"I can take care of myself," Ren said mutinously.

"Like you took care of yourself last night?" Jagger bit out. "Shooting at ghosts?"

Ren remained silent but Declan was glad to see he hadn't emotionally withdrawn himself from the conversation and didn't seem to be on the verge of an episode.

"How long before a ghost turns out to be some innocent hiker who got a little turned around and came to your door asking for directions? How long before some hunter's gunshots put you back in that hellhole and you become the hunter? What happens when you decide you're okay to go back to the city and some guy mouths off to you because you accidentally bumped into him on the sidewalk?" Jagger asked.

"Jagger," Declan said.

"No, Declan, we're not going to tip toe around this," Jagger said as his eyes flashed to Declan for a moment before returning to Ren. "You're a smart man, Ren. You know that you have no hope in hell of beating this thing by yourself. And I know you don't want to hurt anyone but the fact is that even without a weapon, you're a dangerous man."

"Ren," Declan said softly. "I know you're scared. Scared that you'll never be safe again. That you won't ever be the man you used to be. Let Jagger and I take some of that burden off of you. We can keep you safe and we can make sure you don't hurt anyone else by mistake. Maybe if you don't have to worry so much about that shit, you can start figuring out the rest."

Ren remained quiet for a long time and then he started looking around the room. His eyes went to the door and then to the wall where he'd ended up last night after the shooting. It took Declan a moment to realize he was remembering part, if not all, of what had happened.

"You said no one would touch me ever again," Ren finally said.

Ren looked up at Jagger who nodded briefly and then his eyes met Declan's. "Promise me you won't let them take me, Declan," Ren whispered desperately and Declan didn't miss the sheen of tears in his eyes. Declan couldn't stop himself from getting up and going to stand in front of Ren. He waited until their gazes connected before he spoke.

"I swear to God, Ren, no one will ever hurt you again." He wrapped his hand around the back of Ren's neck and squeezed gently and dragged in a breath when Ren finally nodded. And in that moment, Declan knew he wouldn't break his promise to the younger man, no matter what.

~

*D*eclan promised. Ren kept repeating that to himself over and over as he watched the sunlight fade through the kitchen window. He was still working on the plate of food Jagger had slid in front of him and ordered him to take his time eating but with the caveat that he had to eat it all. For most, it wouldn't be considered a huge portion but to Ren it looked enormous. It tasted really good though so at least there was that. And so far his stomach hadn't rebelled though he was starting to get uncomfortable, especially as his anxiety began to notch up.

"When will he be back?" Ren couldn't help but ask as he listened to Jagger working in the kitchen behind him. The logical part of Ren's brain told him he was safe with Jagger but there was something about Declan that was strangely comforting. Which didn't make any sense since he'd spent very little time around the quiet man who always kept to himself at the few family functions they'd attended at the same time.

"A few days," Jagger responded. "He's working tomorrow and has a family thing this weekend." Jagger returned to the table and dropped down in the chair next to Ren.

"I didn't know he had much of a family besides Sylvie," Ren said. At Jagger's silence, Ren stilled. "It's not *his* family, is it?" Ren asked.

Jagger shook his head. "It's an engagement party for Logan's sister and her fiancé."

Ren remembered meeting Logan briefly at Vin's house his first night back in Seattle. Vin had told him about the death of Dom's wife and his newfound relationship with another man but admittedly, Ren had been too preoccupied to give it much thought at that time or even in the past couple of weeks.

"Have you met him?" Ren asked absentmindedly.

"Logan?"

Ren nodded.

"A few times. He comes to the office to meet Dom for lunch," Jagger said.

"What does he do?" It felt strange to be asking someone else the questions he should have asked Dom or even Vin.

"He runs a foundation that helps kids in need. Kids from the street," Jagger explained. "It's named for Declan's sister."

That was a surprise. "Did Sylvie and Logan know each other?"

Jagger shrugged. "Not sure."

"Strange," Ren said.

"What is?"

"That Declan would be close to a man that replaced his sister."

Jagger leaned back in his chair. "Is that really how you see it?"

"What? That he replaced her?"

"Yeah."

Ren considered that for a moment. He'd never known any people that loved each other more than Dom and Sylvie. They'd been perfect for one another and he'd always envied what they'd had. And Dom had loved her too much to just so easily dismiss her memory for someone else.

"Don't you think this thing with Logan is just some way for Dom to deal with losing Sylvie? Like a rebound thing?" Ren asked as he pushed his nearly empty plate away from him.

"No, I don't think that at all. I've seen the way Dom and Logan look at each other. It's the real deal," Jagger said.

Ren must have looked confused because Jagger chuckled. "What, you don't think it's possible to love two people in the same way? Two soulmates?"

"I guess I'd have to believe in soulmates first before I could believe in having more than one in a lifetime."

"You ever come close?" Jagger asked.

The sudden shift in conversation caused a knot to form in Ren's gut but he managed to shake his head.

"Liar," he heard Jagger say softly.

"What about you?" Ren asked.

"No," Jagger said. "I think some people like your brothers are lucky to have found the people they were meant to be with but I've seen the other side of love – the kind that's ugly and cruel. The kind that takes but never gives."

The remark hit too close to home for Ren and he dropped his eyes.

"You know what I'm talking about, don't you?" Jagger asked quietly. The man was either too damn observant or Ren really sucked at schooling his expressions.

Ren snatched his plate off the table and carried it to the sink. He took his time washing it and stacking it in the drying rack but Jagger hadn't moved when Ren was finally forced to turn around. And those unnerving eyes were still on him.

"What's next?" Ren asked. He glanced back at the fading daylight and felt an overwhelming need to examine every shadowy corner and check all the closets.

"How about a walk?"

Was the guy fucking crazy? But just as he was about to voice the question he saw the challenge in Jagger's eyes. And God but if that didn't feel a hell of a lot better than being looked at with pity.

"Okay," Ren managed to get out though even he could hear the fear in his voice. But Jagger didn't call him on it. He just reached into a drawer and pulled out a single flashlight.

"Let's go," he said with a grin but to Ren's dismay, he kept the flashlight for himself.

CHAPTER 4

"We have a problem," Declan said before Jagger could even get a word out. He took one of the grocery bags from Declan and ignored the bout of desire that surged through him as Declan's unique, musky scent drifted over him. Neither of them had spoken since the day Declan had kissed him. After their discussion with Ren, Declan had quickly announced he needed to leave and had called only once later in the day to let Jagger know his whereabouts for the next several days.

Part of Jagger had been looking forward to seeing Declan again just so he could try to get a handle on what had happened between them. He had no idea if Declan was gay or straight or questioning but Jagger couldn't get that fucking kiss out of his head or the feel of Declan's tight ass beneath his palms. Add in his increasing attraction towards the young man he'd spent the last five days with and Jagger was stuck with an endless loop of questions that he couldn't figure out the answers to. But Declan's worried expression and hushed voice had all of those thoughts drifting to the background.

"What is it?" Jagger asked as he watched Declan close the trunk of his car.

"Where is he?" Declan asked, his eyes searching the surrounding glade.

"Still asleep," Jagger said. "He had a rough night."

"Nightmares?"

Jagger nodded. "We ended up doing a couple of perimeter searches before he settled back down. Happened again a few hours ago."

"You okay?" Declan asked.

The question caught Jagger off guard but he managed a nod. "How about you? You look like shit," Jagger said before he realized how obnoxious the words sounded. But Declan actually smiled briefly and Jagger felt his insides jerk at the sight.

"Rafe's back," Declan said.

"I know. Vin said he was hacking their system-" Jagger began to say.

"No, he's actually back. He showed up at the engagement party last night."

"Shit," Jagger whispered.

"No one even knew he was in town and then he was just there," Declan said.

"What happened?" Jagger asked softly as he heard the uneven tone in Declan's voice.

"It was bad, Jagger," Declan whispered.

Jagger couldn't stop himself from reaching out and closing his hand around Declan's upper arm. He was glad when Declan didn't pull away from him. "Tell me," Jagger said.

"The guy who took him – his biological father – he pimped him out," Declan said hoarsely. "Fucker let some trucker rape Rafe in his rig while he was buying beer and a tank of gas."

Jagger felt the bag of groceries start to slip from his lax arm and he quickly lowered it to the trunk next to the bag Declan had set there. "Jesus."

"It sounds like it went on for years," Declan said.

Bile crept up the back of Jagger's throat and he needed to lean against the car to keep himself upright. "He was just a kid…" Jagger said.

"Eight," Declan supplied. "He was eight."

"Vin and Dom?" Jagger asked.

"Destroyed. Rafe blames them for not stopping it – for not coming to get him," Declan said. "I've never seen Dom or Vin like that before..."

"Where's Rafe now?"

Declan shook his head. "He took off. Told Dom and Vin he was done with them. Gave them back the information he stole."

"Fuck," Jagger whispered.

"Ren can't know. Not yet," Declan said.

Jagger nodded. Ren's mental health was already shaky. Who knew what finding out what his baby brother had been through would do? "Agreed."

Declan reached for the bag of groceries he'd put down but Jagger reached out a hand to stop him. "Declan, we need to talk about what happened the other day."

Declan stiffened and pulled his arm free. "It was a mistake, Jagger. You were upset and I said something I shouldn't have..."

Declan brushed past him but Jagger snaked out an arm and grabbed him by the waist. The move had both of them flinching as their bodies brushed against one another. Declan's eyes grew heavy as Jagger let his hand travel down Declan's hip. The muscles in his thigh twitched as Jagger pressed his fingers against it and Jagger glanced down and wasn't surprised to see the outline of Declan's cock against his jeans, the head bulging just inches from where Jagger's hand was resting.

"Declan," Jagger whispered as he began to move his hand but then Declan's eyes flew open and he stepped back. Whatever spell Jagger had managed to weave was broken.

"Why don't you get some rest?" Declan said quickly. "I'll keep an eye on things." And with that Declan hurried to the cabin leaving Jagger to wonder what the hell was going on between them.

∾

"*Y*ou do this a lot?" Ren asked as he stared at the top of the fishing pole in his hands. He'd never actually gone fishing before so he had no idea what he was supposed to be watching for.

"Used to," Declan responded. "I don't get out here as much as I'd like."

"And you find this fun?"

Declan chuckled and Ren found himself enjoying the sound. He glanced at the man sitting on the ground next to him but was disappointed to see that if there had been a smile to accompany the chuckle, it was already gone. The only time he'd ever remembered seeing Declan smile was when he'd been in the presence of his younger sister and even then he'd always seemed grim and withdrawn.

"I find it relaxing," Declan said. "Fun is relative, I guess."

Ren looked around the small lake but saw no sign of movement and a quick check over his shoulder at the trail they'd used to get to the pristine body of water was quiet too. When he'd woken up, his anxiety had been as high as it had been throughout the night before. He'd been certain that someone had been fooling with the outside of the window in his room but subsequent searches of the outside of the cabin had proven fruitless. There hadn't even been any foot prints. It had been Jagger who suggested dumping a light coating of baking soda they'd found in the pantry in the dirt underneath the window.

Ren had been surprised that the other man had even indulged him by taking him outside to check things but when he'd come up with the unusual "security" system, Ren had been touched. And when Jagger had been there each time Ren had been ripped from his sleep by nightmares, something inside of Ren had started to ease. They'd ended up searching the area surrounding the cabin at least three times last night but Jagger had never been dismissive or shown any signs of frustration. He'd simply led Ren to the place where they'd dumped the baking soda to look for footprints or any kind of disturbance and then he'd led him, flashlight in hand, through the dense woods surrounding the cabin. And he'd waited until Ren was satisfied before leading the way back to the cabin.

"How do you know Jagger?" Ren asked.

To his surprise, Declan tensed next to him and he wondered at the cause.

"He works for your brothers," was all Declan said.

"So you two are friends?"

"No," Declan said quickly. Too quickly.

Confusion went through Ren. "Then how did you both end up here?"

Declan glanced at him briefly and Ren saw in that moment that Declan knew he'd been found out. Declan sighed. "He followed me up here."

"I don't understand."

Declan scrubbed his hand over his face. It was a move Ren noticed he often did when he seemed agitated.

"I was drinking in his friend's bar one night last week. I had a little too much and Jagger took me home. I guess I mentioned you at some point so he started following me. He knew your brothers were worried about you so I guess he just wanted to make sure you were okay."

Ren could tell by the fact that Declan refused to meet his gaze that there was plenty he wasn't telling him but he decided to let it go. "Why'd you help me that day, Declan?"

"You mean after the shooting?" Declan asked.

Darkness swept through Ren at the reminder of the man he'd killed. It wasn't so much the man he was thinking about but the reason Ren had been in that deserted parking lot at all. But he didn't want to think about that too much so he just nodded when Declan glanced at him.

"We go a long ways back," was all Declan said.

"You and my brothers go a long way back," Ren corrected. "I can count on one hand the number of times you and I have talked."

"We're family," was all Declan said.

Ren suspected he wasn't going to get anything else out of Declan on the subject and he wasn't sure he really wanted to. He was afraid that the answer might disappoint him.

"I'm sorry about Sylvie," Ren said as his thoughts drifted to the blonde beauty who'd stolen his brother's heart. She'd been full of life and energy and it broke his heart to think about the agony Dom must have experienced when he lost her. And he couldn't even begin to imagine the pain Declan must have gone through at losing his baby sister. "I didn't know she was sick again."

"She got the diagnosis a year ago. June 20th. Her birthday."

Ren felt a wave of pity go through him. June 20th was a week ago. The day before Declan and Jagger had shown up at the cabin. Probably the day Declan had gotten drunk.

"I didn't go to the appointment," Declan continued. "I knew I wouldn't be strong enough this time around."

"This time?" Ren asked softly.

"First one was when she was twelve. She kept asking me if she was going to die. I promised her she wouldn't."

"How old were you?"

"Twenty-two," Declan said.

"Your parents?" Ren asked.

Declan shook his head. "Too busy making all the right political connections to be bothered with a little thing like leukemia – especially when Sylvie had a nanny that once worked for an unnamed royal family in Europe," Declan bit out. "Didn't stop the bitch from hightailing it out of there when she found out she'd be expected to take care of a kid undergoing chemo."

"You took care of Sylvie by yourself?" Ren asked.

Declan nodded. "I was so scared I wouldn't be able to keep my promise," he said. "The vomiting, the hair falling out, the exhaustion, the constant nausea…the doctors tried to prepare us for what to expect but you just can't prepare for something like that. She was so brave. She didn't even cry when I shaved her hair off."

Declan suddenly laughed again but this time the sound was all wrong and it made Ren's heart clench.

"First time she cried was when I shaved my head too. Second time was when she asked our parents to come home and they said they'd try...we both knew what that meant."

"I'm sorry, Declan,"

Declan shook his head. "She got through it. She beat it the second time too. She'd met Dom by then and she was so scared he'd leave her. I guess I was too," he admitted. "Your brother..." Declan started to say. "Your brother was a fucking saint. He was there for every treatment, every appointment."

Ren's insides tightened at the mention of Dom and a flicker of guilt went through him. He'd spent these past few weeks so focused on himself that he hadn't given much consideration to what Vin and Dom had been going through in the past year. Or how his decision might have added to their already heavy burdens.

"Last year when she told me she wasn't feeling well I made an excuse for why I couldn't go with her and Dom to the doctor. Truth was I was too much of a fucking coward to face the truth." Declan reached his hand up to rub at his eyes. "But when she told me she wasn't going to beat it this time around...wasn't going to even try...I lost it. I yelled at her. I begged her. I even gave her the silent treatment like some bratty little kid who doesn't get his way. But she forgave me of course, and I was there at the end."

Ren could feel the man's pain washing off him in waves and the helplessness that Ren felt was overwhelming. So he did the only thing he could think of and closed his hand over Declan's shoulder. He could feel the tremors running through Declan's body as he fought to get himself under control. Ren let his hand coast across Declan's shoulder blade before running it up and down the middle of his back. Declan dropped his hand but kept his gaze focused on the still waters of the lake. It wasn't until he glanced at Ren that Ren felt something other than sadness shimmer through his own body. Something he couldn't put his finger on. Something that should have had him drawing his hand back, not leaving it where it rested against the powerful muscles that rippled beneath Declan's shirt.

"Looks like you're getting a nibble," he heard Declan say but the actual words didn't register as Ren's eyes fell on Declan's mouth as he spoke. His lips were full and looked smoother than Ren would have guessed a man's lips to be. And he had the slightest dimple in his chin...

"Ren, you've got one," Declan said though he didn't yell it. Because he didn't want to scare him.

"Ren," Declan said again and Ren felt his stomach flip-flop when Declan's hand closed gently over his on the fishing pole. What the hell was wrong with him?

"Ren," Declan said a third time and his voice was loud enough to jolt Ren from his wayward thoughts. And when he felt the pole jerk in his hand, reality returned and he instinctively reached for the reel.

"I've got one," he said stupidly as the top of the pole bent.

"Sure do," Declan said with a chuckle. "Reel her in – let's see if she's a fighter."

~

*J*agger stepped back from where he'd been watching Ren and Declan and leaned against a tree. He could still hear them talking excitedly about the fish Ren was trying to reel in but Jagger's mind was swirling with too many thoughts to keep track of everything at once so he tuned them out. He'd awoken about ten minutes ago to an empty cabin and a small piece of paper taped to his bedroom door. It had been a crude, hand-drawn map showing directions on how to get to the lake. There hadn't been any other information except for the words *'Join Us'* written in large, neat penmanship. He'd wondered if that was the way Declan always wrote or if he'd made the letters big and precise to ensure that Jagger could read them. It hadn't mattered – he struggled as he always did - but it was easy enough to type the letters into his phone and let an app read the words back to him. He was just glad as hell that Declan had been thoughtful enough to draw a map instead of writing the directions out.

When he'd reached the lake, the first thing that surprised him was the fact that Ren hadn't heard him coming. From what Jagger had been able to tell, Ren hadn't even been scanning his surroundings like he usually did. His first thought was that maybe Ren just felt more comfortable with Declan but it hadn't taken more than a minute of listening to Declan talk before Jagger realized the truth. Ren was just too engrossed in Declan's words and the immense pain behind them to focus on anything else. And hearing Declan talk about his sister had done the same exact thing to Jagger.

As Declan's voice had grown raspier with emotion, Jagger wished like hell he was sitting on the other side of the man...he wished his hand had joined Ren's in trying to offer silent comfort. And part of him had even wished he hadn't heard any of it because it meant acknowledging that Declan might not be the man Jagger had pegged him to be. It was bad enough that the kiss they'd shared was still fucking with Jagger's head – now he had to process this new information and try to understand what it meant.

It was at the point that Declan had finished his story that Jagger had decided to make his presence known but then he'd seen two things that had stopped him in his tracks. The first had been the way Declan had looked at Ren in that brief moment after Ren had touched him and the way Ren had looked at Declan. Not only was Jagger now one hundred percent certain that Declan was gay, he was almost just as certain that Declan was in love with the younger man. And Ren...

The confused look that had passed over Ren's expression had been the second thing Jagger had noticed and he knew the look had had nothing to do with trying to figure out how to comfort someone and everything to do with coming to terms with some new realization. Declan hadn't seemed to notice but Jagger hadn't missed it. He couldn't have since it was the same thing he was going through whenever he looked at either man. Wanting more but not knowing exactly what 'more' meant.

Before he could dwell on the discovery for too long, he heard it - they were laughing. Not just one of them either. Jagger couldn't see them from his position but the deep rolling chuckles and the slightly higher pitched laughs tugged at something deep inside of him and he was both happy and sad at the same time. He waited for the laughter to die down and then pushed away from the tree.

"You guys out here?" he shouted to make sure they heard him coming.

"Yeah, over here!" he heard Declan say. Jagger forced a smile to his lips as he cleared the tree line. Both men greeted him with brief smiles but whatever closeness had been between the two seemed to have dissipated with his presence. As he made his way down towards them, he realized he should have just left them alone and returned to the cabin but he'd selfishly wanted to be a part of the moment they'd been sharing. But from the awkwardness that suddenly stifled the air around them, they clearly didn't want to share that moment with him.

~

"You sure you don't want to stay for dinner?" Ren asked as he leaned against the doorframe and watched Jagger load the few items he had into a small black bag.

"No, I need to get back and check in on things. Get some fresh clothes."

Ren didn't say that another hour wouldn't change any of that because there was something off with the man. He was sullen and withdrawn and had been since he'd joined them at the lake. They hadn't lingered after Ren had managed to reel in the fish and ultimately convinced Declan they should release it. The walk back to the cabin had been made primarily in silence and Ren had found himself surprisingly comfortable between the two men – like nothing could touch him with Declan leading the way and Jagger at his back. The trek had given him time to think about the feelings that had churned through him after his conversation with Declan but by the time they'd reached the cabin, he'd been no closer to understanding what was going on inside of him. As best he could figure, his mind and body were just trying to adjust to being around two people who were giving him the time and security he needed to try to get his head on straight. It was nothing more than that.

So why did Jagger leaving like this bother him so much? Why did he miss the easy going grin and the rich, deep voice that talked about anything and everything just so Ren wouldn't get lost in his own head? Why did the lack of interaction beyond common courtesy between Jagger and Declan irritate him?

"Are you going to see Dom and Vin?" Ren asked. He didn't miss the slight tensing in Jagger's shoulders as he zipped up his bag.

"Probably. I need to check in and see if they have any jobs coming up for me."

Right. Life hadn't stopped just because Ren couldn't get a grip on his.

"I won't tell them about you," Jagger said as he snagged the bag off the bed.

"I know," Ren responded. And he did. Somewhere along the way he'd grown to trust this man like he did Declan. It still didn't make complete sense to him why they'd go through so much trouble to help him but he wasn't foolish enough to throw away the opportunity. The words of both men had been haunting him since the day they'd pointed out how dangerous he really was. He hadn't believed it at first – he'd been under the naïve assumption that he could control his fear. But then he'd seen the bullet holes in the cabin walls and he'd heard the truth in Declan's voice when he'd told Ren that he'd almost taken Jagger's life. As much as he wished he could deny it, Ren knew that he was sick and that the fear, pain and guilt that had consumed him since the day he lost his team had turned into something dark and cruel that lived inside of him and that would lash out whenever he felt threatened or exposed. He'd proven that when he went after Mia…

Ren realized he must have gotten lost in himself for a moment because Jagger's hand closed over his shoulder. It was something he did often to bring Ren back but he doubted Jagger knew that his touch always left something behind. Something that was as over-whelming as it was comforting.

"I'll be back in a few days."

Ren nodded but didn't move as Jagger brushed past him. It took everything in Ren not to shift his body so there'd be more contact between them – so he could feel that soft warmth flow through him whenever Jagger's skin came into contact with his.

As he watched Jagger disappear into the kitchen, he heard a few brief words exchanged and then the front door was opening and closing. He couldn't make sense of the relationship between Jagger and Declan – they barely spoke and seemed to avoid spending too much time together in one room. But every once in a while Ren would catch them sharing a look between them that made Ren's gut churn with some kind of strange anticipation. Like he was witnessing something that he couldn't quite put his finger on but that he was afraid he would miss if he looked away even for a second.

God, he really was a fucking mess. The whole point of this arrangement had been so that he could start working things out in his head but even in those rare moments where the fear and panic inside of him eased, what he was left with was a mess of emotions he had no idea how to deal with. And they had nothing to do with the hell he'd been through in the last year.

"Ren?" Declan called.

"Be right there," he said. "Just gotta wash up."

Ren went to the bathroom attached to his room and splashed some cold water on his face. He grabbed a towel from the rack and ran it over his face but paused when he saw his reflection staring back at him in the mirror. His hair was slowly starting to grow back and cover the scars on his head where he'd been struck repeatedly with the butts of several guns. He'd always been amazed that his captors had tempered their blows enough to keep from killing him. The scars on his face would eventually start to fade but he knew they'd never disappear entirely. For some reason the men who'd tortured him hadn't shredded his face with the box cutters like they could have. Maybe so that he'd still be recognizable for the countless pictures they'd taken of him. But the pictures had been worthless since they'd never managed to get his name out of him. It was the one thing he'd been able to hold on to.

"Ren?"

Ren turned to see Declan watching him with concern. He forced himself to finish drying his face and put the towel away. Declan's sharp eyes never seemed to miss anything so Ren pasted a smile to his lips and hoped to hell it reached his eyes because he didn't want the questions that he knew would someday come – the questions about what exactly had happened down in that hole and why he'd been the only one to walk out alive.

"Dinner ready?" Ren asked lightly but when he made a move to leave the bathroom, Declan stepped in his path.

"You know you can tell me anything, right?" Declan said softly.

God, how he wished that were true. But no man, not even one as kind hearted as Declan Hale, would be able to offer Ren forgiveness for the things he'd done. And the idea of Declan looking upon him with judgement...recrimination. No.

"I'm really hungry, Declan," Ren lied. The pain in his gut had nothing to do with hunger and everything to do with the man standing in front of him.

"Okay," Declan said as he stepped aside. "Just remember we could have been having fish tonight."

Ren had no idea if he managed a smile or not but from the worried look in Declan's eyes, he suspected it wouldn't have mattered either way.

~

*A*ny guilt Declan had felt in not telling Ren about Rafe's return disappeared as he watched Ren pick at his food. It had been foolish to hope that the brief, fun moment they'd shared down at the lake as Ren had reeled his catch in would have been indicative of some kind of miraculous recovery on Ren's part. But seeing the old Ren, the one with the infectious laugh and bright smile - even for the briefest of moments - had given Declan hope that the man he'd fallen in love with so long ago was still in there. Not that it would change anything for Declan either way because the feelings that had plagued Declan for years hadn't wavered. If anything, they grew stronger the more time he spent with Ren. And if that wasn't confusing enough, fate had decided to be the cruel bitch that it was and throw Jagger into the mix.

In the hours it had taken to drive to the cabin from Seattle the morning after Rafe's stunning appearance and admission, Declan's main thought had been to get to Jagger. Get to Jagger because he'll know how to handle this. He'll know if not telling Ren is the best way to go. He'll be there to lean on...to draw strength from.

And damn if Declan hadn't been right. Just seeing Jagger stride from the cabin towards him had had Declan wishing he could wrap his arms around Jagger and cry. Cry for Rafe and what had happened to him. Cry for Vin and Dom and the hell that was just starting for them. Cry for Ren and the truth he would need to someday face.

Although Declan had been too much of a coward to actually seek the comfort of Jagger's hold, Jagger had done what Declan needed him to do anyway. The powerful hand closing around his arm had done what no words could have. But everything had changed again when Jagger had tried to talk to him about that kiss. That one amazing, too brief kiss. What he wouldn't have done to give in to Jagger's hold on his waist, to feel his big hand sliding farther across his thigh to his aching flesh. To claim Jagger's mouth and take his time exploring every surface and drinking in his sweet taste.

"What do you know about Mia?"

Declan glanced up from the food he'd been moving around on his plate and saw Ren watching him. He was surprised at the question since Ren hadn't shown any interest in Vin's girlfriend since the day Ren had shot her stalker. Even when he'd had the opportunity to talk to Mia in person after the incident, Ren had gotten agitated and shut down when she'd attempted to convince him to return home.

"She's an incredibly strong woman. I think she's really good for your brother."

Ren continued to pick at his food but didn't put any into his mouth.

"She said something about being prisoner the night I..."

A flush of shame crossed Ren's features and Declan guessed what he'd been about to say. The night Ren had attacked her. Declan remembered the phone call he'd received from Dom that night telling him that Ren was on the run and armed. The thought that Ren would have attacked an innocent woman was beyond comprehension for Declan but it had just been further proof that the damage to Ren's psyche was extreme and beyond his control.

"Your brother didn't tell you how he met her?"

"He may have," Ren said quietly. "I don't remember," he admitted

"Mia's father was a rapist and serial killer. He murdered 13 women after he raped Logan's younger sister."

Ren lowered his fork and Declan knew he had his complete attention.

"About a year ago he found out Logan's sister, Savannah, had returned to the state after finishing school in the Midwest. He tried to abduct her and shot Logan in the process. We thought Hamilton had died in the fire that he'd set in Logan's bar but he'd managed to escape and kidnapped a couple of Dom and Logan's friends last January. He was about to kill them when Mia beat him to death with a pipe. Turned out he'd been holding her prisoner for two years."

Declan pushed his plate away and took a long swallow of his soda as he studied Ren. The young man was clearly trying to process what he was hearing.

"There were marks on her neck," Ren said.

"Her father put shock collars on the women he abducted. Mia too. It was linked to an underground fence but had been modified with a small charge that would detonate if the person wearing the collar passed over the perimeter of the fence. The man you shot, Owen Pritchett, was Hamilton's accomplice. He modified Mia's collar so the charge wouldn't go off because Hamilton had promised her to Pritchett in exchange for services rendered."

Ren suddenly pushed back his chair and moved to the kitchen. His hands gripped the kitchen counter hard as he leaned against it, his eyes boring into the laminate countertop.

"Go on," Ren said though he didn't look up. When Declan didn't immediately continue, Ren did look up and said, "I'm okay, Declan. I need to hear this."

Declan watched him closely for another long moment and was satisfied when Ren didn't drop his gaze again. "Mia managed to escape her room but she didn't have a way to get the collar off. But it didn't matter because her father had told her if the collar was removed it would go off. She didn't know Pritchett had disabled the charge when she chose to cross the fence," Declan said slowly and waited for his statement to register.

Ren's eyes slid closed. "She wanted to die."

"After she killed her father she was hospitalized. She refused to eat or drink so they ended up institutionalizing her. A reporter got into the psych ward and took her picture so Dom decided to hide her at Vin's house since he was out of the country searching for you."

Ren straightened and walked the length of the kitchen and combed his hands through his hair. His back remained to Declan when he whispered, "I didn't mean to hurt her."

"You didn't, Ren. Yes, you scared her but you didn't hurt her."

"I wanted to protect him."

"Vin?" Declan asked.

Ren nodded. "He was always the one watching out for us but no one ever watched out for him. When I saw her there, in his house…I thought she was going to do what all the other women did to him."

Declan knew he was treading on shaky ground so he carefully said, "Was it just about protecting him, Ren?" When Ren tensed, Declan knew his instinct had been right. "Who was she?"

Ren remained quiet for so long that Declan figured he wasn't going to get a response.

"She was an aid worker. Her name was Geraldine. Geri. She was sweet, pretty. Everything else over there was so ugly and cruel. She was refreshing to be around." A good two minutes passed before Ren continued but Declan just waited.

"I thought I was in love with her. The group she worked for did a lot of their relief work in some of the hardest hit areas and I was always afraid for her. A year ago my team was tasked with escorting some tactical weapons - high value cargo. Even though our route wouldn't be decided until the day of transit, I knew the chances were good that her group would be working in one of the villages nearby."

"You warned her," Declan said softly.

"I didn't give her specifics. I just told her to tell her superiors to pick a different place to work that day. About a week after the ambush I was being moved to a different location. When I saw her with them I thought she'd been taken prisoner too."

"She wasn't," Declan observed.

Ren shook his head. "My Pashto wasn't the greatest but I understood enough to realize she was making a deal for the weapons we'd been moving. When she saw me she started yelling that no one was supposed to have been left alive. They shot her in the head before she even finished her sentence."

"You were trying to protect her, Ren. It's understandable."

The harsh, ugly laugh that erupted from Ren's throat made Declan cringe.

"I sold out 20 good men for a pretty face and a nice ass."

Declan was out of his chair before he could think better of it and he was turning Ren around to face him before he even realized what he was doing. "You trusted her," Declan said.

"Exactly," Ren snapped. "And look where that got me."

Ren's bitterness was so profound that Declan released his hold on him when Ren tried to pull free of him.

"Ren," he said as Ren brushed past him.

"Leave me alone, Declan. Just leave me alone."

But Declan grabbed his arm before he could escape. "I can't," he said quietly. When Ren began struggling against him, Declan gently forced him back against the counter and used his body to keep him from escaping. As slight as Ren still was, Declan knew the man had the skills to disable him if he really wanted to so Declan quickly reached into his pocket.

"Let's go for a drive," he said as he opened his hand so Ren could see the contents. Blue eyes lifted to meet his and when Ren nodded, Declan felt a surge of relief go through him and he carefully opened Ren's hand and placed the fuses for his GTO in them.

CHAPTER 5

"Mom, you home?" Jagger called as he stepped into the small house. He knew the answer before his mother spoke because the scent of cinnamon hit him just as he was closing the door.

"In here," came the response but Jagger was already on his way to the kitchen. All the excitement at seeing his mother had fled when he'd smelled that sickening spice and it came as no surprise when he saw his mother hovering over a three-layer cake covered in streusel. She was carefully drizzling the thick, white icing in precise lines along the top of the cake and didn't look up until the last drop fell into place.

"Hi baby," she said as she came around the counter to where he stood in the doorframe.

"Hi," he said softly as he leaned down to kiss the top of her head as her arms wrapped around his waist. Even towering over her petite, 5-foot frame, Jagger never felt more like a kid then when she hugged him and called him 'baby.'

"Can I fix you something to eat?" she asked as she rubbed a flour covered thumb over his unmarred cheek. Just once he wished she'd touch the scarred one the same way. Not because he actually needed her touch but because he wanted her to stop pretending like the jagged, raised flesh wasn't there.

"No," he answered and she quickly released him to return to her cake. Jagger wasn't surprised to see her carefully carry it to the refrigerator and put it inside. *He* liked his coffee cake to be slightly chilled, not room temperature.

His mother finally seemed to relax and a bright smile covered her face as she began untying her apron. Her dark brown hair was fashioned into a simple twist at the nape of her neck and bits of flour clung to the few strands that had escaped. Brown eyes darted between him and the dirty counter and he could see the indecision in her gaze. She was clearly on a timetable but didn't want to disregard his presence. Jagger decided the course of action for her and began collecting some of the dishes she'd used to make the cake and dumped them in the sink. When he began washing them, he felt his mother's small hand brush over his back. The small gesture of appreciation took the sting out of knowing his mother was having company tonight.

"Where have you been this week?" she asked as she began drying the dishes he placed on the counter next to sink.

"Work stuff," he answered. He didn't really like lying to his mother but he sure as hell couldn't tell her he'd been holed up for the better part of a week in a remote cabin in the mountains with a man who'd nearly taken his life with one almost perfectly aimed bullet.

"Did you make any new friends?"

Jagger bit back a laugh at the odd question. To his mother he was still the scrawny little boy who had had trouble connecting with others in class. He'd never had the heart to tell her that the kinds of kids she'd always hoped he'd befriend in school were the same kids who had tortured him with endless taunts about how stupid he was. Well, until he'd turned twelve and towered over all of them anyway. After that, one hard punch to the ringleader's upturned nose was all it had taken to make sure the shit kids said about him was done behind his back and not to his face.

"A couple," he answered and cursed the image of Ren and Declan arguing heartily over the fate of the fish that hung from the end of

Ren's pole. The look on Declan's face when the huge fish had been dropped back into the water had been priceless.

"And how's Connor?"

"Good," he answered simply.

"That poor boy," she whispered and he wasn't surprised to see her make the sign of the cross against her chest. "I will pray for him," she said softly.

He wanted to tell her that if God had been listening to any of her prayers, Connor sure as shit wouldn't have ended up with an asshat like Jason Sutter. Nor would he be struggling with the after effects of a war that had nearly destroyed him.

Jagger finished the last of the dishes and watched his mother carefully dry each and every one. Her eyes shifted to the clock above the stove and her hand came up to push a stray hair behind her ear.

"What time is he getting here?" Jagger finally asked.

His mother kept her eyes downcast when she said, "Half an hour."

Jagger knew she wanted all of that time to make sure she looked her best. It was on the tip of his tongue to say that after twenty years the fucker shouldn't care that she had a few hairs out of place or a couple of wrinkles in her dress. But he didn't because it wouldn't matter. It never mattered. His mother was in love and Jagger was smart enough not to ask her to choose between the son who thought she deserved better and the man who kept her hidden in the shadows. Because he already knew what her answer would be.

"I'm going to be out of town on and off over the next couple of weeks so if you need anything and can't reach me, call Connor, okay?"

"Okay, baby," she said softly. "Stay safe."

"Love you," he said as he leaned down to brush another kiss over her head. He didn't look back as he left the house because that would just make him want to stay and try to talk some sense into her. But between the fucking cinnamon and the look of anticipation in his mother's flushed expression, he knew nothing he said would change anything and he just needed to get the hell out of there.

∽

"What's going on between you and Declan?" Ren asked as he took a swing at Jagger. Even though his question had clearly caught Jagger off guard if the surprised look on his face was anything to go by, Jagger still managed to deflect the punch. It had been Jagger's idea to do some boxing, sans boxing gloves, after their normal hike had failed to ease the tension in Ren's system.

"Nothing," Jagger responded as he landed a blow to Ren's stomach. If they hadn't been training, Ren knew the strike would have taken him to his knees.

"It's like you guys can't stand to be around each other," Ren said as he took a few steps back and used the hem of his T-shirt to wipe his brow. Jagger went to the porch and grabbed their bottles of water and handed one to him.

"I guess we just don't have a lot to talk about."

"Besides me, you mean?" Ren said before he took a long swallow of the icy water. Although the mountains were typically cool this time of year, a heat wave had struck the region and even at the higher altitude they were feeling it.

"Yeah," Jagger said.

Jagger had returned the day before yesterday but his mood hadn't seemed to have improved in the time he'd been gone. In fact, he'd been even quieter than usual. And his interaction with Declan as they'd exchanged a few words outside of the cabin before Declan left was nothing less than ice-cold. Ren hadn't been able to make out any of the words from his spot on the porch but the whole conversation had taken less than a minute and then Declan's car was disappearing down the dirt road that led down the mountain.

"You want to tell me what your nightmare was about last night?" Jagger asked as he put his water back down and raised his arms in a defensive stance.

Ren sighed and got rid of his water, then dragged his shirt off over his head. It was becoming far too routine that his questions went unanswered but Declan and Jagger had no issue with wringing out every one of his thoughts and feelings whenever they could.

"If I say no?" Ren asked as he took a jab at Jagger's mid-section.

"You say no and we do three miles tomorrow."

"You know, some day I'm going to get my full strength back and you won't be able to pull all your he-man shit on me," Ren said sourly. He'd like to think his foul mood had to do with the terrible images that had ripped him from sleep at three this morning but the fact was that there'd been other things bothering him long before he'd drifted off.

"Understood," Jagger responded. "Talk."

"Well, Doctor," Ren said as he sidestepped Jagger's next swipe. "I was in this airplane and it started to go down-"

Ren's words died in his throat when Jagger suddenly grabbed his arm and yanked him forward several steps.

"Bullshit," Jagger said, his eyes completely serious. "The truth," he ordered.

The anxiety that went through Ren at the feel of Jagger's fingers pressing into his skin had absolutely nothing to do with being afraid and everything to do with something else. Something he'd been trying to deny since the day Declan and Jagger had stormed into his life.

Since for whatever reason Jagger could read him like a book, Ren opted for the truth. "I was trying to climb out of my hole. It was hard because my hands were covered in blood."

"Did you make it to the top?" Jagger asked.

Ren nodded but shame coursed through him and he closed his eyes. No way could he be looking at Jagger when he admitted what he'd done. It didn't fucking matter that it was a dream. "You and Declan were there. I reached for you but you both fell. You grabbed on to me as you went over but I couldn't hold onto you and the edge too so I..."

"You let us go," Jagger finished for him.

"You were both screaming my name as you fell," Ren whispered. Disgust coursed through him and he tried to pull his arm free of Jagger's grip.

"That's it?" Jagger asked.

Ren could only manage to nod his head.

"Look at me," Jagger said. Ren tried to keep his eyes closed but when Jagger repeated the words they popped open of their own accord.

"That is fucking horseshit," Jagger declared.

"I'm telling you the truth."

"I know that," Jagger said. "The problem I have is that you're actually even giving it a second thought."

"I did some stuff over there," Ren started to say but Jagger cut him off.

"What you did was survive. A year, Ren. A whole year in that Godforsaken place. I can count on one hand the number of men I know who could live through what you did."

Ren yanked his arm free. "Don't put me on some God damn pedestal, Jagger. I wished for death...prayed for it."

"Yet you're still here," Jagger said as he straightened and crossed his arms.

Fury went through Ren. "Yeah, I'm still here! For what? To hurt the people who love me most? To put them and everyone I come into contact with at risk?"

"If that's all you can see then it'll be like you never got out of that hole," Jagger said quietly.

"Maybe it would have been better if I hadn't," Ren finally admitted, though the words sounded wrong even as he said them out loud.

"Tell that to Vin," Jagger responded. "And not just because it would have cost him a brother, but the woman he loves too."

"Mia-" Ren began to say.

"Would have been in that parking lot that day no matter what. She's alive because of you. It doesn't matter why you were there – what matters is you stepped up. So don't bother feeding me any more bullshit about people being better off if you weren't around. And if you truly wanted to die you would have done it the moment you got your hands on Vin's gun. Now either take a fucking swing at me or start heading for the lake because I'm hot as hell and we're either going to fight or swim. Your choice."

Ren couldn't understand the lightness that suddenly went through him but maybe it didn't matter. Maybe Jagger was just telling him something he'd been trying to tell himself since the day he opened his eyes and saw his brother leaning over him. He'd been too afraid to hope that day or even in the days that followed but maybe that's what the feeling inside his chest was. Maybe there was a way to live with the past but not in it. To forgive himself for the things he'd done even if he could never forget them. And if he could do those things it meant he had a future…it meant he could someday go home. The idea was too overwhelming so Ren did the only thing that made sense. He turned and began walking towards the lake.

~

J agger jolted awake and was scrambling out of the bed before the second gunshot shattered the silence. Even as he processed that the sound was coming from a ways off and was likely the result of a rifle, concern filled him and he ran down the short hallway to Ren's room. When he saw that the door was open, he knew in his gut that Ren wouldn't be curled up in his corner on the thin sheet that was all that separated his body from the hard floor.

"Ren!" he called as he turned on the light and scanned the room. The room was indeed empty so he rushed to the kitchen, turning on lights as he went. His only solace was that the front door alarm hadn't gone off so that meant Ren was still in the cabin. Another gunshot cracked through the air at the same moment that Jagger flipped on the living room lights. Both relief and concern went through him at the sight of Ren standing frozen in the middle of the room, his eyes closed. Another shot had Ren flinching before Jagger could reach him.

"Ren," Jagger said softly as he closed his hands over Ren's upper arms. He wasn't wearing a shirt and his skin was chilled despite the warm air.

"I'm okay," Ren managed to get out though his voice was strained. Jagger realized Ren was fighting to not lose himself to his panic and a surge of overwhelming pride went through Jagger.

"It's probably just a hunter," Jagger offered as he rubbed his hands up and down Ren's biceps. Ren was still too thin but in the nearly three weeks they'd been holed up in the cabin, he'd managed to put on some weight and his strength and stamina were slowly returning. His pale skin had lost the sallow tint that had been evidence of the malnutrition that had ravaged his body and his face no longer had that sunken appearance that had made him look like a walking skeleton. "It'll be over soon."

Ren nodded at Jagger's statement but didn't open his eyes. He kept sucking in deep breaths as the minutes passed.

"At least it's not the fourth again," Ren finally said as his breathing evened out and Jagger felt the tension start to drain out of him.

Jagger chuckled. They'd known that the Fourth of July would be rough on Ren so both he and Declan had watched Ren together that day. Even high in the mountains, they'd still heard the remnants of fireworks and no amount of distraction had been able to prevent a few instances of panic on Ren's part. But between the two of them, they'd managed to talk Ren down each time and by the time the end of the holiday weekend had rolled around, Ren had been so completely exhausted that he'd actually slept through the last few hours of the festivities. Declan and Jagger hadn't fared much better in the sleep department and Jagger hadn't even woken up when Declan left the following morning.

"You okay?" Jagger asked as Ren finally opened his eyes. He tried to ignore the punch of lust that went through him but his traitorous body hardened as Ren's tongue darted out of his mouth to briefly run over his lower lip before disappearing again.

"Yeah," Ren said.

Let him go. Jagger's brain was screaming the command at him but his hands refused to obey and his grip on Ren's arms actually tightened. Warning bells went off in his head as he realized he was crossing a line he'd been trying to avoid for a while now but his body didn't give a shit. It knew what it wanted and it didn't care that Ren was vulnerable. It didn't care that any confusion Ren was facing regarding his sexuality had nothing to do with Jagger and everything to do with Declan. And it didn't care that there was another man it wanted just as much as the one standing before him.

"Jagger?" Ren whispered.

If he'd heard only confusion in the way Ren said his name, Jagger would have been able to drop his hands and step away from Ren but the thread of desire as his name slipped from Ren's lips had Jagger pulling him closer. A shred of sanity managed to push its way to the forefront of his brain but before he could even consider it, Ren's head lifted and the last couple of inches of space that separated them fell away and warm, soft lips coasted tentatively over his for just an instant before covering his mouth completely.

Jagger groaned as a hot, wet tongue met his and he didn't even realize he'd wrapped his arms around Ren's body until he felt the heated skin of Ren's back rippling beneath his fingers. Ren's hard chest brushing his nearly stole Jagger's breath as their tongues dueled but when a stiff cock brushed against his, Jagger lost it and plunged his tongue deep into Ren's mouth. His whole body shook as long fingers skimmed over his scalp and settled at the back of his head as if to keep him from pulling away. But he had no intention of going anywhere as Ren returned his kiss with fervor.

～

*R*en's entire body drew tight as Jagger's mouth explored his and when he was finally forced to come up for air, Jagger's lips dragged across his jawline and then skimmed down his throat. Every soft kiss was punctuated with a sensuous lick and when teeth closed gently over the place where his neck met his shoulder, Ren was sure he would come in his pants. His fingers dug into Jagger's skin as he desperately tried to hold on to some shred of control but the hot flesh flexing in his grasp only made the fire inside of him burn hotter. And then that talented mouth was back on his.

Ren didn't recognize the ragged moan that fell from his own lips or the desperation that swept through him as he skimmed his hands down Jagger's wide back, each muscle rippling in response to his touch.

"Ren," Jagger breathed against his lips. Lust surged through Ren at how breathless Jagger sounded but when Jagger's hands closed over his ass, Ren froze as a tremor of unease went through him. Before he could work through it, Jagger's hands were shifting up and closing over his hips and pushing him back. Regret washed through him as Jagger's mouth pulled free of his.

"Jagger," he started to say.

"It's okay," Jagger interjected. "Go back to bed, Ren."

That was the last thing Ren wanted but he could tell just by looking at Jagger's hooded gaze that the other man was withdrawing emotionally as well as physically from what had just happened. Confusion swamped Ren as he nodded and quickly brushed past Jagger. His whole body was wound up as he hurried into his room and shut the door. But he bypassed his makeshift bed on the floor and went into the bathroom. He had the shower going within seconds and eased his sweats over his turgid cock where it lay pressed against his abdomen. His need had him climbing into the shower stall before the water was even lukewarm and his hand began jerking up and down his dick relentlessly. It took just minutes for his balls to draw up tight against his body and with the sound of Jagger's voice whispering his name, Ren came hard and fast.

Panting heavily, Ren kept stroking his cock as he leaned his head against his arm. The amazing beauty of his first kiss with another man was tempered by the fact that he'd fucked it up by freaking out when he'd felt Jagger's touch on his ass. It hadn't been that he didn't want the contact – it'd just been such a foreign sensation that he'd been caught off guard by it – or what it meant, rather.

Ren released his dick and turned around so his back was pressed against the smooth tiles. He'd been so caught up in trying to stave off an episode after hearing the gunshots that he hadn't even noticed Jagger was touching him at first. And when he finally had, whatever fear that had remained had disappeared and was replaced with a raw, aching need. The same need he'd been plagued with since the day he and Jagger had sparred and then gone swimming. It was exactly the same as what he'd felt around Declan too after the other man had shared his heartbreak over the loss of his sister.

Letting his body slide down to the floor, Ren closed his eyes and let the water pelt his face. While he knew there was nothing wrong with being attracted to another man – or in his case, two – he wasn't sure what to make of it since he'd only ever been attracted to women. Though, if he were being honest, there had been one man in his life who'd stirred something deep within him that he'd been unwilling to examine. But comparing what he'd felt for that man to the all-consuming need that Declan and Jagger brought out in him was like comparing the flame on a match to the inferno of a bonfire. And no matter what angle he looked at it from, in all likelihood, he was going to end up getting burned.

~

*D*eclan put his car in park but couldn't find the energy to get out. Between the extended hours at work and the long drive back and forth to the cabin, Declan was definitely starting to feel the strain. Add in the fact that every day he kept Ren's location a secret from his brothers was another day he continued to lie to the only family he had left, as well as the never ending lust that wracked his body, and he was nearing his breaking point. He'd briefly considered reaching out to Zane earlier today but something he didn't want to think too much about kept him from making the call. Not that Zane would necessarily even be willing to meet him since their last interlude hadn't exactly ended on the best note.

A knock on his window had Declan turning to see that Jagger was waiting for him. They hadn't spoken since the day Declan had told Jagger about Rafe beyond a few necessary words to coordinate their schedules and give updates on Ren to one another. The man looked as shitty as Declan felt.

"Bad night?" Declan asked as he climbed out of the car.

"I've got a job so I'm not sure when I can get back," was all Jagger said as he turned and began walking to his car.

"No problem," Declan said as he followed, his eyes taking in the tension that was rolling off of Jagger in waves. "I've got a lot of vacation time saved up. I'll tell my Captain I have a family emergency."

Jagger opened the door to the backseat of his car and tossed his bag in. He had yet to look at Declan and that fact bothered Declan more than it should. "You okay?" he asked.

"There was a hunter in the area last night. Ren did great – he kept it together on his own."

Something in the man's voice was wrong and when he opened the car door to get behind the wheel, Declan stepped forward and slammed it shut before he could get in.

"What's going on with you?" Declan asked softly.

"I'll text you when the job's done and I'm on the way back."

It wasn't the wisest thing to do but Declan grabbed Jagger's arm. "Talk to me."

"Talk to you?" Jagger said with a harsh laugh. "Now you want to talk?"

Declan didn't really have a response to that so he kept his mouth shut.

"Yeah, that's what I thought," Jagger muttered as he tried to open the door once more.

An irrational fear went through Declan that whatever was driving Jagger to leave like this would be the same thing that kept him from coming back. "I don't know if I can do this without you."

That got Jagger's attention and his steely eyes met Declan's.

Declan fidgeted as the truth of his own words sank in. "He needs you...I need you," Declan whispered. He forced his eyes to stay on Jagger even though his nerves had him wanting to drop his gaze. He couldn't even remember the last time he'd admitted such vulnerability to anyone, let alone a man he couldn't deny his attraction to.

"I don't get you, Declan," Jagger finally said.

"If it makes you feel any better, sometimes I don't get me either,"

Declan admitted. "Drive safe," he added as he reluctantly turned and headed back to his car to get his stuff.

"Declan."

Declan forced himself to turn around and tried to mentally prepare himself for whatever Jagger was going to say.

"I'll see you soon," Jagger said. And then he was getting in his car and driving away leaving Declan in his wake.

~

*R*en bit back the combination of disappointment and desire that went through him at the sight of Declan reaching into the cabinet to pull out a couple of coffee mugs. Disappointment because Declan's presence meant Jagger was gone and had left without even saying goodbye and desire because Declan's jeans were drawn tight over his ass. Declan hadn't noticed him yet so Ren took his time studying Declan's muscular build and the way his clothes lovingly hugged his body. Biceps bulged beneath a gray T-shirt that clung to Declan's broad chest and he had a heavy gold watch on his right wrist which meant he was likely left-handed. His thick, caramel streaked blonde hair had just the tiniest bit of curl near the nape of his neck and Ren couldn't help but wonder what it would feel like if he ran his fingers through it.

"Morning. Coffee?"

Ren jerked out of his daze and hoped like hell Declan hadn't noticed him staring.

"Please," Ren said as he went to the refrigerator and pulled out the milk.

"Jagger told me what happened last night - he said you did great."

Ren nearly dropped the milk at Declan's words but then he realized Declan was talking about the gunshots.

"I did okay, I guess," he said as he placed the milk on the counter and reached for the mug Declan had filled for him.

"I'm really proud of you, Ren," Declan murmured just before he took a sip of his coffee. Ren nearly moaned at the sight of his lips caressing the mug.

"Thanks," Ren managed to say. "So Jagger left?"

"Yeah, he had a job. Not sure when he'll be back."

Ren managed to pour some milk into his coffee but had to force the bitter brew down since it suddenly tasted like sawdust in his mouth. So Jagger hadn't even stayed long enough for them to talk about what had happened last night. Maybe he'd lost interest after Ren's momentary freak out. Maybe he'd never really even been interested.

"Any idea what you want to do today?" Declan asked.

Ren lifted his eyes to meet Declan's and another flash of lust went through him. He wondered what would happen if he reached out and took the mug from Declan's broad fingers and then dragged him down for a kiss. Would his lips be as firm as Jagger's? Would his hands electrify Ren's skin wherever he touched it? Would he moan Ren's name against his lips like Jagger had? He highly suspected the answer to all three questions would be yes.

What the hell was wrong with him? It was unlikely that Declan was even gay. Hell, was he even gay himself? Or bi? Growing up, he'd had his fair share of girlfriends and he'd been attracted to Geri from the first time he'd met her. He'd always thought the sex was pretty good but the few stolen moments with Jagger last night had made him harder than he'd ever been and jerking off in the shower with an image of Jagger had made him come so hard that he'd been unable to remain standing afterwards. And he'd never obsessed over a woman the way he did with Jagger and Declan.

"Ren?"

"Sorry, what?" he asked as he struggled to remember what he and Declan had been talking about.

"I asked if there was something in particular you wanted to do today."

"Right," Ren said. His whole body itched and felt restless and he knew he wouldn't be able to sit still long enough next to Declan to do any fishing. And he sure as hell didn't want to go hiking and watch

Declan strip off his shirt as he was often inclined to do as the sun's rays beat mercilessly down on them.

"Can we go somewhere?" he finally asked.

Declan looked at him with concern but finally nodded. "Sure. Did you have a place in mind?"

"Town." His response surprised even himself since the whole point of coming up here had been to get away from people.

"You sure?" Declan asked worriedly.

Ren nodded. "I need this, Declan."

Declan swallowed the rest of his coffee down and put his mug into the sink. "Let's go."

~

*D*eclan leaned back against the seat as the GTO's engine rumbled as he let the car roll to a stop at the last light on the way out of town. It was the first time Ren had let him drive the car though he suspected that stemmed more from the fact that driving seemed to relax Ren in a way that nothing else could. And with the stress he'd put himself through this past week, Ren had needed to take advantage of anything that would help him remain in control. But today it seemed like everything had caught up with Ren and he'd handed the keys to Declan with a tired smile. And within minutes of Declan putting the car in gear, Ren had fallen asleep.

Declan glanced over at the young man whose head lolled to the side. Warmth spread through Declan at how at peace Ren looked and Declan had to resist the urge to reach out and run his fingers across his cheek. Since the day Jagger had left, they'd been following the same routine of driving into the small town at the base of the mountain but Ren had pushed himself a little more every day. The first day had just been parking the car near the small harbor and sitting there while Ren tried to process the noise and commotion as cars and tourists accessed the marina. After that, they'd driven to the coast and walked along the beach before hiking to a small bluff that overlooked a lighthouse at the entryway to the Strait of Juan de

Fuca, a waterway that led from the Pacific Ocean to the San Juan Islands.

Day two had been a repeat of day one but by day three Ren had insisted on getting out and walking around the harbor. He'd tensed up as people walked towards them and had always looked over his shoulder as they passed but he hadn't had any episodes. Day four had been walking around the town itself but the sound of a car backfiring had almost destroyed the progress Ren had made. Declan had managed to talk him down before his anxiety caused him to react violently to the people that moved past them, completely unaware of the danger they were potentially in. And today...today had been a fucking miracle because Ren had insisted that they sit in a restaurant and eat a meal. The sound of several dishes crashing to the floor as two wait staff collided had put Ren on edge momentarily, but then he'd smiled at Declan and said he was okay before Declan could even ask. They'd still walked along the beach but Ren had been so relaxed that Declan had actually felt tears sting his eyes. Because for the first time since this nightmare had started, Declan saw a glimpse of the old Ren. The Ren that smiled for no reason. The one whose eyes shone with pleasure because of something as simple as a beachgoer's friendly dog coming up to say hi.

"You like the car," Declan heard Ren murmur. Declan gave him a brief glance and felt his stomach drop out at the soft look on Ren's face. He looked...content.

Too overwhelmed to speak, Declan managed a nod.

"It looks good on you," Ren said. His silky smooth voice had Declan's whole body tightening up and it wasn't until the car behind them honked its horn that Declan realized he'd been staring at Ren... or rather, they'd been staring at each other. Declan managed to press the gas pedal down enough to get the car moving.

"I always wanted a car like this," Declan admitted.

"Why didn't you get one?"

"Too flashy I guess."

"You think I'm too flashy?" Ren said with a laugh and the sound actually caused goosebumps to skitter across Declan's skin.

"No," Declan responded with a chuckle. "I think you can pull this kind of car off. Even when you were a kid."

"You didn't know me when I was a kid," Ren said with confusion.

"I guess you seemed that way when we first met."

"I remember. It was at Sylvie and Dom's wedding."

A flicker of pain went through Declan at the mention of his sister but he forced it away. "You were the life of the party," Declan said softly.

"And you stayed in the shadows," Ren countered.

Ren had him there. The only pleasure he'd found that evening among a group of virtual strangers had been in watching Ren.

"Crowds have never really been my thing," Declan said.

"I guess we have something in common now," Ren said. Declan gave him a quick look but relaxed when he saw that Ren didn't seem upset by the observation.

"You'll get there," Declan said. "You're making amazing progress."

Ren was quiet for so long that Declan looked over at him once more. He was startled to see Ren's blue eyes studying him with curiosity.

"What?" Declan asked, unnerved by the intensity in Ren's gaze.

"If I get back there…back to who I was – will you still be there?"

Declan had no clue what Ren was talking about so he said, "We'll always be friends."

"Friends?" Ren said quietly. "Is that what we are?"

Was that disappointment in Ren's eyes? Declan's phone rang suddenly and whatever tension had been in the air was broken. He glanced at the Caller ID but didn't recognize the number. As much as he wanted to clear up whatever confusion was going on between him and Ren, Declan knew he couldn't risk missing a call from work. He'd handed most of his cases over to Adam Dwyer and he didn't want something to get thrown out of court on a technicality because the new guy didn't follow protocol.

"I need to take this," Declan said as he reached for the phone and pulled the car over to the side of the road.

"Hello?"

"Detective Hale?"

"Yes, who is this?"

"Detective Hale, this is Connor Talbot."

Declan's gut seized as he recognized the name. Jagger's friend.

"I'm not sure if you remember me," Connor started to say.

"I do. Is Jagger okay?"

Ren went on alert next to him but Declan didn't dare take his attention off the call.

"Um, he told me not to call you but I think he needs some help." The man's voice was unsteady and Declan forced himself to keep his own tone calm and collected.

"It's okay, Connor. Tell me what happened."

"He's in jail. He shot someone."

CHAPTER 6

"Where is he?" Declan snapped as he shot past Dwyer and began searching Dwyer's desk until he found the file he was looking for.

"Lock up."

"What are the charges?" Declan asked just as he found the file. When Dwyer didn't answer him immediately Declan looked up. "What the fuck are the charges, Dwyer?"

"He hasn't been charged with anything."

Rage went through Declan as he pulled up a program on Dwyer's computer and began typing. "Then what the hell is he doing in lock up?"

"Captain…" Dwyer began to say but stuttered to a stop.

"Spit it out Dwyer," Declan shouted as he quickly scanned the screen in front of him before closing the program out. He strode towards the back of the building and wasn't surprised when Dwyer fell in step behind him.

"Captain Mitchell said to put him there. He said he'd deal with him in the morning."

"And you didn't think to speak up?" Declan bit out. "The prosecutor tells you the shooting was justified and he's not pursuing charges yet you still put the guy in lock up."

"Captain said-"

"Fuck, Dwyer. You ever going to grow a pair?"

"Captain said the guy's bad news. He's going to talk to the prosecutor about additional charges – evading arrest, leaving the scene..."

Declan slammed through the door leading to the cells and flipped open the file in his hand. "Did you get his statement?" he snapped.

"He wouldn't give it to me."

Declan shoved the file at Dwyer and didn't wait to see if he would take it. He found Jagger in the last cell and winced at how wrong it looked to see him confined to the small space. How the hell had he ever thought Jagger was the type of guy who belonged in a place like this?

"Open it," he said to Dwyer though he kept his eyes on Jagger. He had no doubt that Jagger wasn't pleased to see him.

When Dwyer didn't move fast enough to suit him, Declan grabbed the key from his lax fist and opened the cell.

"Detective," Dwyer began to say.

"Let's go," Declan said to Jagger. Jagger didn't argue with him but he knew that the second they had more privacy, all hell was going to break loose. Little did Jagger know that Declan was more than ready for the fight.

"Sir, you can't-"

"The hell I can't," Declan snarled. "This man is in my custody now. If Mitchell wants to try and press some bullshit charges, tell him to contact Mr. Varos' attorney."

Declan stomped past Dwyer and led Jagger from the room. He was glad Jagger kept his mouth shut until they reached the car but he was surprised at how calm the man sounded when he finally spoke.

"Where's Ren?"

Declan started the car. "With Connor."

"You shouldn't have come here, Declan. I was handling it," Jagger said with obvious irritation.

"Is that what you were doing in that jail cell? Handling it? Did you even think to call a lawyer at least?"

"I don't need a lawyer. Mitchell would have backed off," Jagger stated.

"Oh yeah? Like all the other times?"

Jagger's head whipped around and he finally looked as enraged as Declan felt.

"What the hell did Connor tell you?"

"Just that Mitchell's had it in for you for years. He wouldn't tell me why. I looked up your record. Multiple arrests for shoplifting and vandalism when you were a kid. Two for disorderly conduct and assault after you turned eighteen. One of those assaults was against Mitchell himself."

Jagger turned his head away and stared out the window but kept silent.

"So that's it? I don't get any explanation?"

"I don't owe you anything," Jagger responded.

The comment both infuriated and stung Declan at the same time. It had been ridiculous to think that he and Jagger would ever be anything other than enemies to one another. Declan put the car in gear.

"I need to go back to the hospital," Jagger said when they reached the parking lot exit.

"Tell me about the shooting," Declan said.

"You know Cade Gamble?"

"He's one of Dom's men. He was protecting Logan last year when we realized Hamilton was still alive." He and Cade hadn't really gotten along, especially since Declan had initially struggled with the knowledge that Dom had moved on from Sylvie so quickly – something he knew now not to be true because he had no doubt that Dom continued to love Sylvie even as he built a future with Logan.

"Cade found Rafe in L.A. and brought him back to Seattle a couple weeks ago after someone took a shot at him. He asked me to watch Rafe this past week while Rafe did some volunteer work at Logan's foundation."

Declan couldn't help but be surprised not only that Rafe was back, but that he was working with his brother's lover. He had a ton of questions that he wanted to ask but kept silent as Jagger continued.

"Cade had me shadow him and Rafe this weekend when they went to Friday Harbor. We got back a few hours ago. I guess Dom and Vin were waiting for them in Cade's apartment when we got back but I don't know what happened – I just saw them leaving. Less than an hour later I see Cade come running out of the building yelling Rafe's name. Turns out Rafe took off on Cade and had exited the building through the garage so I wouldn't see him. He was crossing the street when a car came out of nowhere and tried to run him down. Cade got to him in time and took the brunt of the impact."

"Fuck," Declan whispered. "Is Cade okay?"

Jagger shook his head. "He was unconscious after the car hit them. Rafe was banged up pretty bad too. Fucker got out of the car and pointed a gun at Rafe. I got him before he could pull the trigger."

"Jesus."

"The ambulance got there before any cops did so I followed it to the hospital so I could stay with Rafe until I was able to reach his brothers. I asked the security guard in Cade's building to stay with the body and to let the cops know who I was and where I'd gone. Rafe was a fucking mess when he got out of the ambulance – I guess Cade had a seizure on the way there. Dom and Vin got there about a half an hour later. Cops showed up a few minutes later and arrested me."

Declan's phone rang and he glanced at the Caller ID. "It's Vin," he said to Jagger. "Yeah," he said into the receiver. "No, I already got him out. I'm bringing him to the hospital now. How's Cade?" he asked. He felt Jagger's eyes on him.

"And Rafe?" It took only another minute to get the information he needed and when he hung up he spared Jagger a glance. "Cade's in surgery – they needed to relieve the swelling in his brain. Rafe's okay but he's pretty fucked up about Cade."

Jagger sighed and nodded. As Declan pulled into the hospital parking lot and stopped in front of the Emergency Room entrance,

Jagger gave him an odd look...regretful almost. "You shouldn't have put Ren at risk to come here."

Disappointment went through Declan at the criticism. "You know what, Jagger? Fuck you," he snapped. "You want to handle this shit by yourself, you go right ahead. Get yourself a lawyer because you're going to fucking need it because I'm done."

Jagger didn't respond and the second he was out of the car and the door slammed closed, Declan hit the gas. Maybe Jagger didn't need him but Ren sure as hell did.

$\sim$

*R*en watched Connor move slowly behind the bar as he stocked bottles of liquor in the rack behind the bar. Something about the man's gait wasn't quite right.

"Lost it to an IED," Connor said and Ren looked up and realized he'd been staring.

"Sorry," he said.

Connor shrugged. "I find it easier just to get it out there instead of watching people try to figure it out for themselves."

"When?" Ren asked.

"Two years ago. One minute I'm doing a sweep of some shitty little building on the outskirts of Kabul, next minute I'm waking up in a hospital bed and the doctor's telling me my leg's gone below the knee and that I'm lucky to be alive. The two guys doing the sweep with me weren't so lucky."

Ren studied Connor and figured they were close to the same age. He was quite attractive but Ren didn't feel the same sexual pull that he did towards Declan and Jagger which served only to confuse him more. The man had been extremely welcoming when Declan had dropped him off, but it had been his boss, Mags, who'd caught Ren off guard when she quickly told the few patrons in the bar to get out. There had been a few grumbles but no one had argued with the big woman when she shoved them out the door and locked it and then turned off the *Open* light. She'd then made herself scarce, but not before telling Connor she'd be in the back if he needed her.

"How did you and Jagger meet?" Ren asked. Part of him really wanted to know but another part of him was concerned he wouldn't want to hear the truth.

"We met in Iraq about a year before he was discharged."

"You served in the same unit?"

"No, just on the same base. The only thing we had in common was that we were both gay. But somehow it just worked out and we hit it off. It was easy to keep in touch after he left the service. I didn't have any place to call home after I got out so I picked Seattle in case he ended up coming back here after his merc days were over."

It was the first time Ren had heard confirmation that Jagger was gay and the fact that Connor was too only made Ren wonder more at the true nature of their friendship.

"We've never been together," Connor suddenly said and Ren glanced up from the countertop he'd been idly rubbing circles into with his finger.

"None of my business," Ren murmured though the relief that went through him was ridiculous.

"You sure about that?" Connor asked as he slid a few wet glasses across the bar and handed Ren a towel.

He automatically began drying them as he contemplated how much to say. The man across from him was a stranger but the fact that Jagger clearly trusted him had Ren already feeling comfortable around him. When Declan had told him that Jagger was in jail, Ren had been beside himself with worry and he'd been the one to insist that they go and get him. But he'd been smart enough to know that he wasn't in any shape to go into a busy police precinct or to even wait in the car so when Declan had suggested they ask Connor to keep an eye on him, he'd readily agreed. He hadn't expected to like the guy and he certainly hadn't thought he'd be contemplating discussing something as sensitive as his sexuality with the best friend of one of the men he was obsessed with, but maybe having someone to talk to about it would help him figure out the jumble of emotions he couldn't seem to escape.

"Can you tell something about me?" Ren finally asked and he winced at how childish the question sounded, especially since he was asking it in such a roundabout way.

"You mean is my gaydar going off?" Connor said with a chuckle.

Ren couldn't help but laugh. "Yeah, I guess so."

"I didn't need gaydar to see the worry in your eyes when you told Declan to go get Jagger. Or the jealousy when you thought he and I were something more than friends to each other."

"Shit," Ren muttered. "Connor, I'm sorry…"

"Sorry for what?" Connor said. "It's about time that Jagger found someone who cares enough about him to be jealous. But that's not the only problem, is it?"

Fuck, he *was* completely transparent. Except to the two men who mattered apparently.

"It doesn't matter. I don't think they'll ever be able to see me as anything other than damaged and broken. And that's not even taking into consideration the fact that Declan is probably straight. Or that Jagger's loyalties lie first and foremost with my brothers."

Connor began collecting the glasses Ren had been drying. "So let me make sure I've got this straight," he began. "You managed to join one of the most elite units the armed forces has to offer and spent the better part of ten years completing missions that saved countless lives. You lived through what I can only imagine was pure hell for more than a year and when you finally escaped, you had the guts to walk away from the only family you have to keep them safe. But you won't fight for what you want with Jagger and Declan? Hell, fight's not even the right word considering you're not even willing to step into the ring."

Why did the way Connor said it make it sound so simple when the emotions that were running through him were anything but?

Ren handed Connor the last glass and shook his head. "I gotta say Connor, your talents are wasted behind that bar." He'd meant the comment as a compliment but the sudden sadness that came over Connor's features caught him off guard.

"Hey man, I'm sorry-"

His words were interrupted when there was a sharp rapping on the door. Ren instantly jumped to his feet and automatically put his back against the bar so he'd have both his hands free to defend himself.

"Ren, it's Declan," he heard Connor say from behind him, his voice low and soft.

The panic in Ren's chest eased somewhat but he couldn't make himself fully relax. Footsteps came around the bar but he was glad when Connor didn't touch him.

"I'm going to go let him in now, okay?" Connor said quietly though he didn't actually move until Ren managed to nod. Then Declan was standing in front of him, his big hands running up and down his arms.

"Shit, Ren, I'm sorry. I should have called to say I was here," Declan said.

Ren's voice finally returned to him and he willed himself to calm down. "So much for thinking I'd made progress, huh?" he said.

"You fucking amaze me every day, Ren," Declan said and Ren's body jolted when Declan's hand briefly caressed his cheek. God, how he wanted to believe the move wasn't just about offering comfort.

"Where's Jagger?" he asked when he realized Declan was alone. Declan's expression hardened at the mention of Jagger and he dropped his hand.

"I'll tell you in the car," Declan said. "Let's get going. We have a long drive back."

Ren nodded. Before Declan's arrival he'd been thinking that maybe they could stay in the city overnight but one look at Declan's tired features had him rethinking that plan. Being around the hustle and bustle of a neighborhood, no matter how quiet, would mean that Declan would have to be on a higher level of alert to make sure Ren didn't have one of his moments. And despite the strides he'd thought he'd made this past week, his reaction a moment ago made it clear that he still had a ways to go. At least at the cabin he'd be more relaxed which meant Declan could get the rest he clearly needed.

~

"*J* thought I made it clear you weren't welcome here anymore."

Jagger wasn't surprised to see that Declan was sitting on the living room couch since he'd seen the lights on as he'd driven up the dirt road that led to the cabin. He also wasn't surprised at the anger that lingered in Declan's tone. Jagger had been hoping they could hash this shit out in the morning but he doubted Declan was going to go for that. Not that Jagger could blame him – not after the way he'd treated Declan today.

"You said you were done but that doesn't mean I am," Jagger said as he dropped his bag to the ground and locked the door.

"How's Cade?" Declan asked.

"He made it through surgery but he hasn't woken up yet. Doctors are worried about possible brain damage."

Declan fell silent and Jagger used the moment to study the man on the other side of the room. He looked worn out.

"Why are you still up?" Jagger asked.

"Go home, Jagger," was Declan's response as he stood and began moving towards the kitchen. Jagger stepped in front of him to cut him off and was satisfied to see Declan suck in a sharp breath. The man might be pissed at him but he still wanted him.

"You said you needed me," Jagger whispered. "You said you couldn't do this without me."

He reached out to touch Declan but he stepped back before Jagger could make contact.

"So is that what this is about, Varos? You like being needed but you're such a big, tough badass that you don't need anyone or anything?" Declan snapped.

Declan tried to move past him again but Jagger grabbed him by the arm. Before Declan could utter a protest or pull free of him, Jagger yanked him forward and crushed their mouths together. Declan fought him briefly but as soon as Jagger ran his tongue over Declan's lips, his mouth opened and Jagger surged inside. The kiss was raw and carnal but before he could explore any farther, Declan shoved him away and wiped at his mouth. The pain at seeing Declan try to wipe away the evidence of what had just happened between them went bone deep and Jagger didn't know if he wanted to walk away or grab Declan again and show him how good it could be between them.

"Get out," Declan said harshly. The fact that he wasn't raising his voice meant Ren was likely asleep and Declan feared waking him. Jagger had no issue with using that fact to his advantage.

"Is that really what you want, Declan? Because that's not what your body is saying," he said as he looked pointedly at Declan's crotch and the outline of the erection pressed against his jeans.

"Is this just a game to you, Jagger?" Declan asked, his voice losing all of its anger. "Did you come all the way out here to spite me or something? To force me to admit that I'm attracted to men? Or is it that you want to hear me say I'm attracted to you?" Declan looked so dejected that Jagger didn't stop him when Declan went to move past him once more.

"Frank Mitchell is sleeping with my mother," he forced out just before Declan stepped around him. Humiliation flooded through Jagger as he felt Declan stop next to him but he forced himself to continue. "It's been going on for almost twenty years...since the first time he arrested me on a bogus shoplifting charge when I was fifteen."

This time it was Jagger who moved. He stepped farther into the living room but kept his back to Declan.

"Does your mother know Mitchell is married?" he heard Declan ask.

"She knows. She's known from day one but she believes him every time he says he's getting ready to leave his wife for her. In the beginning he needed to wait till his wife gave birth to their kid. Then it was waiting till the youngest kid was in high school, then college. His latest thing is he needs to retire first."

"Why does he have it in for you?"

Jagger forced himself to turn around though he found it difficult to raise his gaze. He couldn't even remember the last time he'd been unable to look another man in the eyes.

"Because I was always a threat...someone who knew his dirty little secret. He also knew I was trying to convince her to break things off with him so he kept pinning shit on me to drive a wedge between me and her."

"Did she believe him?" Declan asked softly.

"She said she didn't but I was never really sure. It had been just me and her for so long...anyway, when I was seventeen I threatened to tell his superiors. He lost it and came after me. He did this," Jagger said as he trailed his fingers over the jagged scar on his cheek. "Beer bottle," he added. "I thought for sure I had enough to get him out of our lives after that but he threatened to call Immigration and have my mother deported back to Greece if I said anything."

"But if your mother's been in this country since you were born-"

"She was too afraid to apply for citizenship after her work visa expired. The only family she had back in Greece had disowned her when they found out an American tourist had gotten her pregnant so she had nothing to return to. We moved around a lot until I was five and then settled here."

"Your father?" Declan asked.

"He brought her over here when she told him she was pregnant but he didn't want to marry her. He left her just before I was born and died in a car accident a year later. She named me Jagger because it was what he'd talked about naming me before he left her."

"What happened with Mitchell?"

"I knew my mom wasn't going to leave him and that she'd believe whatever lies he told her. I didn't want to force her to choose between us so I dropped out of high school. The dyslexia made it hard for me to keep up with my classes and I knew I wasn't going to graduate anyway, so I enlisted. The recruiter had a quota to fill so he lied about me having a diploma and the dyslexia. I only came home a half a dozen times in the past fifteen years. When Vin offered me a permanent role after we found Ren, I decided to give this place another try."

Jagger finally managed to lift his gaze and was surprised to find that Declan had moved closer. He wanted so badly to reach for him that he had to clench his fists at his side.

"Why didn't you call me when you were arrested today?"

"I didn't want you to see me like that. I don't ever want you to see me like that."

"Like what?" Declan asked gently.

"Like a loser," he admitted. He couldn't help but drop his eyes again as he forced himself to say the name Frank Mitchell had so often referred to him as in front of his mother...the name she'd never openly refuted to her lover.

"Declan, I'm sorr-"

The last word never made it past his lips because Declan was suddenly kissing him. He groaned as Declan's tongue slipped into his mouth and he couldn't help but wrap his arms around Declan's waist to keep him from retreating again. The kiss was slow and sweet and so very different from either of the two kisses they'd shared previously. It felt like Declan was worshipping him and he fucking loved it. It was all he could do to beg Declan not to stop this time but his words weren't necessary because Declan's hand wrapped around the back of his neck to hold him in place and Jagger knew in that instant that Declan wasn't going anywhere.

CHAPTER 7

*D*eclan backed Jagger up until he hit the wall and breathed a soft "yes" when Jagger's hands palmed his ass. It felt so good to feel the life surging through Jagger once again after watching all of it seemingly drain away as he admitted the truth about Frank Mitchell and his mother. It didn't surprise Declan one bit that Mitchell was an adulterer as well as an all-around bastard but to know what the cruel man had put Jagger through had enraged Declan. And that the man continued to wield his power over Jagger by using his mother's immigration status against him was just mind boggling.

As Jagger's hands coasted up his back, Declan closed his eyes and let Jagger take control of the kiss. But when he suddenly broke it off and held Declan back when Declan tried to push forward, Declan hesitated. Had he done something to turn him off? But a quick glance up at Jagger's face told Declan everything he needed to know and horror went through him as he realized they were no longer alone. He turned and saw that Ren was watching them from the entryway to the kitchen.

"Ren," he whispered stupidly as he dropped his hands from where they'd been resting on Jagger's waist.

He couldn't gauge the expression on Ren's face as he looked back and forth between him and Jagger but the silence was unnerving.

"Ren," Jagger started to say but Ren raised a hand as if to silence him and a chill went through Declan when Ren's bright eyes came to rest on him. Ren had yet to speak but since Declan was at a complete loss for words, it didn't matter at the moment.

Ren finally began moving and Declan was caught off guard when Ren didn't stop until he was almost completely in Declan's space. Their bodies were mere inches apart.

"Ren, I should have told you..." Declan began to say but Ren cut him off by placing his thumb over Declan's lips. To his shock, the rough digit began slowly dragging back and forth over his lower lip as if testing the texture.

"Are they as soft as they look?" he heard Ren ask.

"Yes," Jagger whispered, though his voice sounded even huskier than it usually did. "But you shouldn't take my word for it."

What the fuck? Declan opened his mouth to ask what was going on but the words died in his throat when Ren suddenly leaned forward and replaced his thumb with his lips. The kiss was soft and quick – a mere brush of one mouth against another, but it sent shockwaves through Declan's entire system. And before he could even register that Ren had indeed just kissed him, it happened again. But where the first kiss had been chaste, this one was not. It was all consuming just like Jagger's had been and he could only stand there as Ren's tongue stroked over his for the first time. It felt so amazing that Declan had to lock his knees to stay upright and he let his eyes drift shut just so he wouldn't be forced to wake up from what had to be the most spectacular dream of his entire life. And then it got better because he felt Jagger's hard body lining up along his back and a pair of firm lips sought out the nape of his neck.

Declan's whole body lit up as Jagger's hands disappeared beneath his T-shirt and explored his back while Ren's kiss grew more and more desperate. And then Declan did what he'd longed to do for so long – he took control of the kiss and plunged his tongue into Ren's mouth. Ren's whimpers of need were driving Declan insane and he wrapped his arms around Ren to keep him from backing away. But it was Ren who dragged him closer and began grinding against him. He was already so close to exploding that he knew it wouldn't take much to send him over.

"Beautiful," he heard murmured in his ear. "Fucking beautiful." Jagger's voice skittered over his skin and Declan bit back a moan when he felt blunt fingers disappearing beneath the waistband of his pants. Jagger's touch was hot and hungry and when a long finger brushed his crack, Declan tore his lips free of Ren's and reached behind him to drag Jagger's head down for a searing kiss. A hand began rubbing his dick through his jeans and Declan was too far gone to figure out whose it was. And it didn't matter because they were both giving him exactly what he'd needed for so long...what he'd been searching for his entire life. And then just like that his world came crashing down as a voice from the past reminded him that he couldn't be this man – this man that Jagger and Ren would need him to be.

"I can't," he whispered as he pulled free of Jagger's mouth and extricated himself from between the two hard bodies that had wrapped around him as if trying to protect him from the outside world. Jagger and Ren both released him, though they looked equally confused.

"Declan," Jagger began to say.

Declan shook his head violently. "I can't!" he shouted as his body grew cold inside.

Escape. He had to escape because even now he could see their questions and he knew that one more touch from either of them and he'd be unable to walk away. But instead of walking, he ran. And by the time his car reached the main road, the sounds of Ren shouting his name finally began to fade and he allowed the first tears to fall.

$\sim$

*D*eclan's fingers shook as he opened the motel room door but the sight of Zane sitting in his usual spot brought him absolutely no relief. But he forced the unnamed feeling that was rolling through him away and began tugging his T-shirt over his head. The drive back to the city from the cabin had done nothing to ease the feeling of loss that had overtaken him, so he'd called Zane from the road and asked him to meet him at their motel. As soon as he'd hung up the phone, a sour taste had permeated his mouth and a voice in his head had screamed at him to turn around. But he'd ignored it and continued on in the hopes that a few minutes with Zane would finally silence it.

Declan's desperation grew as he fumbled with the snap on his holster and by the time he got the gun free and had placed it on the nightstand, he knew in his gut that nothing Zane did to him would relieve what was happening to him. A ragged sob escaped him and he covered his mouth with his hand in an attempt to stifle the next one. As he lowered himself to sit on the bed, he heard Zane shift in his chair.

"Sorry," Declan whispered as he felt Zane come to a stop in front of him. To his shock, he felt Zane run his fingers through his hair. The comforting move was so unexpected that Declan closed his eyes and actually leaned into his touch.

"When are you going to stop punishing yourself, Declan?"

Before Declan could answer, someone pounded on the door so hard that it rattled against the frame. He felt Zane release him.

"Should I answer it?" Zane asked.

"Declan, open this God damn door or I'm going to open it myself!"

"Asked and answered," Zane said dryly.

"Open it please," Declan said as he forced his eyes open and dashed away the few tears that had begun to blur his vision. Zane gave him a concerned look and then went to the door and opened it. He seemed unsurprised when Jagger burst in, took one look at Declan's damp face and grabbed Zane by the shirt and slammed him against the wall.

"What the fuck did you do to him?" Jagger snarled.

"Let me guess," Zane quipped as he looked Jagger up and down and then glanced to where Ren stood in the doorway. "Jagger and Ren."

"Jagger, let him go," Declan said softly.

Jagger didn't immediately release Zane, though his hold loosened somewhat when he seemed to realize that Declan wasn't hurt. Ren moved past Jagger and Declan dropped his gaze when he saw the mix of betrayal and confusion in Ren's eyes as he took in the scene. Warm fingers brushed under his chin and he allowed Ren to tip his head up so that their eyes met.

"Are you okay?" Ren asked gently.

Declan brought his fingers up to close around Ren's wrist, but he didn't try to remove the hand that was now caressing his cheek. He managed to nod and the move seemed to be what Jagger needed to finally release Zane.

"Out!" Jagger snapped at Zane but Declan wasn't surprised when Zane didn't move. Zane's eyes shifted to his and Declan gave him a quick nod of ascent.

"Thank you, Zane," Declan whispered. Although he and Zane would cross paths on occasion as a result of their day jobs, Declan knew that no matter what happened tonight, his and Zane's liaisons were over. Zane left without another word and Jagger slammed the door behind him.

"How did you find me?" Declan asked as he reached for his T-shirt and pulled it over his head.

"I remembered this was one of the places you went the day I followed you. We decided to drive by on the way to your apartment just in case you were here and saw your car," Jagger said. His anger was clear in his tone and in the way his body simmered with tension as he hovered near the door. Declan wondered if he was just trying to get himself under control or if he was half expecting Zane to come back into the room.

"Why did you leave?" Ren asked as he lowered his hand from Declan's cheek and sat down on the bed next to him.

Declan dropped his head into his hands and rested his elbows on his knees. He'd been avoiding this moment his entire life but it hadn't done any good. His body was done denying what it wanted and his brain wasn't far behind.

"The cabin belonged to my grandfather. My parents traveled a lot when I was little so I spent almost every weekend there with my grandfather during the school year after my grandmother died when I was four. He taught me how to fish, hunt...everything. He was the only one I had until Sylvie came along."

Pain wracked Declan's body as images of his grandfather and Sylvie bombarded him. God, he missed them.

"I had trouble making friends in school and the kids used to pick on me because they thought I was weird. 'Socially awkward' the guidance counselor told my parents on one of the few times they actually made it to a parent-teacher meeting. My parents told me I should try harder to be normal like the other kids. My grandfather said I should tell the kids to fuck off," Declan said. A small smile flitted across his lips as he remembered his grandfather's gruff and endearingly simple declaration. He'd been so surprised to hear his grandfather using the F word that it had taken him a while to process that his grandfather was sticking up for him when his parents hadn't.

"I worshipped him," Declan whispered. "I didn't even think twice about telling him I was attracted to boys instead of girls. I just expected him to tell me it would be okay...that I was okay."

Ren's warm hand began to rub up and down his back and Declan stifled the need to beg Jagger to touch him too. But words were unnecessary because Jagger's hands came up to wrap around Declan's and force them away from his face. Jagger's fingers laced with his and Declan focused on the man who had squatted down in front of him.

"What happened?" Jagger asked softly.

"He told me it was wrong. That it was unnatural. He said I'd go to hell because God hated fags and that's what I would be. He made me promise I wouldn't ever act on it or mention it again. I was so afraid of losing him that I swore I wouldn't. I hoped things would go back to the way they'd been, but he started making excuses that he was busy when I was supposed to go visit him. Whenever I did see him, he asked me if I was a queer."

"How old were you?" he heard Ren ask.

"Thirteen," Declan said. "He died just after I turned seventeen. When I found out he left me the cabin, I saw it as some kind of sign that he really did love me but I convinced myself I had to keep my promise. He was the only one besides Sylvie who'd ever really loved me but he hated that part of me so I decided to hate it too – to pretend it didn't exist. So I never told anyone else, not even Sylvie, and I dated a few girls here and there when I started at the police academy. Then Sylvie got sick and it just didn't seem important."

Declan fell silent as he tried to regain control of his muddled breathing. Ren's soothing touch continued and Jagger made no move to release him. And neither man pressed him to finish his story.

"After Sylvie got better, I went back to work and found out the officer I was assigned to train under was gay. His name was Mac and the other officers in the department used to say some pretty bad shit about him and treated him like dirt. I was afraid that by working with Mac that they would suspect I was gay too so I asked to be reassigned. My request was granted," Declan said. Tears began to flow down his cheeks.

"I ran into Mac in the locker room the day my request came through. I was so embarrassed but he told me it was okay and that he understood. He told me he thought I was going to be a hell of a cop. That was the last time I saw him. He died that night in a shootout with some home invasion suspects because the backup he called for never showed up. The guys were joking about it the next day – they kept saying that the best kind of fag was the dead kind. Maybe if I hadn't asked to get reassigned..."

"You were young and scared, Declan," Jagger whispered. "It's not your fault."

"He had a boyfriend," Declan said. "I saw him at the funeral. It was just him and me – Mac's family had disowned him. I watched them lower his casket in the ground and I knew that if I ever said anything that that would be my future...Sylvie's future. Me in a box and Sylvie standing alone over my grave."

Declan reached up to wipe at his tears and a tissue was gently placed in his hand. "I wasn't with another man for the first time until I was almost twenty-seven. I went down to a gay club in Portland and let some guy pick me up. After that I went to different clubs in different cities when I couldn't deny the cravings. But the pressure of being discovered was too much so I stopped. I met Zane last year. He's a defense attorney so we'd seen each other a few times in the court-house and when he came to the precinct to meet with clients. He must have seen something in the way I looked at him because he confronted me one day in the parking lot – said we could give each other what we needed. He had as much to lose as I did so I agreed."

At the mention of Zane, he felt both Ren and Jagger tense up but neither withdrew from him. "We never kissed or really even touched," Declan admitted shamefully. "We barely even talked."

"Why did you come here tonight?" Jagger asked. "Is it because Ren and I both-"

"No," Declan quickly said. "No. I wanted what happened at the cabin. I wanted it so badly."

"Then why did you leave?" Ren asked.

"Because I wanted it too much," Declan said again. "And because I'm scared that one time won't be enough."

"You're afraid you'll have to choose between us and the lie you've been living," Jagger offered. Declan almost smiled at Jagger's blunt-ness. Though what Jagger said was true, it was only a half truth and even though his brain was warning him to keep his mouth shut, Declan's gut refused to start whatever this new aspect of their rela-tionship was off with a lie.

"I'm afraid I'll end up with even less than what I have now and what I have now isn't much."

"Declan," Ren whispered. Declan forced himself to turn to look at Ren. "This whole thing scares the shit out of me and I have no idea what any of it means but it feels right." Ren's hand came up to circle around his neck and Declan sighed when Ren's lips brushed over his. "Give this a chance, Declan."

Ren released him and Declan turned to Jagger. "Nothing happened between me and Zane tonight. He can't give me what I need," he said and he glanced at Ren to make sure he'd heard him too.

Jagger nodded and rose to his feet and pulled Declan up with him. A deep, hungry kiss followed and then Jagger and Ren were kissing and Declan was sure he'd never seen anything more stunning then the two men wrapped around each other. Where there should be jealousy, there was only a burning hunger.

As Jagger reached for him to pull him into their embrace, Declan held back and said, "Not here."

There was no way in hell he'd tarnish the memory of what was about to take place between the three of them by having it happen in this ugly motel room that had only ever served as an escape from his self-imposed prison…this place that had always left him a little emptier every time he left it.

"Your place," he said to Jagger and then he reached for Ren's hand and laced their fingers together before he dragged Jagger down for one more kiss.

∾

*J*agger reached up to adjust the rearview mirror and bit back a groan at the sight of Declan and Ren kissing as their hands roamed over each other's bodies. Thank God his townhouse was only a few minutes away because at this rate he'd either end up getting into a car accident because he couldn't keep his eyes on the road or he'd get arrested for the second time today for speeding and indecent exposure. He hadn't been willing to risk Declan changing his mind, so he'd insisted that Declan ride with them and they'd return to the motel to get his car later. But he hadn't considered the fact that Ren would climb in back of the car and that the two men wouldn't be able to keep their hands off each other.

A sliver of doubt went through Jagger that he was the odd man out and that Declan and Ren didn't really want or need him tonight but his next glance in the mirror nearly stopped his heart. Declan's eyes connected with his in the reflection as he kissed Ren and they stayed with him as his long, thick fingers began stroking over Ren's cock through his jeans. Ren's moans and whimpers filled the car and Jagger bit back a curse as his own dick pressed uncomfortably against his pants. Jagger forced his eyes back to the road but couldn't stop himself from checking the mirror every few seconds and each time he did, he saw that Ren's legs were splayed open on the seat bench as Declan rubbed him. But what caught Jagger off guard was that Ren was watching him now too and every time Jagger drove underneath a street lamp, the light illuminated the pleasure that shone in Ren's eyes as Declan's caresses drove him higher. And then Declan's hand slipped inside of Ren's pants and Ren cried out.

"Declan, please," Ren whispered harshly.

"Please, what?" Declan asked.

"Please, I need to come."

"Jesus," Jagger muttered as he shifted desperately against the seat but the move provided absolutely no relief.

"Should I let him come, Jagger?"

"No," Jagger said softly. "Keep him there," he ordered.

"Jagger!" Ren nearly yelled. But before he could say anything else, Declan's mouth closed over his once more and Jagger pushed down on the gas. He was pulling the car into the garage less than three minutes later and he was out of the car before he'd even jammed it into park. He barely remembered to the hit the button to close the garage door before he was striding to the back door and yanking it open. He dragged Ren out and slammed the door closed, then pushed Ren up against the car and crushed their mouths together. He felt Ren's fingers clutch his shirt and he barely registered the door on the other side of the car opening and closing. As he shoved his tongue down Ren's throat, he felt fingers working between his and Ren's hips and then he heard a zipper being dragged down. Ren cried out against his mouth and punched his hips forward and Jagger glanced down to see that Declan had closed his hand around Ren's length and was stroking him slowly.

As Ren writhed against him, Jagger turned and sealed his mouth over Declan's. Their kiss turned languid and slow but Ren's escalating moans told Jagger that Declan's hand had increased its pace. Jagger tore his lips free of Declan's and dropped to his knees. He looked up and saw that Ren's eyes were closed.

"Ren, look at me," he said firmly. It took Ren several long seconds to respond and he actually didn't until Declan stopped moving his hand. He seemed surprised to see Jagger on the floor and his mouth parted in anticipation as he registered what was about to happen.

"Tell me you want this," Jagger said. As overwhelmed as Ren was by the all the new sensations bombarding his body, Jagger needed to be sure that he was okay with what was happening.

"Yes," Ren whispered.

Jagger held Ren's gaze as he bypassed Declan's hand which was still wrapped around Ren's nearly purple cock and instead licked over one of Ren's lightly furred balls. He gave the other the same treatment and then sucked it into his mouth.

"Fuck," Ren whispered, but he kept his eyes open. Jagger saw that one of Ren's hands was hanging on to the door handle of the car while the other encircled Declan's wrist on the hand he had resting on Ren's hip.

Jagger licked and sucked each testicle over and over and then dragged his tongue up Ren's length. Declan removed his hand and Jagger shuddered when he felt it stroke over his head and finally come to a stop on the back of his neck. Jagger traced the ridge around the head of Ren's cock and then flicked his tongue into the slit on the top. He repeated the slow torture and then added to it by sucking just the tip of Ren's cock into his mouth and making love to it as if it were Ren's mouth. Ren groaned and tried to punch his hips forward but Jagger used his hands to keep him from moving. He shifted his eyes up and saw that Declan and Ren were going at it with rushed, desperate kisses.

"Jagger, please!" Ren shouted as he ripped his mouth from Declan's. Declan's mouth immediately began sucking on his neck and his big hands closed over both of Ren's wrists to keep him from reaching for Jagger like he clearly wanted to. Jagger decided to take pity on Ren and sucked him in to the root, automatically relaxing his gag reflex. He took in a deep whiff of Ren's musky scent as he pressed his nose against the wiry hair on Ren's groin and then dragged back up, applying suction as he went.

"Declan, I can't! It's too much," Ren cried out.

Jagger swallowed Ren back down and began bobbing up and down on him relentlessly. He released his hold on Ren's hips and was rewarded with a hard thrust that had him gagging as Ren pushed in as far as he could.

"Come for us, baby," Jagger heard Declan command and the husky order had Jagger almost coming in his pants. Seconds later, he felt the first splash of Ren's release hit the back of his throat and Ren's shout of pleasure ricocheted through the garage.

"Fuck!" Ren kept repeating the word over and over as his orgasm consumed him. When Ren's release finally began to slow, Jagger gave him one final lick and then stood and reached for Declan. As they kissed, Declan licked the remnants of Ren's come off Jagger's tongue.

"I need you," Declan said against his mouth. "Inside me," he added and before Jagger could answer, Declan's mouth was on his again.

~

*R*en couldn't believe that his sated body was capable of feeling anything after what Jagger had just done to him but sure enough, the sight of Declan and Jagger kissing had his dick stirring once more. And then Declan spoke his words to Jagger and a whole new bout of lust pooled in Ren's belly.

"Inside," Jagger said and he reached for Declan's hand and snagged his arm around Ren's waist.

By the time Jagger had dragged them into his bedroom, Ren's original nerves returned. From the moment he'd covered Declan's mouth with his back at the cabin, Ren knew what he wanted, but the unknown of being with another man, let alone two, had had anxiety mixing with his desire. When he'd first heard Declan and Jagger talking after Jagger's return to the cabin, he'd feared he'd have to intervene because the anger in Declan's voice had been palpable. And then Jagger had made his crushing admission about his mother and from Declan's side of the conversation Ren had figured out that the man who'd put Jagger through so much hell growing up was another cop, someone Declan knew. Learning that Jagger had also been dealing with dyslexia since he was a child had caused several things to click into place for Ren including his mention of wanting to be a fighter pilot when he enlisted but not being able to and the fact that he always used an app on his phone to read texts back to him. Ren could only imagine how vulnerable the disorder must have made Jagger feel growing up or the challenges he faced in the adult world.

When he'd heard the pain in Jagger's voice after he'd told Declan he didn't want to be seen as a loser, Ren had nearly gone into the living room himself so that he could offer comfort. But it had only taken a few seconds of silence followed by soft moans to tell Ren what was going on and he hadn't been able to stop himself from turning the corner and entering the kitchen where he had a perfect view of Declan pressing Jagger against the wall. The sight of the two men in each other's arms had meant so many things to Ren...it had provided confirmation that Declan was into men as well as proof that whatever tension existed between Declan and Jagger hadn't been about disliking each other.

They were utterly beautiful together and as passionate as their kisses had been, the emotion behind them had been something he'd never forget. And something he absolutely needed to be a part of. So when Jagger had seen him, Ren had remembered Connor's words about fighting for what he wanted and he'd stepped into the living room and finally done just that. And when Declan had run, he'd been the one to tell Jagger they were going after him. The drive to the city had been done mostly in silence but when Ren's nerves started to get the best of him, he'd reached his hand across the console and Jagger had been there to take it. But the last thing Ren had expected was to find Declan with another man and he'd felt a betrayal streak through him that was nearly as profound as when he'd learned Geri had used him.

Ren had never thought he'd see someone as strong as Declan look so broken as he sat there in that cheap motel room on the ugly, stained bedspread. And at that point Zane's presence hadn't mattered to Ren, nor had the fact that Declan had sought the other man out instead of choosing to be with him and Jagger. All he'd cared about was taking away Declan's pain and after hearing about his grandfather's cruelty, Ren prayed he and Jagger could do just that.

As he watched Jagger reach for the hem of Declan's T-shirt, Ren stifled a moan at the sight of the two men's bare chests pressing against each other. He wasn't sure when Jagger's shirt had been removed, but between the rippling muscles and seeking hands, Ren's own body began to come alive again and he quickly stepped behind Declan and began trailing his fingers down Declan's spine. Declan turned his head enough to seek out Ren's mouth for a kiss and then Jagger was reaching over Declan's shoulder and stealing a kiss for himself.

"Off," he heard Jagger say as he reached around Declan and tugged on Ren's shirt. Ren had never considered himself someone who would get a thrill out of taking orders in the bedroom but from the second Declan and Jagger had inflicted their game of sensual torture on him in the car, Ren knew he wouldn't protest a single thing that either man wanted to do to him. He yanked his shirt off and began working on his pants which he'd managed to zip up but not button before Jagger had dragged them from the garage. As he toed off his shoes, Declan's pants suddenly dropped to the floor and were quickly followed by his underwear. The sight of Declan's perfectly round ass had Ren's heart in his throat and he couldn't help but stop what he was doing and reach out to run his palms over it.

Declan froze up at the contact but pressed back against Ren's hands a moment later. At some point, Jagger had gotten Declan's shoes off and the pants were completely gone but Ren was too focused on the flesh beneath his fingers. When he let his pointer finger slip down Declan's crease, he felt Declan's hands reach behind him and search out Ren's thigh. Another hand grabbed one of Ren's and then a glob of lube was placed on his finger.

"Get him ready," Jagger whispered an instant before he dropped to his knees and sucked Declan's cock into his mouth.

"Shit!" Declan shouted and slammed his hips forward.

Ren watched Jagger's fingers wrap around Declan's ass, the tips biting into Declan's pale flesh. And then he was pulling Declan's cheeks apart and Ren got his first glimpse of Declan's hole. It flexed over and over as Jagger worked Declan's dick down his throat and it wasn't until a bit of the lube dripped onto the floor that Ren woke up from his haze of lust. The second his slick finger brushed over Declan's opening, Declan whispered a harsh "yes." It was all the encouragement Ren needed and he began massaging the lube around the hole. He'd never had anal sex with any of the women he'd been with, but he knew Declan would need more preparation so he sucked in a breath and gently began pressing his finger into Declan's body. The pressure and resistance that he met with were unexpected and a shimmer of uncertainty went through him. He was about to tell Jagger that he couldn't do this for fear of hurting Declan, but Declan took the decision away from him and pressed his body back against Ren until his hole collapsed and Ren's finger glided inside to the first knuckle.

"Yes," Declan moaned and he pulled forward almost to the point that Ren's finger slipped free of him, then shoved back again, sucking Ren's digit deeper this time around. Declan's whimpers of pleasure finally registered with Ren and he took over and pushed his finger in as far as it could go. Declan's body was like a vise and his channel rippled around Ren's finger as he worked the lube around.

"Jagger," Declan said.

Jagger must have heard something in Declan's voice because he let Declan's cock slip from his mouth and then he was standing and pulling off his own pants even as he kissed Declan over and over again. Ren pulled his finger from Declan's body and wasn't surprised when Declan turned in his arms and began kissing him. Ren felt the bed hit the back of his legs as Declan walked him backwards and then the mattress was cradling his body. Declan quickly tore away the pants that had been wrapped around Ren's feet and then he was lowering his weight on to Ren's body. Ren automatically made room for him by opening his legs and he sighed when their cocks brushed. He'd long since gotten hard again and the feel of Declan's flesh on his had his dick dripping. But he couldn't help the niggle of fear that went through him. Would Declan want to be inside him while Jagger was fucking him? What if it hurt too much? Would all this come to an end?

Would he be left to watch Declan and Jagger lose themselves only in each other because Ren couldn't be what they needed?

"Hey," Declan whispered.

Ren forced his eyes up to meet Declan's and the gentleness he saw there was humbling. "Nothing happens that you don't want," Declan said.

Ren nodded and forced the lump of emotion in his throat back so he could speak. "I don't think I'm ready for you to…" Jesus, he was too much of a fucking coward to even finish the statement. He wanted so badly to be an equal partner but he just couldn't get past his fear of the unknown.

"Just hold me, Ren," Declan breathed against his lips before he kissed him. "I just need you to hold me."

That was something he could absolutely do.

~

Jagger's fingers trembled as he rolled the condom down his cock. The sight of Declan and Ren wrapped in each other's arms and exchanging kisses had Jagger's knees feeling weak. What was supposed to be a night of simple fucking was turning into something entirely different and even though he knew it was too fast and it wasn't something any of them could sustain, he wanted it more than he'd ever wanted anything else in his entire life. He finally had a chance to be part of something amazing and even if it was for only one night, he sure as hell was going to take full advantage.

As he listened to Declan reassure Ren, Jagger stepped forward and knelt on the bed and settled himself between Declan and Ren's legs. He let his hands roam over Declan's back as he enjoyed the sight of Ren's hands drifting down to knead Declan's ass. The two men were grinding their cocks together desperately and Jagger knew he'd come long before he ever got inside of Declan if he didn't speed things up because just listening to their heavy pants and soft whimpers was killing him.

"Open him for me," Jagger said to Ren as their eyes connected and he saw the lust flash in Ren's eyes as he got Jagger's meaning and much like Jagger had done earlier, Ren used his hands to split Declan's cheeks open. The fluttering, lube slickened hole greeted him with hungry anticipation and Jagger quickly guided his cock to it. He placed his palm on Declan's lower back to hold him steady as he pushed forward and bit out a curse when Declan immediately bore down on him. The heat and pressure that welcomed Jagger had him groaning in relief and he reveled in the feel of Declan's body pulling him in. By the time he was fully seated, Declan's body was shaking beneath him and he felt a momentary pang of concern.

"Declan, am I hurting you?" he asked as he reached up to close his hands over Declan's shoulders. Declan's face was buried in Ren's neck and Ren was peppering him with soft kisses.

Declan shook his head but didn't respond otherwise and it was then that Jagger realized Declan was too overcome with whatever he was feeling to speak. Jagger slowly pulled out a bit before pushing back in and Declan moaned in pleasure. With every surge into Declan's body, Ren and Declan groaned as their cocks slid against each other. Jagger tried to focus on slow, steady strokes that he knew would build up the tension in Declan's body but when he felt a hand close over his where he had it resting on Declan's hip, Jagger looked up to see that Ren was watching him with a combination of wonder and something else that went so deep that Jagger was terrified to put a name on it. His control snapped and he began driving into Declan over and over and he quickly used his free hand to pull Declan up enough so he could squeeze his hand between Declan and Ren's bodies. He wrapped his hand around both their cocks and began stroking them so the pace matched his thrusts.

It took just minutes until he felt his balls draw up tight against his body. As fire began to shoot up his spine, Jagger's measured plunges became choppy and uneven and every time he slammed into Declan, his own body pressed Declan farther onto Ren. He finally gave up the battle and lay flat over Declan as he humped into him repeatedly. He managed to keep his hand on both cocks that pulsed and surged in his hold but it was his hips pushing Declan against Ren that provided the friction that had both Ren and Declan begging for relief. He had no idea who went over first but it didn't matter because both men beneath him shouted and he felt liquid fire spurt over his hand in endless jets. It was enough for Jagger's own body to let go and he actually bit into Declan's shoulder as his release claimed him. His hips jerked endlessly against Declan as blissful agony tore through every nerve ending. And as Declan's inner walls continued to milk his still pulsing dick, he closed his eyes and smiled when he felt a pair of lips brush over his. He had no idea whose they were and the fact that it didn't matter scared the shit out of him. But he did the only thing he could do and returned the kiss with everything he had left in him.

CHAPTER 8

Something was wrong. No, not wrong...different. Not bad different – just different. It took Ren a moment to figure it out as his eyes slowly came into focus and then he realized what it was. He was in a bed instead of the floor. And not just any bed but a fucking huge one with soft sheets and a heavy comforter. And the pillows...when was the last time he'd used a pillow?

Ren glanced at the clock on the nightstand and saw that it was almost eleven. He had no idea if it was eleven at night or in the morning since the curtains were closed. The light on the nightstand was on so he was able to examine his surroundings. The first and most disappointing thing he realized was that he was alone. The next thing he noticed was how warm and inviting the décor of the room was. Everything looked new including the oak bed and dresser as well as the leather chair in the alcove on the far side of the room. There was a flat screen TV on a stand across from the chair and he saw a box sitting near it that said *DVDs*.

There were no pictures on the wall but he did see a few on the dresser including a couple of Jagger with men in military garb. There was also a picture of Jagger with a tiny woman with dark hair. He almost smiled at the thought of someone as big as Jagger coming from a woman as petite as the woman Ren was certain was his mother.

Ren pushed the covers back and swung his legs over the bed. His body still had that pleasantly sated feeling that had overtaken him once his orgasm had worn off. He wasn't sure how long the three of them had lain there after Jagger had brought them to an explosive climax but he remembered the feel of Declan's warm breath drifting over his neck as he'd tried to slow his breathing. There'd been no desire to move even as the weight of the two men pressed down on him and he'd actually been disappointed when Jagger had lifted his weight onto his arms. But he hadn't just disappeared like Ren had thought he might. No, he'd simply locked his arms and began kissing his way along Declan's neck and shoulders. Then he'd leaned down and stroked his tongue over Ren's mouth before slipping inside. Not once had any of them spoken and at some point Ren had nodded off because he had no idea what had happened from that point on. A glance at his stomach and dick showed that someone had been thoughtful enough to clean the proof of his and Declan's release off of him.

A sudden sound jerked Ren from his thoughts and he tensed when he heard a computerized woman's voice saying his brother's name. He realized it was Jagger's phone and his eyes settled on Vin's name as the strange sounding ringtone repeated it over and over. A sudden sadness came over him as he realized it would only take one swipe of his finger to hear his brother's voice. He felt tears sting his eyes as the unexpected longing went through him.

"You okay?" he heard Jagger say.

Ren looked up and saw that Jagger was leaning against the door-frame of the attached bathroom. A white towel was slung around his hips. If he hadn't been so distracted, he would have enjoyed the sight of Jagger's wide chest and broad shoulders.

"I miss them," Ren admitted.

A second later Jagger was standing in front of him, his fingers skimming over his short hair. He could tell Jagger could feel the scars on his scalp because he would skim each one as his fingers caught on them.

"You can answer it," Jagger said.

Ren smiled as he imagined Vin's shock at hearing Ren's voice out of the blue and then the look on his face as he registered what it meant that it was Jagger's phone he was answering.

"Vin was always the most levelheaded of all of us but I think he'd blow a gasket if he knew what I'd done."

He felt Jagger drop his hand and was surprised when he stepped back. It was when he saw the look of disappointment on Jagger's face that he realized the other man had misunderstood him. He grabbed Jagger's wrist before he could retreat any farther and stood as he pulled Jagger flush with his body.

"I meant he'd be upset that I dragged you guys into my disappearing act, not because of what happened last night."

Jagger smiled. "Maybe don't go into the details about last night. Vin's a pretty understanding guy but you're still his kid brother."

Ren chuckled but his humor quickly faded as he realized there was only a thin towel separating his and Jagger's cocks. "Where's Declan?" he asked as he released Jagger's wrist and let his hand travel up Jagger's arm. His fingers pressed against the intricate tattoos that covered the surprisingly smooth skin and he reminded himself that someday he'd need to ask Jagger what they meant.

"Making breakfast. Or lunch rather," Jagger said. His voice had grown heavy and Ren could feel Jagger's cock pressed against him.

"Can I touch you?" Ren asked as his other hand hovered over the spot where Jagger had tucked the towel into itself to keep it on.

Jagger only nodded and Ren hoped it was because he was too turned on to do anything else. It took only a flick of the wrist to release the towel and then it was gone. Jagger's cock stood long and thick against a thatch of dark hair and as he studied it, drops of pre-come leaked from the head. The sight had Ren licking his lips and before he could reconsider it, he swiped a finger over the liquid and sucked it into his mouth.

"Christ," he heard Jagger mutter and then Jagger's mouth was crushing down on his. He let Jagger take control of the kiss but the second he wrapped his hand around Jagger's dick, Jagger sucked in a breath and looked down to where they were connected. Ren had seen plenty of dicks in his life since the army didn't exactly offer privacy but he'd never touched one besides his own. And he sure as hell hadn't experienced the rush of power that was now surging through him as Jagger watched his hand with hungry anticipation. As he began stroking Jagger, he wondered if his inexperience would be a turn off but from the shallow pants coming from Jagger, he guessed it wasn't. And when he dropped to his knees and briefly touched his tongue to the weeping crown, the grunt Jagger let out had the last of Ren's hesitation dissipating.

The salty, musky flavor came as a surprise to Ren as he licked Jagger over and over but it quickly grew on him and when he reached the head of Jagger's cock on his fourth pass, he experimentally closed his mouth over it. Jagger let out a loud curse which only encouraged Ren to take more of him in. Hands closed around his head but didn't push him down or try to control him in any way. Jagger's girth was impressive and Ren's cheeks began to ache as he added suction. He tried to take more in but his gag reflex kicked in and he couldn't quite get the hang of relaxing it enough to pull Jagger any deeper. So he settled on what he could do which was suck as hard as he could as his tongue swirled around the flared tip. He remembered how much he'd liked it when a girl had once hummed around his own dick when she'd been giving him a blowjob so he tried the same thing and smiled around Jagger's cock when he felt the grip on his head tighten. But before he could do it again, Jagger was dragging him up and kissing him and then he was being lowered to the bed.

Hands explored his body as Jagger's lips trailed a path down his neck but when he felt Jagger begin licking over the scars that covered his chest, Ren tried to sit up. But Jagger's hands closed around his wrists and gently pinned him to the bed as he leaned up and kissed Ren once more.

"They don't bother me," Jagger said against his lips.

"They're ugly," Ren said.

"Nothing about you is ugly," Jagger said firmly. "You're fucking perfect."

"I was weak."

"We all carry scars, Ren. Maybe not on the outside but they're there. It doesn't make us weak."

Ren fell silent as Jagger again began moving down his body but he didn't move his arms when Jagger released him and began kissing the scars once more. Jagger didn't miss even one and by the time he'd reached Ren's navel, Ren was beyond caring about the scars. He bit back a moan when Jagger took him into his mouth and began sucking him gently. But it wasn't enough so he reached down and grabbed Jagger's head to hold him in place as he surged upwards. Jagger took every thrust that Ren gave him but he pulled off and crawled back up Ren's body before Ren could protest.

"I want you to fuck me," Jagger said. Excitement slammed into Ren at the thought but the disbelief in his eyes must have shone through because Jagger said, "I want everything you and Declan can give me."

Ren managed a nod. Jagger pulled him to his feet and then he was reaching into his nightstand and pulling out a condom and a bottle of lube. Ren managed to get the condom on but his mouth went dry as he watched Jagger pour some lube on his finger and reach behind himself.

"Turn around," Ren heard himself order. "I want to see."

Jagger sucked in a breath at the demand but he quickly spun around and bent over. His finger was working between his cheeks and Ren stepped forward and used his hands to separate them so he could watch. The sight of Jagger's entire finger jammed into his hole had Ren's cock hardening to epic proportions. Jagger's moves were rough and jerky and as his finger popped free, Ren actually groaned at the sight of Jagger's entrance flickering as if in invitation. Jagger started to stand, probably to move to the bed, but Ren's impatience got the best of him and he placed a hand on Jagger's back to keep him from moving. Jagger hesitated only for a moment before he reached a hand out and gripped the corner of the nightstand to brace himself. As Ren stepped closer, he sensed another set of eyes on him and a thrill went through him at the sight of Declan standing in the bedroom doorway, his eyes glittering with lust. He wore only a pair of jeans but the button had been released and Declan's hand was jammed deep down his pants.

Ren returned his gaze to Jagger's beautiful ass and guided his cock to the opening. Just like the night before when it had been his finger breaching Declan, the feel of Jagger's body opening to his invasion was all consuming and it took everything in him not to just shove his dick in as far as it could go. As he watched the head of his dick disappear inside of Jagger, Ren closed his hands around the man's hips and held him place as he kept up the pressure. Jagger groaned and the tight hole suddenly gave way, allowing Ren to sink all the way in to his base. His thighs brushed the back of Jagger's as he hung there for a moment before slowly pulling back out. He could already tell that he wouldn't last long because it just felt too damn good and he hoped like hell he could last long enough to bring Jagger his pleasure. But Declan seemed to sense his dilemma because he stepped into the room and went around to Jagger's front.

Jagger didn't seem surprised to see him and he opened instantly to the kiss Declan gave him. The sight was enough of a distraction to have Ren slowing his pace but as Jagger straightened just a little and Declan dropped to his knees, Ren's grip on Jagger tightened because he knew what was coming. He couldn't see Declan but felt Jagger's whole body jerk as Declan took him into his mouth. Any hope Ren had of keeping things slow disappeared and he began gliding in and out of Jagger. Jagger's moans increased as Ren's thrusts pushed him forward and Ren shifted his stance just enough so that he could see Declan. And sure enough, Declan's mouth was open wide as Jagger's dick shuttled in and out of the perfect O his lips had formed. Declan didn't even have to move because it was Ren's powerful lunges that were forcing Jagger's dick deeper and deeper into Declan's welcoming mouth.

Ren canted his hips slightly when Jagger straightened a little more and he heard Jagger shout as if in pain. Ren forced himself to slow his pace in case he'd inadvertently hurt Jagger but Jagger quickly yelled, "Again!"

When he did it again, it elicited the same reaction and suddenly Jagger was desperately meeting every thrust. He cursed every time Ren slammed into him and Ren finally realized he was nailing Jagger's prostate. It took just three more strokes before Jagger's orgasm hit him hard and the overwhelming pressure on Ren's dick sent him over the edge. Stars danced before his eyes as he shot into the condom and he heard Declan moan at almost the same exact time. Ren's convulsions went on and on and he continued to pump his dick into Jagger long after every last drop of his release was wrung from his body. When he finally had nothing left, he began to pull free of Jagger's warmth but Jagger reached behind him and grabbed Ren's thigh. Ren got the silent message and stayed exactly where he was.

~

"*D*etective Hale, thought you were on leave," Declan heard the desk sergeant say as he strode past the main desk.

"Captain in his office?" Declan asked.

"Uh, yeah, but I think he's on a call with the mayor-"

Declan ignored whatever else the man had to say and climbed the stairs to the second floor. He bypassed his desk and headed for Mitchell's office. He ignored the secretary who told him the Captain was busy and threw open the door. Mitchell was leaning back in his leather desk chair, his feet on the desk and his arms behind his head. His thin smile faded as Declan entered.

"Uh, Your Honor, I'm going to have to call you back," Mitchell said calmly though his eyes flashed with fury. The sight had Declan's blood firing.

"Everything okay?" came the voice on the phone.

"Everything's good, Bill," Declan said as he leaned over Mitchell's desk and spoke just above the speakerphone that Mitchell had been using. "Just a minor emergency," Declan added.

"Declan, that you?" the mayor asked and Declan smiled coolly as Mitchell's eyes widened in surprise.

"Yeah, it's me. How are you?"

"Good, real good."

Mitchell slowly pulled his feet off the desk and straightened in his chair. His eyes never left Declan's as Declan spoke.

"How's Monica?" Declan asked.

"Keeping busy," the mayor chuckled. "Keeps reminding me to invite you to dinner. You haven't met our newest grandbaby yet, right?"

Declan enjoyed the sight of Mitchell tensing up.

"No, I haven't," Declan said. "Monica showed me pictures a few weeks back though. He's a good looking kid, Bill."

"That he is. How about next Saturday for dinner?"

"Sounds good. I'll let you know for sure in a couple days, okay?"

"Great. I'll let you get to it then."

The line disconnected and Declan jammed his finger down on the speakerphone button. It was all he could do not to reach across the desk and grab Mitchell by his scrawny throat when he snarled, "You go after Jagger one more time and it won't just be the Barrettis you'll have to deal with, do you hear me?"

Mitchell gaped at him before his skin turned bright red. "Clean out your desk, Detective. You're done!"

Declan chuckled as he straightened. "Do you really think it's going to be that easy, Captain?" Declan drawled. "Didn't you ever stop to ask yourself why none of the Powers that Be have entertained your efforts to get rid of me in the last twelve years?"

At Mitchell's look of surprise, Declan shook his head in amusement. "Maybe we should just ask the Chief what he thinks about all this," Declan said as he pulled out his phone. "I'll make sure to also ask him how he feels about you locking up a man without cause," he added as he found the contact he was looking for. He reached across the desk and hit the speakerphone on Mitchell's phone again and dialed a number. A woman answered on the second ring.

"Good afternoon, Chief Gorman's office."

"Hey Sally Ann, it's Declan."

Mitchell paled and wiped a hand over his mouth nervously.

"Hi Declan, how are you?"

"I'm good, thanks. Hey listen, is Henry available?"

"Let me check. Hold on."

Music came on over the speaker.

"How do you think the Chief will like hearing how you seduced the mother of a fifteen-year-old kid you pinched and then planted evidence on? How you blackmailed him for years by threatening to have his mother deported. Assault, false arrest, harassment-"

"What do you want?" Mitchell snapped.

"As far as you're concerned, Jagger Varos doesn't exist. You even look at him wrong and I will rip you apart. And if I even get a whiff of Immigration sniffing around his mother, you're done."

"Declan? How are you?" said a thick voice over the phone.

Mitchell gave him a quick nod and Declan enjoyed the satisfaction of watching all the blood drain from his face.

"I'm good, Henry. I just wanted to make sure you and Denise were going to make it to the benefit next month. Nadine's trying to finalize the seating arrangements and she hadn't heard from you yet."

Declan only half-listened as the Chief answered him. As much as he would have liked to watch Mitchell squirm for a while, what he really wanted to do was get back to his men.

~

*D*eclan couldn't help but smile as he glanced in the rearview mirror at the seat he and Ren had been making out in last night like a couple of kids as Jagger had driven them to his place. He'd been too pissed about Mitchell to consider the memory when he'd borrowed Jagger's car this afternoon after he'd declined the invitation to join Jagger and Ren in the shower after their most recent encounter. He'd said he needed to rescue the food he'd been cooking before he had joined in on the fun but his need to confront Frank Mitchell had overridden all other thoughts and he'd grabbed Jagger's keys without considering the consequences. There was no doubt in his mind that both Jagger and Ren would be pissed at him for not answering the texts and phone calls he'd received in the hour it had taken him to get to the Precinct and bring Mitchell down a couple of notches, but he was more than willing to take whatever anger they threw at him because his only desire had been to end the torment that Mitchell had put Jagger through.

Last night had somehow been one of the most painful and one of the most incredible of his entire life at the same time. As hard as it had been to confront the truth about himself and the impact his grandfather's emotional withdrawal had had on him, he'd felt lighter than he had in years after they'd left the motel. And while he'd expected the sex to be incredible, he hadn't been at all prepared for it to change his entire life. But from the moment his eyes had connected with Jagger's in the rearview mirror, he'd known that his future would include both men because there was no way he could choose between them.

His fear that one night wouldn't be enough had come true and he'd known it the moment he felt Jagger slip completely inside of him. Between Ren's soothing touch and Jagger's strength, Declan had never felt safer or more wanted. His insides had no longer felt hollow and the ache that had plagued him since Sylvie's death had eased. Words hadn't even been possible in that moment so he'd just clung to Ren and marveled at the feel of their bodies lining up perfectly as Jagger made the rest of the world disappear.

Declan pulled the car into the garage and got out. He tried not to linger as he recalled how beautiful Ren had looked when he'd come apart against the passenger door but he couldn't stop himself from letting his fingers slide over the cool metal as he walked around the car.

"Where were you?"

Declan looked up to see Jagger standing just inside the doorway that led from the garage to the townhouse. His eyes were dark with fury and Declan felt his stomach sink. He'd hoped to avoid this conversation for a little longer but his gut was telling him that Jagger suspected where he'd gone.

"I went to talk to Mitchell," Declan said.

Jagger slammed his hand against the garage door opener on the wall and turned around and disappeared into the house. By the time Declan had followed him in, Jagger was pacing back and forth in front of the living room couch. "You had no right," he snapped.

Ren appeared in the doorway of the bedroom but he remained silent. The look of disappointment in his eyes tore at Declan but he kept his focus on Jagger.

"I knew he'd never stop coming after you," Declan said quietly.

"Jesus, Declan, what the fuck did you do?" Jagger bit out. "I had it under control!"

Anger went through Declan. "And that's all that matters, right? Always the protector but never the protected."

"What the fuck does that mean?" Jagger snapped.

"Never mind," Declan responded. Anxiety went through him as he felt everything he'd had an hour ago slipping away.

"No! You don't get to shut down again," Jagger yelled. "Say what you mean!"

"Jagger," he heard Ren say.

"No, Ren!" Jagger said sharply though his eyes remained on Declan. "I want to hear this."

"She never stood up for you, did she?" Declan whispered.

Jagger stilled at the words as his arms dropped to his sides.

"Every time he came after you, harassed you, hurt you...she sided with him, right?" Declan held Jagger's gaze as he moved towards him. "Even when he did this," Declan said as he stroked his fingers over the scar on Jagger's cheek. He felt Jagger tremble beneath his touch but he wasn't sure if it was because of anger or something else. Declan caressed the raised flesh for a moment before running his hand down Jagger's face and settling it around the back of his neck. "You can hate me. You can curse the fact that you ever met me. You can tell me to fuck off. But I will always" – he tightened his hold on Jagger's neck - "always protect you when I have the chance."

Disappointment went through Declan as Jagger pulled free of him. He seemed agitated as his eyes shifted back and forth between him and Ren and he finally strode to the kitchen counter and snatched up the car keys Declan had deposited there.

"I need to get to the hospital to check on Cade. I'll take you and Ren to the motel so you can get your car."

Declan felt Ren move past him to follow Jagger to the garage. None of them spoke on the way to the motel and Jagger didn't say anything as Declan and Ren climbed out of the car. He just drove off like they weren't even there.

"I'm sorry," Declan said softly to Ren before turning to unlock his car. He was surprised when Ren's hand closed over his arm and turned him around and even more surprised when Ren kissed him. The fact that they were in a very public parking lot didn't seem to bother Ren as he reached up to clasp Declan's face as his tongue slipped into Declan's mouth.

"I would have done the same thing," Ren whispered briefly against his lips before giving him another kiss. "Next time though, leave a fucking note saying you're coming back."

Ren's words startled Declan and guilt went through him as he realized what it must have looked like for him to have taken off without a word.

"God, Ren, I'm sorry. I didn't think-"

Ren cut him off with another kiss and kept doing it until Declan got the message that Ren didn't need any more apologies. He smiled against Ren's lips after the fourth or fifth interrupting kiss.

"I'll drive," Ren said as he took the keys from Declan. "You drive like a little old man."

～

"What the hell are you watching?" Ren heard Declan ask as he came into the living room.

"I think it's some kind of cooking competition," Ren answered.

He glanced over his shoulder to see Declan drying off his hands with a dish towel and then he was tossing it on the kitchen table. "Maybe it will teach you something," Declan quipped as he came to stand next to the couch Ren was sprawled out on.

"Shut up. That was some damn fine lasagna."

"Sure," Declan said. "You do know you're supposed to boil the noodles first, right?"

Ren chuckled as he reached out and gave Declan a light punch in his gut. Declan caught his hand and held it against his stomach. Even with the light banter, Declan's expression still held the same haunted look it had had since they'd left Jagger's townhouse. They hadn't spoken much in the car or during dinner because they were both acutely aware that something was missing, but as the hours passed and there was no word from Jagger, Ren's hopes had begun to fade that the two men would be able to move past what had happened that afternoon. Jagger's temper typically ran hot, so it had been unnerving to see him so quiet after Declan's declaration.

"Come sit with me," Ren murmured as he drew Declan down to the couch and made room for him by folding up his legs. Declan sat but then he was pulling Ren up until he was kneeling next to Declan. But the contact didn't seem to be enough for Declan because he dragged Ren closer until he had no choice but to straddle Declan's lap. Ren lowered his weight down as Declan rubbed his palms up and down Ren's thighs. It was Ren's first real chance to explore Declan so he did what he'd been wanting to do for so long and ran his fingers through Declan's hair. It was as soft as he'd thought it would be and he found that the length was perfect because there was just enough hair to grip to hold Declan still for a searing kiss. Declan's hands moved from his thighs to his ass but instead of fearing the contact like he had the night he'd kissed Jagger, Ren welcomed it.

"What's it like?" he asked as he pulled back from Declan's kiss.

"What?" Declan asked.

"To have another man inside of you."

"You mean does it hurt?" Declan said.

Ren nodded

"I think it depends on the guy you're with. You have to trust him to take care of you."

"Is that why you were with Zane?" Ren asked. He felt Declan tense beneath him.

"I was with Zane because I knew it would only be about physical pleasure. I didn't have feelings for him and he didn't have them for me. He helped me forget..."

"Forget what?" Ren asked as he ran his fingers over Declan's cheeks. He hadn't meant for the conversation to get this heavy but there was so much emotion built up in Declan's gaze that he had to know the cause.

"Don't you know, Ren?" Declan whispered.

Ren froze and he felt his chest seize up. His mouth suddenly felt dry and he had trouble swallowing as he shook his head.

"You. I was trying to forget you."

Oh God. Was Declan saying what he thought he was? Ren's fingers trembled as he tried to process Declan's words.

"When?" he asked.

"When did I know I loved you?" Declan asked softly.

Jesus. Ren could only nod.

"The wedding."

The wedding? "But that was the first time we met."

"Right," Declan said.

Ren couldn't believe what he was hearing. Declan had been in love with him for more than ten years? How was that even possible? How could he have not known? Not even suspected? Did he love Declan back? Was that what the endless ache in his chest was? Was that the reason he'd felt so broken this morning when he and Jagger had discovered that Declan had disappeared on them again? And what about Jagger?

"Ren," Declan said gently. He felt Declan's hand cup his chin and he realized he'd been silent for too long because he saw the fleeting disappointment in Declan's eyes. "I didn't tell you just so you'd say the words back."

"Why did you tell me?" Ren asked.

"Because I'm done lying to myself about it or hoping it will go away. But you need to know that what I feel for you I feel for Jagger too. I didn't expect it but I can't change it. I won't."

"Declan," Ren began to say but Declan silenced him with a kiss.

Declan loved him. His brain kept repeating the phrase over and over as Declan worshiped his mouth. But a chill went through him as he realized that Declan didn't know the truth yet. About him. About what he'd done.

"Tell me again," Ren whispered. He knew it was cruel to ask Declan to say something he couldn't say back but he needed the words anyway. Maybe if he heard them enough, he'd find the strength he needed to admit what he'd done in the darkness of his prison.

"I love you, Ren," Declan breathed against his lips. He said it again before Ren silenced him with a kiss but as he reached for Declan's shirt, Declan froze and grabbed his hands. It was then that Ren heard what sounded like a door slamming shut. Declan pushed him to his feet and quickly rose. "Stay here," he said before Ren could argue.

Declan didn't even manage to reach the door before it flew open. Jagger's haggard gaze connected with Ren as he strode towards Declan. The apology was there clear as day but Ren knew that he wasn't the one that needed it.

～

*D*eclan hadn't even heard the sound of the car coming up the road because he'd been too caught up in the fact that he'd admitted not only his love for Ren but for Jagger as well. Neither admission had been on his agenda tonight but it had felt so right to finally tell Ren the truth. Even as hard as it had been to know he wouldn't hear the words back, he'd still felt lighter then he'd felt in a long time and he had no regrets. Nor did he have any desire to take back the admission that he was in love with Jagger too. The latter hadn't even hit him until he'd watched Jagger's car drive away from the motel. The loss he'd felt had been a hundred times worse than the pain his grandfather had inflicted upon him with his heartless defection but he didn't regret what he'd said to Jagger either about always protecting him.

Hope went through Declan as Jagger closed the distance between them and he didn't hesitate for even a second when Jagger's lips covered his.

"I'm sorry," Jagger whispered raggedly and then his mouth was back on Declan's. Jagger released him long enough to give Ren a scorching kiss and then Declan lost track of everything else besides the two men whose hands freed him of his clothes and whose mouths set his skin on fire with kiss after blazing kiss. He wasn't even aware they'd made it to the bed in his room until the mattress hit his back and Jagger's mouth was wrapped around his cock. He cried out at the sensation but Ren was there to swallow the sound.

"Will you show me, Declan?" Ren asked against his lips. "Will you show me how you feel?"

Declan didn't understand what Ren was asking until he felt a condom being rolled down his cock. "Do you trust me, Ren?" Declan asked.

"Yes. Always yes."

It was all Declan needed to hear and he quickly rolled Ren onto his back. He immediately searched Jagger out for a kiss.

"Missed you," he murmured against Jagger's mouth. "Get our boy ready for us."

Jagger's nostrils flared as he licked over Declan's mouth once more and then he pulled Ren to the edge of the bed. Ren's eyes widened with confusion as Jagger lifted and separated Ren's legs just before he dropped to his knees on the floor. Jagger gave Ren little time to contemplate what was about to happen but the second his tongue licked over Ren's hole, Ren shouted his name and then his hand reached for Declan's.

∿

*R*en's moans were slowly driving Jagger insane with need as he licked and bit at the pulsing hole beneath his mouth. But when Ren suddenly bucked beneath him and let off a string of curses, Jagger smiled and confirmed what he'd already suspected – Declan was leaning over Ren and had sucked his leaking cock deep into his mouth. Their eyes actually connected as they worked Ren in tandem but it was over too soon because Declan pulled off of Ren after just a few merciless drags. He guessed Declan could tell that Ren was already on the edge and they definitely needed him to stay there until Declan could get inside him. With that in mind, Jagger eased his mouth from Ren's opening and reached for the lube he'd dropped on the bed. Ren's body tensed up the second he felt Jagger's finger press against him but when he looked up, he saw that Declan had laid down next to Ren and was murmuring something to him. Whatever he said seemed to work because he felt Ren's body relax somewhat and when Jagger gently pressed against him, Ren bore down.

Jagger's own body felt like it was burning up as he watched his finger disappear into Ren's body and he couldn't believe his pride had nearly caused him to miss this moment. The betrayal he'd felt when he had figured out that Declan had likely gone to confront Mitchell had been brutal and his anger had only grown as time went by. Ren had tried talking him down on more than one occasion but Jagger had done exactly what he'd accused Declan of doing – he withdrew and shut Ren out. But when Declan had voiced what Jagger had been trying to deny for so long – that his mother had never protected him – Jagger had felt blindsided.

The fact that his mother had chosen her twisted version of love for Mitchell over her devotion to him had been a truth he'd been hiding from for a long time and to hear someone else say it brought it all that pain back to the surface. But Declan's next words had scared the hell out of him because they'd been the last thing he expected. Jagger was always the protector because he was bigger and stronger than the people around him. They needed that from him. It was the only role he knew how to play. But he'd believed Declan when he'd said he'd always protect him and the hated vulnerability he'd felt had him needing to escape. It had taken him hours to come to his senses and he'd spent the whole drive to the cabin overcome by the fear that he wouldn't be forgiven this time around. That he'd fucked up the best thing in his life before it had really even gotten started.

Jagger felt his cock stir in anticipation as Ren's body began to accept the smooth gliding motion of his finger and he carefully added another.

"Fuck," Ren muttered and Jagger stilled his movements until he heard Ren's breathing even out from the ragged pants that had over-taken him. Jagger lifted enough so that he could run his tongue over Ren's cock which had started to soften and he was rewarded with a loud groan. He kept up his attention on Ren's dick as he slowly eased the second finger in and as Ren's length thickened under his ministra-tions, his hips began pushing down onto Jagger's fingers. Jagger slowly eased them from Ren's body and then rose to his feet and leaned over Ren and kissed him hard. Declan's mouth joined his and they took turns kissing and stroking Ren's body all over with their hands until he was writhing beneath them, begging for relief. While Jagger pulled Ren farther up the bed, Declan moved into position.

~

*R*en couldn't help but tense up again as he felt Declan's cock start to push into his body. He knew it would make the discomfort worse if he couldn't manage to relax but no amount of telling himself that changed his body's response. But he reminded himself that the pain he'd felt at Jagger's fingers piercing him had eased and had started to turn into something else that hadn't felt all that bad. Except that even as thick as Jagger's fingers were, they didn't match the size of the dick that was impaling him.

"Ren, do you want Declan to stop?" Jagger whispered against his ear.

Ren shook his head violently. There was no way he was giving up on this – no fucking way.

"You know how beautiful you two are together?" Jagger asked as his palm began caressing Ren's chest. The warm, rough skin felt good against his and Ren felt a stab of pleasure jolt through him every time Jagger's fingers brushed his nipples. "I dreamed of this," Jagger said huskily. "Last night when I was inside of Declan, I imagined him inside of you – the three of us connected."

Ren moaned at the image and he felt Declan sink farther inside of him. Jagger's hand slid over his hip but skirted around his dick which lay painfully hard against his groin.

"And when you fucked me this morning I began to wonder if I could take both of you at once. Your cock rubbing against his so deep inside of me that I wouldn't be able to breathe without both of you feeling it."

The next moan Jagger heard was Declan's and he shot him a quick glance. Dark blue, glittering orbs met his as Ren's body finally relaxed enough to allow Declan to slide all the way in. He hung there as he slashed his mouth over Jagger's for a moment before dropping it to Ren's to steal a kiss. Jagger wasn't surprised when Declan settled his weight onto Ren completely and kept kissing him as his hips began to move.

Jagger was content to watch the two men make love but then Declan's eyes sought his out. "Do it," Declan whispered. "Take me."

"Declan," Jagger started to say, but Declan cut him off.

"Please, Jagger. I need it to be the three of us…just like you said."

As much as this moment was supposed to be about Ren, Jagger could see the truth in Declan's eyes. For whatever reason he needed more. In truth, Jagger needed more too. So it took him just moments to get a condom on and prepare Declan's body. And then they were exactly what Jagger had been telling Ren they'd be – connected.

~

*D*eclan shuddered as Jagger's hips began to increase their pace and every thrust had him sliding deeper into Ren. They'd both given up on kissing since they were panting too hard to actually keep their mouths together, but Ren's eyes had never left his and his hands had wrapped around Declan's back the moment Declan had leaned over him. The only thing that could have made the moment any better would have been to be able to see Jagger's eyes but he'd have to settle for Jagger's breath against his neck and his endless words of how good they both felt beneath him.

"It's so good, Declan," Ren whispered.

Declan wished like hell he could tell Ren how much he loved him but he knew that in the throes of passion, Ren would likely say it back and as much as he wanted to hear the words, he wanted them to be said when Ren truly meant them.

It took some effort but Declan managed to get a hand between their bodies and he began jerking Ren off as Jagger ruthlessly slammed into him. He couldn't stop the scream that erupted from his lips when Jagger suddenly changed the angle of his entry and hit his prostate. He yelled Jagger's name over and over as Jagger pounded into him and he could hear Ren grunting in unison to his shouts. When he finally came, he managed to open the eyes that had squeezed shut and watched in awe as Ren's release hit him. He heard both his and Ren's names fall from Jagger's lips as he came and the heat of Jagger's come burned his insides even through the latex barrier that separated them. Jagger's lips sought his out as his dick continued to pulse inside of Declan and each convulsion had Ren's body jolting beneath his. The words again threatened to burst free from his throat but at the last second he managed to keep them inside and settled for whispering Ren and Jagger's names one last time before he drifted off.

CHAPTER 9

*J*agger closed his eyes as he listened to the sounds of the woods waking up around him. The air was cool on his skin and the breeze was strong enough to have the old trees surrounding the cabin creaking.

"It's beautiful, isn't it?" he heard Declan say and then he was dropping down next to Jagger on the top stair of the porch steps.

"I can see why you liked coming here as a kid," Jagger murmured. He took the cup of coffee Declan handed him and then leaned over and brushed his lips across Declan's. "He still asleep?"

Declan nodded. "I think you wore him out last night," Declan said with a chuckle. "He'll be lucky if he can even walk today."

Jagger smiled. In the week that they'd been at the cabin, none of them had spent much time outside the bedroom other than to eat or go for a swim. Even the swims usually ended up with someone on their knees in the sand. Jagger had ended up taking Ren the same night Declan had even though it hadn't been his intent since he'd known that Ren was likely sore. But he'd been woken up in the middle of the night with whisper soft kisses on his chest and silky tongues licking up and down his dick. He doubted he'd ever see anything as erotic as his two men's tongues dueling with each other with his dick

139

between them. And then Ren had climbed on top of him and made love to his mouth. Within minutes, Declan was guiding Ren down onto Jagger's cock and he'd lost the ability to speak as Ren rode him.

Since that night it had been a free for all and it didn't matter where they were or if they were even all together. They gave and took whatever the other needed in that moment. And last night Jagger had needed to take Ren to the edge over and over. He and Declan had edged Ren until his pleas were no longer comprehensible and only then had they given him relief. He'd passed out before the last of his orgasm had even left his body.

"Vin called this morning. Cade's awake," Jagger said.

"Thank God," Declan murmured.

"He'll probably be in the hospital for a few more days so they can make sure there's no permanent damage to his brain. His leg's broken in a couple of places and he cracked some ribs but they think he'll be okay."

"We need to tell Ren about Rafe," Declan said.

"I know," Jagger said softly. "He's still having nightmares and this morning I found him sitting on the floor in his room. He was rocking back and forth and saying he was sorry."

Jagger saw Declan run his hand over the back of his neck. "Brandon again?"

Jagger nodded. It was a name they'd both often heard Ren say during his sleep but the way in which he'd said it made it clear that whatever had happened to Brandon hadn't been good.

"I wonder who he is," Declan said.

"He was my friend."

Jagger and Declan both turned to see Ren standing in the cabin doorway.

"And I killed him."

∾

*D*eclan shifted on the step and Jagger did the same as Declan reached his hand up. Ren took it and it Declan gently pulled him down to sit between them. He watched as Jagger drew Ren up against his chest. Declan kept their hands intertwined and draped his arm over Ren's leg. Neither of them pressed Ren to speak and at least five minutes passed before he finally did.

"We met in basic training. He was the same age as me and grew up in small town in Indiana. We hit it off right away – probably because we had so much in common. Cars, football. I didn't even realize things had changed for me until a few years ago. I found myself thinking things about him that didn't make sense to me. We were as close as two best friends could be but it didn't seem like enough."

"You were attracted to him," Jagger offered.

Ren nodded. "It took me a while to realize it and I tried to deny it because I'd never once been interested in other men. I passed it off as the stress of being in combat. But when he came back from leave and told me he'd gotten engaged to his girlfriend, I was heartbroken. I felt like I'd lost him even though he was right there. Nothing had changed – he was still my best friend."

"What happened?" Declan asked gently.

"I ignored what I felt. I knew he loved his girlfriend – they'd been together since high school – and he'd never once shown any interest in me beyond our friendship. So when I met Geri I threw myself into the relationship. I convinced myself that I loved her. The day of the ambush I lost track of Brandon so I thought he'd died in the attack. It wasn't until a week after they put me in that hole that I found out otherwise."

Tears began to flow down Ren's cheeks and Declan saw Jagger tighten the arm he had wrapped around Ren.

"They...they threw him down the hole one day. I didn't know it was him at first because it was too dark but then he said my name. He couldn't move so I pulled him onto my lap. He kept telling me it hurt over and over again. He was covered in blood – they'd stabbed him at least a dozen times. I thought if I could stop the bleeding he'd be okay but he was in so much pain. But he said he couldn't feel his legs..."

Declan swallowed hard and lifted his eyes to meet Jagger's. He knew the pain he saw there mirrored his own.

"I realized the fall must have broken his back. I guess he did too because he...he began begging me..."

Ren seemed unable to continue and he turned his face into Jagger's chest and howled in agony. Declan released Ren's hand long enough to shift his position so that he could wrap around Ren's back.

"Shhh, it's okay," he murmured against Ren's ear.

"I didn't know what else to do. I held him for hours but he kept begging me to take away his pain. He asked me to tell his parents he hadn't been afraid and to tell his fiancée how much he loved her and that he'd always be with her. And then he told me he loved me and I did it...I broke his neck."

"He wouldn't have made it out of there, Ren. He knew that. You did what he needed you to do," Jagger whispered as he dropped his chin to Ren's head.

"They left him in there with me for three days. When they finally came to take him away I begged them not to. It was the only time I ever asked them for anything."

"It's going to be okay," Declan whispered. He felt Ren shake his head.

"I never even gave his parents or his fiancée his messages."

"You will," Jagger responded. "Someday when you're ready, you will."

~

*R*en let his eyes drift shut as he felt Jagger's cock slip all the way inside of him. The tile felt cool against his cheek but he didn't feel any of the water from the shower on his back because Jagger's body was covering his from shoulders to ass. But he didn't need the water to provide the warmth he craved because Jagger's skin sliding over his as he thrust in and out of Ren's body gave him all the heat he needed. He doubted this had been Jagger's plan when he had coaxed Ren into the shower and started gently washing him but it hadn't taken much urging on Ren's part for Jagger to concede. In fact, it hadn't taken anything beyond saying Jagger's name a certain way. It had been like that for the past two weeks since his impromptu confession about Brandon. He didn't remember much about the first few days other than having Declan and Jagger holding him between their bodies as he'd alternated between fits of crushing sorrow and bitter silence. When the pain became too much, he would beg them to take it away for a little while and they did. And when his body was sated from their lovemaking, he slept. When the sound of Brandon's neck snapping had him jolting upright in bed, they soothed him with soft words.

"Don't stop," Ren said when he felt Jagger's still hard dick slip from his body.

"I don't have a condom," Jagger whispered against his ear. When he felt Jagger's hand close around his dick, Ren reached down and forced Jagger to release him. He quickly turned around in Jagger's arms and wrapped his hand around Jagger and began stroking mercilessly.

"Please Jagger, I need you inside of me. All of you."

Jagger's eyes pinned his and Ren saw the indecision there.

"I trust you to take care of me," Ren whispered.

The words had the desired effect because Jagger reached beneath Ren's thighs and lifted him. For once Ren was grateful that he hadn't regained all his weight back because the feel of Jagger pinning him to the wall while he angled his cock into position excited Ren like nothing else. And then Jagger was surging into him. With every upward thrust, Ren's body slid up the slick tile and as soon as gravity brought him back down, Jagger rammed into him again. But Jagger quickly seemed to grow impatient with the pace and wrapped his arm around Ren's waist to hold him in place as he pistoned into him. The burning friction and sheer pressure of being stuffed full had Ren closing his eyes.

"Look at me," Jagger ordered.

Ren managed to open his eyes and he instantly got lost in the emotion in Jagger's gaze.

"Tell me who you belong to."

"You and Declan."

"Always," Jagger said.

"Always."

Jagger kissed him hard and then shifted just enough to hit Ren's gland. Electricity surged through his entire body as his climax rolled over him in waves and every spurt of Jagger's seed coating his inner walls had him shouting with pleasure. The aftershocks were still curling through him when he found himself being carried out of the shower and placed on the shaggy bathroom mat in front of the huge tub. He started to protest as Jagger released him but then Declan was there and sliding into him. He had no idea where Declan had come from or if he'd been watching but he didn't care either way. All he cared about was Declan gliding into him over and over as Jagger kissed him. It could have been minutes or hours later for all he knew but another, smaller orgasm overtook him as Declan shoved into him one last time and hung there. More liquid heat bathed his insides and he moaned as he realized that he now carried a little bit of each of his men inside of him.

～

*R*en's body ached as he pulled his shirt on. His ass was still pleasantly sore from what had happened in the bathroom just a few hours earlier but it was his heart that had taken the brunt of the encounter because he'd finally begun to understand that as much as he'd cared for Brandon, the feelings he had for Jagger and Declan went a thousand times deeper. Not once had either man condemned or judged him for what he'd done to Brandon. And though he couldn't agree with their opinions that he'd done the right thing, he'd accepted that they weren't going to walk away from him because of it.

He found both men in the kitchen. Declan was cooking something – for dinner probably – and Jagger was setting the table.

Declan noticed him first and quickly turned off the stove and came up to him. "Ren, Jagger and I are both negative. We each went and got tested at a clinic in town when we went to get supplies. We should have told you before we-"

Ren cut him off with a kiss. Declan kissed him back of course and he didn't hesitate to follow Ren when Ren grabbed his hand and led him to where Jagger was watching them by the table. He stopped in front of Jagger but turned to face Declan.

"Declan, I love you so much,' Ren whispered. "Thank you for not giving up on me. I have a future because of you." He brushed a brief kiss over Declan's lips but Declan seemed too shocked to kiss him back. When he turned to Jagger he was surprised to see how anxious he looked – like he was expecting bad news.

"Jagger, I want you to belong to me the way I belong to you. The way we both belong to Declan and he to us. I have no idea how this thing between the three of us will work or what people will say but I don't care. I love you."

Relief flooded Jagger's features and Ren realized he had indeed been expecting Ren to say something different. Jagger kissed him hard before dragging Declan forward and kissing him too. When they separated, Ren stepped free of both of them and made sure their eyes were on his when he said, "I'm ready to get help. I want to go home."

CHAPTER 10

*D*eclan impatiently tapped on the edge of the keyboard in front of him as he glanced at his cell phone. He cursed himself and pushed the button but nothing but the time appeared on the screen. He'd been doing the same thing for the past thirty minutes. He turned his attention back to his computer but couldn't focus on what he was looking at so he finally reached for the phone again. Before he could even dial, the phone lit up, but it was Dom's name that appeared. The rush of guilt that he always felt when he saw or heard any reference to Dom or Vin went through him but he knew he couldn't keep avoiding the men forever. He and Jagger had decided to hold off on telling Ren the truth about Rafe's reappearance after Ren's admission about Brandon. The two weeks they'd watched Ren spiral into a haunting depression had scared both of them to death and they'd been on the verge of reaching out to Ren's brothers when Ren finally seemed to snap out of it. And then he'd said those words... those amazing, fucking perfect words.

"Hey Dom," Declan said into the phone.

"Hey, how are you?"

"Good. How are Cade and Rafe?"

"Doing good. Cade's happy to finally have the cast off and he'll be back at work next week. Rafe's been volunteering at the foundation and has even consulted on a few jobs for me and Vin."

Declan felt another jolt of guilt go through him at how good Dom sounded. The man was finally getting back on track after the devastating truth about Rafe's childhood and Declan was going to end up shattering it again when Dom found out about his betrayal.

"That's great. Glad to hear it."

"So I never heard back from you about the party this weekend."

Shit, he'd completely forgotten about the invite to the party Logan and Dom were throwing for Riley and Gabe to welcome their new baby girl into the world.

"Right, sorry. I've actually got some things I need to do this weekend."

Dom's silence was heavy on the other end of the phone.

"Declan, I'm worried about you."

"What?" Declan asked. "Why?"

"Hale!"

Declan snapped his eyes up at the sound of his name being shouted from across the room and saw Mitchell striding towards him, file folder in hand. The man hadn't spoken to him in the week since he'd returned to the office but he'd gotten his fair share of murderous looks in every time he stalked past Declan's desk.

"Dom, I gotta go. Give Gabe and Riley my best, okay?"

"Okay."

Mitchell dumped the file on Declan's desk. "Some kids found a body down by the docks. Go check it out."

"Sure thing, Captain," Declan said, making sure to let the disrespect drip from his voice. Mitchell's ruddy face tightened but he kept his mouth shut as he stomped back to his office and slammed the door.

Declan grabbed the folder and his jacket and made his way to his car. He hit the speed dial on his phone and waited anxiously for Jagger to pick up.

"How is he?" he asked before Jagger could even say hello.

"Still in with the doctor," Jagger said.

"Fuck, is that good or bad?"

"How the hell do I know?" Jagger muttered. After a moment he said, "Sorry."

The apology wasn't necessary since Jagger was undoubtedly as anxious as Declan was. It had been Connor who'd helped them find a therapist for Ren since he'd interacted with several as part of his volunteer work at the VA.

"I've got a case I need to work tonight so I'll be home late. Will you ask him to call me later?"

"Yeah. Stay safe."

"I will. See you soon."

Declan hung up the phone and couldn't help but smile when he realized he'd said "home." How long had it been since he could say that he'd actually looked forward to going home? Easy. Never.

~

*J*agger pushed the plastic container across the bar to Connor.

"What is it?" Connor asked curiously as he eagerly pulled the top off.

"Païdakia."

"Yes," Connor muttered. "Your mom makes the best lamb chops," he added as he began searching behind the bar for something.

"I made them," Jagger said.

Connor stilled and then carefully put the lid back on the container and slid it back to him. "Uh, no thanks."

"Fuck you," Jagger laughed. "Try it."

Connor frowned but then pulled out the fork he'd been searching for and reached for the container.

"Holy shit, this is amazing," Connor said as he stabbed his fork into another piece of the meat. "Since when do you cook?" Connor asked.

Jagger couldn't hide the smile that spread across his face. He wanted to say since he had two men living with him whose strength he needed to keep up since none of them could stop fucking each other's brains out night after night, but he figured that was TMI even for his best friend so he kept his mouth shut.

But Connor let out a loud laugh in between bites. "Don't tell me you're playing house?" he finally managed to get out. "Jagger 'Fuck 'em and leave 'em' Varos?"

"Bite me, asshole," Jagger responded.

"Would there even be enough room for me?" Connor quipped.

"Things keeping you pretty busy around here?" Jagger asked even though the nearly empty bar answered that question for him. He really hoped like hell that Mags had another source of income.

"Nope, no subject change. A soldier and a cop – how the hell did someone who hates taking orders as much as you do end up with guys like that?"

Jagger felt heat flood his face as he remembered the orders he'd taken last night. He'd done every single thing Ren and Declan had demanded of him and he'd been handsomely rewarded.

"Mags, get out here. You gotta see this!" Connor suddenly yelled.

Jagger bit off a curse and took a slap at Connor who managed to step back in time.

"What is it?" Mags responded as she appeared from the back room.

"Jagger's blushing."

"No shit," Mags said in awe as she walked behind the bar.

"Fucker," Jagger growled.

Connor laughed heartily until Mags saw what he was eating. "What the hell is this?" she asked. Connor swallowed hard.

"Lamb," Jagger answered for him.

"So you'll try this nasty shit but not my Haggis?"

"Mags-" Connor began to say.

"He loves it Mags. My mom's been making it for him almost every week since he moved here."

"Asshole," Connor muttered under his breath.

Mags gave him a dirty look and turned her back on him before storming towards the back.

"Fuck, that one's gonna cost me," Connor said as he shoved

another piece of meat into his mouth. "So how are things going besides you finding your inner chef?"

"Better than I thought possible."

"They're both still staying with you?" Connor asked.

Jagger nodded. It was funny because the topic of the three of them staying together once they'd returned to the city hadn't even come up. His townhouse had been the easy choice because of the extra space and Declan had gone to his apartment only long enough to get more clothes.

"How's Ren?"

"He's making progress. He seems to like Dr. Barnes."

At first Jagger had been worried after Ren's first meeting with the therapist because he'd been surprisingly quiet about the whole thing after the session ended. But he'd gone back two days later and hadn't balked when the doctor had suggested group therapy as well.

"Glad to hear it."

Jagger fell silent for a moment before asking, "Sutter been bothering you at all?"

Connor shrugged but didn't answer him.

"Tell me," Jagger said.

Connor sighed and put down the fork. "He calls. Leaves messages."

Jagger felt himself tensing up. "What kind of messages?"

"Jagger, stop, please. Go home. Be with your men."

"Damn it, Connor, tell me about the messages!"

"No," Connor said firmly. "Go home."

Frustration went through Jagger. "Why won't you tell me?"

Connor sighed and reached his hand out to cover Jagger's. "Because I need to deal with this myself. I love that you want to protect me but I need to know that I can take care of myself – that I can still be the man I was before this happened," Connor said as he tapped the side of his head.

"Let me at least talk to Declan about getting a restraining order."

Connor smiled and shook his head slightly. "I already got one. Now go home. I've got customers."

Jagger looked down the bar and saw that the only other patron was passed out with his forehead pressed against the top of the bar.

"Right," Jagger said with a chuckle. As much as he hated not being able to take care of the shit with Sutter, he understood what Connor was asking of him. He climbed off the barstool but turned to glance at Connor. "Promise me you'll call me if you need me."

"Promise," Connor said. "And thanks," he added as he held up the half empty container.

Jagger nodded and headed towards the door.

~

*R*en left the building and walked towards his car. It felt strange to be alone for the first time in the nearly three months that had passed since Jagger had broken down that cabin door and he and Declan had changed the course of Ren's life forever. He'd half expected Jagger or Declan to follow him this morning when he'd gotten in his car to head to his therapy session but if they had, Ren hadn't seen them. Not that he could blame them considering the gamut his emotions had run since their return to the city.

While his nightmares had lessened and he didn't jump at every strange sound, he still struggled with the fear that he would have an episode where he ended up hurting someone. It was the one thing still holding him back from reaching out to his brothers. In the end, it had been his therapist who had convinced him that he was ready to do something as simple as driving himself back and forth to his sessions. Jagger and Declan had both been supportive but hadn't rushed him either. They'd continued to manipulate their work schedules so that Ren was never alone at home but Ren knew that was something he needed to put an end to as well.

The drive to Jagger's townhouse took less than ten minutes and he quickly pulled his car into the garage and hurried into the house. He knew it was silly to be excited over something as simple as having made it through a few hours on his own but it was so much more than that to him. It was the first step to getting his life back – to getting his family back. But more importantly, it meant maybe he'd finally start to feel like an equal member in his relationship with Jagger and Declan. He'd no longer be the weak link that needed protecting and coddling...he'd be able to give as much to his men as he took.

As Ren entered the kitchen, he saw Jagger sitting at the kitchen table. He could tell by the fact that Declan's car hadn't been parked on the street that only Jagger was home but he was surprised when Jagger didn't seem to notice his entry. In fact, Jagger was completely still as he stared at what looked like some folded up papers on the table.

"Jagger?" Ren said as he reached his side.

His voice seemed to snap Jagger out of his reverie and he looked up at Ren and smiled. "Hey, how did it go?"

"Good," Ren said absently. "Are you okay?" He wasn't surprised when Jagger pulled him down to sit astride him and kissed him.

"Tell me what's wrong," Ren said as he ended the kiss. He tensed when he felt Jagger's arms go around him and he dropped his head to Ren's chest but didn't speak. Ren held him there for a moment as he stroked his hand over Jagger's head.

"I love you," he heard Jagger whisper. "More than I ever thought possible."

Ren sucked in a breath at the words. In his gut he'd known that Jagger loved him but to finally hear the words...

"I love you too," Ren said as he lifted Jagger's head and kissed him. But something was still off with Jagger and it was scaring the hell out of him. "Did something happen?"

Jagger reached past him for the papers on the table and then handed them to him. "What is it?" Ren asked.

"I don't know. I can't read it." The shame in Jagger's voice was crushing. "A guy delivered it an hour ago."

"Do you want me to see what it is?" Ren asked carefully. Jagger's dyslexia wasn't something they'd ever talked about but he knew it had to be a painful topic for Jagger.

Jagger nodded.

Ren opened the document and scanned it and then felt his heart sink. "You're being sued," he said. "Some guy named Jason Sutter is suing you for battery. Jesus, he wants four million dollars in damages."

Jagger took the document from him and tossed it back on the table. He seemed unconcerned by the news.

"Who is he?" Ren asked.

"Connor's ex. He went after Connor a few months ago outside my place. I stopped it. Fucker's got no case. The cops took pictures of Connor's injuries and there were witnesses that saw Sutter assault Connor."

"You're not worried about this?" Ren asked.

Jagger shook his head. "Does it bother you?"

"That someone's coming after you like this? Hell yeah, it bothers me," Ren said angrily.

"Does it bother you that I can't read?"

"What?" Ren asked in surprise, all thought of Jason Sutter disappearing from his mind. "No. No!" Ren grabbed Jagger's face to make sure he couldn't look away. "Is that what you think?"

"I never even finished high school-"

"I don't give a shit about that," Ren said, cutting him off. "You're fucking perfect, do you hear me?"

He felt Jagger relax beneath him and Ren leaned down to kiss him softly. A second later he was flat on his back on the table and Jagger was braced above him. "You're so hot when you get all protective," Jagger whispered before he seized his lips. "What do you say we find out if this table is as strong as it looks?"

Instead of answering, Ren reached for the hem of Jagger's shirt.

~

*R*en closed the shower door so the steam wouldn't escape and began drying himself off. He smiled as a bare ass pressed against the tempered glass but when Declan's moans began resonating through the large bathroom, Ren felt his own cock stirring. He was half tempted to climb back into the shower but decided against it since it was his turn to cook tonight. As he quickly dried off, he saw the ass disappear and then a pair of hands was pressed against the glass. Jagger's familiar shout of satisfaction had Ren reaching for his dick and jerking it hard as the sound of skin slapping on skin increased.

"Harder," he heard Jagger order. Ren could tell Declan complied with the order because suddenly Jagger's whole body was plastered up against the side of the shower and the door began rattling in its frame. Ren couldn't stop himself from reaching for the door and pulling it open. The sight of Declan pumping into Jagger's tight ass had Ren's dick hard again within seconds and he matched his strokes to the deep, twisting motion of Declan's hips. Neither man had noticed him since Jagger's face was turned away and Declan's was buried against Jagger's neck. It wasn't often that Ren got to enjoy the show and he took full advantage of watching the passion that consumed the two men. They were so very different but yet somehow perfectly matched.

"Please, Declan," Jagger whispered as Declan's plunges turned to long, slow glides. On every up stroke he pushed his body into Jagger's as far as it could go and then rotated his hips fully before sliding back out until he slipped almost completely free of Jagger. Declan's arms were wrapped around Jagger's chest and had curled over his shoulders so that he could hold Jagger in place for his gentle assault.

"What, baby? Tell me what you want."

"I want" – Jagger cried out as Declan flexed into him once more – "I want it to always be like this."

"It will," Declan whispered. "I promise." And then Declan was kissing Jagger and increasing his pace.

"Love you, Declan," Jagger said hoarsely. "Love you so much." And then Jagger was screaming in pleasure and Ren felt his orgasm take him. He managed to stifle a groan and was glad he did because otherwise he would have missed Declan whispering his own words of love into Jagger's ear just before he gave in to his release.

❧

"Jagger, baby, are you here?"

"Up here Mom," Jagger said as he glanced around the room once more.

"What are you doing?" he heard his mother ask and he looked up and saw her standing in the doorway of the bedroom. "You should have called," she said nervously.

"I won't be long," he said. "Why do you keep it this way?" Jagger asked as he studied the bedroom that had once been his. It looked exactly the same as he'd left it when he was seventeen and the fact that it was completely dust free meant his mother was still cleaning it when she did the rest of the house. There was even fresh tape on some of the half-dozen fighter jet posters that had started to yellow with age.

"Because it's your room," his mother answered in confusion.

Jagger shook his head in frustration. "It stopped being mine the minute he came into our lives."

"That's not true-"

"It is, Mom. It is."

"Jagger-"

"Did you really believe all the things he said about me or were you just too afraid of losing him?"

His mother dropped her gaze and he had his answer. He was surprised to realize that it actually hurt more to know she'd believed him but had still chosen Frank.

"You were always such a good boy," his mother murmured. "I knew you'd be okay."

Jagger let out a sad laugh. "You know what's ironic? I didn't get it until now. How being in love with someone else can consume you like that. How the idea of losing them..." The idea of a future without Ren or Declan was too disturbing for Jagger to even finish the thought.

His mother lifted her eyes. "Have you found someone, baby?"

"Two someones, actually."

His mother looked confused but he wasn't in the mood to clear it up for her. His sexuality wasn't something they'd ever talked about beyond him telling her over dinner when he was sixteen that he was gay. She hadn't condemned him or supported him – she'd simply reached for his plate and started piling more food than he could possibly eat on it and they'd never discussed it again. But since Frank had started calling him fag and queer shortly thereafter, he knew she'd talked to him about it.

"If Frank loved you, he wouldn't hide you away, Mom. If he loved you, he'd want to spend every moment with you, share every part of his life with you. He'd accept you for who you were and he'd do anything to protect you. He'd cherish you."

"He does love me like that. He's just not free to show it yet."

Jagger felt tears of frustration sting his eyes. A little part of him had always hoped he'd be able to free his mother from the hold Mitchell had on her but it was a battle he just couldn't fight anymore.

"Here," Jagger said as he stood and handed her the papers that he'd been holding in his hand.

"What is it?" she asked as she glanced at it.

"Citizenship papers. You're already approved - all you have to do is fill them out and send them to the address on the bottom."

His mother flipped through the pages. "How did you do this?" she asked in shock.

"I didn't. One of the men who loves me did it because he knew how important it was to me," Jagger said. He leaned down to kiss her cheek and started to leave but she grabbed his arm.

"This man – he makes you happy?"

"He does. His name is Declan."

His mother nodded slowly. "And there is another man?"

"Ren."

He was surprised to see his mother start to cry and he mentally prepared himself for the rebuke he knew was coming. But instead, his mother leaned into him and wrapped her arms around him. "You'll bring them both to dinner sometime?"

"Lucia!"

Jagger flinched as he heard Mitchell's voice bellowing from down-stairs and his mother tensed in his arms.

"You here honey? I only have half an hour."

Jagger clenched his fists and he stepped back from his mother as he heard footsteps on the stairs.

"Jagger, please don't," his mother whispered.

Mitchell froze when he saw them and then sneered. But to Jagger's surprise, the man didn't say anything.

"Bye, Mom," Jagger said as he left the bedroom and forced himself to brush past Mitchell without wrapping his hands around his throat and squeezing the life out of him. He wasn't surprised when he heard Mitchell mutter something to his mother that included the word "faggot" but he didn't stick around long enough to see how his mother would respond.

~

*J*agger fumbled with the key as his dick tightened with anticipation. He'd seen Declan's car parked on the side of the street in front of his townhouse but he had no idea if Ren had returned from his appointment yet since the garage door was closed. They'd decided to have Ren park his GTO in the garage since the distinctive car would be recognizable on the off chance that Vin or Dom dropped by unexpectedly. It was getting harder and harder to keep the truth from the two brothers, especially now that Jagger had returned to work, but hopefully it would just be a few more days until the deception was over. He'd learned from Declan that Rafe had started doing some consulting around the office though he hadn't seen the young man himself. But whatever was happening between Rafe and his brothers seemed to be a good thing because he'd finally seen some of the life returning to Vin and Dom's eyes. If all went as planned, they'd have more reason to celebrate with Ren's reappearance. He just hoped like hell that Dom and Vin would forgive him and Declan and that they'd accept them as being a part of Ren's life...and that Ren would forgive them for keeping the truth about Rafe from him for so long.

Jagger finally managed to get the door open and hurried inside.

Even if Ren wasn't home, he and Declan could start without him and let him catch up. Maybe he'd bend Declan over the kitchen table so that would be the first thing Ren saw when he walked in the door. Jagger was so preoccupied with the image that he didn't even notice Declan or the man sitting across from him at the table until he was almost on top of them.

"What the fuck?" Jagger snarled when he recognized Zane.

Zane's green eyes flashed with amusement as Declan immediately got up and placed his body between Jagger and Zane.

"Jagger-"

Jagger tried to push past Declan. Seeing Declan's former lover sitting at *their* kitchen table – the very one he'd been contemplating making love to Declan on – had him seething with rage. The idea that this man had used Declan when he'd been vulnerable…

"Get the fuck out of our house!" Jagger snarled.

"Jagger, stop it!" Declan ordered. "I asked him to come here."

"Why?" God, did Declan want Zane back? Had he not meant it when he'd told Jagger he loved him?

Declan's hand came out to close over Jagger's cheek and Jagger allowed him to draw his gaze away from Zane. "Don't you dare think it! I love *you*."

Jagger forced himself to draw in a breath and then another one. He finally nodded and relaxed as Declan drew him down for a quick kiss.

"Why is he here?" Jagger asked stonily.

"I asked him to take a look at Sutter's lawsuit," Declan said.

Jagger hadn't given the lawsuit much thought since he'd been forced to ask Ren to read it to him. He'd mentioned it to Declan that night but hadn't considered how to deal with it.

"It's bogus."

"I assure you Mr. Varos, it's very real," he heard Zane say. Jagger forced himself to release Declan and focus on Zane.

"Are you saying he has a case?" Jagger asked.

Zane stood. "I'm saying you need a plan of attack. Declan tells me the Barrettis terminated their contract with Lionel Sutter because of you and your friend."

"Connor."

"Lionel Sutter doesn't enjoy losing and from what Declan tells me about what Jason did to your friend, his kid doesn't like it much either. This" – Zane held up the document outlining the suit – "is two bullies trying to get their power back."

"Can you fix it?" Jagger asked.

Zane eyed him for a moment. "Yes," he said simply. God, the guy was arrogant. "With your permission, I'll start drawing up a countersuit."

Jagger nodded briefly. He didn't like the guy but he trusted Declan and if Declan thought Zane was the best man to take care of the shit with Sutter, then so be it.

"Declan, I'll need the police reports like we discussed," Zane said crisply as he reached out a hand. Even the sight of Declan touching the other man had Jagger's blood boiling but he managed to remain where he was. Zane was smart enough not to try to shake his hand and it took just moments for Declan to show him out.

"I don't like him," Jagger snapped as he tossed his keys on counter.

"I think the feeling is mutual," Declan said. "How did things go with your mom?"

Jagger shook his head. He was still too raw from the conversation with his mother to share the details just yet so he said, "Mitchell showed up."

Declan's anger was instantaneous. "Did he say anything to you?"

"Surprisingly, no," Jagger said. "At least not to my face anyway."

"Good," Declan said in satisfaction.

When Declan turned to go towards the bedroom, Jagger reached out and pulled him back. "Want to tell me how you got him off my back exactly? Or how you managed to get those papers for my mother?"

Declan remained mute and Jagger felt his insides jump at the unspoken challenge. He used his arms to cage Declan between his body and the kitchen counter and leaned down to run his tongue over Declan's lips. Declan instantly opened for him but Jagger pulled back.

He let one of his hands close over Declan's cock and smiled when Declan's eyes closed and his body shuddered.

"How'd you do it, Declan?" Jagger whispered as he ghosted another kiss over Declan's lips. Declan tried to follow his mouth when Jagger pulled away but a hard tug on Declan's cock had him biting back a moan.

"Bastard," Declan muttered as he caught on to the game. "I know some people."

"What people?" Jagger asked as he continued to stroke Declan. He waited until Declan was writhing against him before he stopped.

"Fuck," Declan bit out. "Mayor, Chief of Police. We're on a first name basis."

"I'm going to need more than that," Jagger said.

"Really? Now?" Declan asked in frustration.

Since Jagger's own body was tight with need, Jagger said, "Promise you'll tell me everything afterwards."

Declan's hand tried to wrap around his neck to drag him down for a kiss but Jagger grabbed his wrist.

"Yes, damn it, I promise."

Jagger instantly released Declan and moaned at the hungry assault on his mouth. But he only let it go on for a few seconds before he grabbed Declan and dragged him to the table and did exactly what he'd been planning to do.

"You better hope Ren comes home soon," Jagger whispered as he bent over Declan and rubbed his cock against Declan's ass. "Because I'm going to keep fucking you for as long as it takes for him to walk through that door and see you like this."

He cut off Declan's strangled groan with a kiss and then reached for his zipper.

～

"*N*ice car."

Ren froze as he watched Zane climb out of the luxury sedan that had pulled up behind his car in front of the bar where Connor worked.

"What are you doing here?" Ren asked in irritation.

"Between you and that boyfriend of yours, I'm starting to think you guys don't like me very much," Zane drawled as he walked around the car. He was wearing an expensive suit and looked every bit the lawyer that he was. In truth, the guy was gorgeous but he had nothing on Declan or Jagger.

"You're an observant guy. We'd probably like you a whole lot better if you hadn't used Declan like you did."

Zane seemed like he was about to say something but then a strange look came over his features before he shuttered them with a mask of indifference. He took a few steps towards the bar and opened the door. "You coming?" he asked.

"Why are you here?"

"I came to speak to Mr. Talbot about the lawsuit your boyfriend managed to get himself caught up in."

"Jagger hired you?"

"I guess you could say that. Right after Declan kept him from ripping my throat out."

"I thought you were a criminal lawyer," Ren said as he walked past him.

"Winning's winning," he thought he heard Zane say.

The bar was dark compared to outside and it took a moment for Ren to focus. "He must be in back," Ren murmured.

"I don't give a shit about some restraining order! You're mine!"

Ren tensed at the raised voice coming from the back of the bar. The pitch was higher than Connor's. He felt Zane right behind him as they hurried towards the commotion.

"Baby, I'll drop the lawsuit against your friend if you come back. I love you so much."

"My backpack, have you seen my backpack?" a confused voice said.

Connor's voice.

"God, you are such a retard," the first voice snarled.

"My backpa-"

The words were suddenly cut off and Ren heard what sounded like a struggle. A second later there was a resounding slap.

Ren and Zane reached the storeroom at the same time. Connor was pressed back against the shelves, his hands pinned above his head. He was struggling against a slightly larger man who was kissing him and grinding his hips against him.

"Get your fucking hands off him," Ren yelled but Zane beat him to it and grabbed the guy and dragged him off Connor. Ren managed to catch Connor as he lost his balance.

"My backpack. I need it or I'll be late for school again," Connor whispered brokenly as he looked around in confusion.

"Connor, it's Ren," Ren said softly as he gently lowered himself and Connor to the floor.

Connor flinched over and over again and it took Ren a moment to realize that he was reacting to Zane's fist connecting with the man's face. Blood was pouring from the guy's nose and he wasn't fighting back against Zane at all.

"Zane, stop!" Ren shouted. "Zane, for God's sake, stop!"

Zane finally stopped and the man slid in a heap to the floor. Zane's fists were bruised as he turned around and there was blood on his face and suit. None of it appeared to be his though. Ren turned his attention back to Connor.

"Connor, can you hear me?" Ren asked.

"Ren?" Connor asked as his eyes suddenly seemed to clear from the fog he'd been in. His eyes darted up to meet Ren's and then came to rest on the unconscious man at Zane's feet.

"What happened?" Connor asked. His eyes settled on Zane and his eyes widened as he noticed Zane's battered fists. "What did you do to Jason?"

～

"Jagger, don't!" Declan heard Connor yell as Jagger slammed through the bar door. He was right behind Jagger as they'd entered the bar but his view had been obstructed. But within seconds of walking through the door, Jagger had sped up and Declan saw Ren step in his path just as Connor shouted at him. Zane was there too and grabbing Jagger's arm as he lunged for a man being treated by paramedics. They'd gotten the call from Zane only fifteen minutes ago but a patrol car and ambulance had beaten them to the scene.

"Jagger, Connor needs you," Ren said firmly but it wasn't until Ren grabbed Jagger by the face and forced him to look at him that Jagger finally calmed down. He pulled free of Zane and went to where Connor was sitting in a chair near the bar.

"What happened?" Declan asked Ren as he took out his badge and flashed the officer flanking the man being loaded onto a gurney.

"We found him assaulting Connor," Ren said.

"Sutter?" Declan asked and Ren nodded in in response. Declan looked Ren up and down quickly to make sure he wasn't injured. One look at Zane had him asking, "Do you need medical attention?"

Zane shook his head but didn't say anything. His eyes kept flashing to Connor.

"Stay here," he said to Ren and Zane. He hurried over to where Jagger was kneeling in front of Connor.

"You okay, Connor?" Declan asked.

Connor nodded but his eyes were on Jagger. They were filling with tears. "I had another one," Connor whispered. "I don't remember anything after he came into the storeroom."

"It's okay," Jagger said softly. "Ren's going to sit with you for a bit, okay?" Jagger motioned to Ren who came over and pulled up a chair next to Connor.

Declan pulled Jagger aside and said, "What did he mean?"

"The bombing that took his leg also left him with permanent brain damage. He has episodes where he starts saying things that don't make sense or he forgets where he is. They don't last long but he never remembers them. Sometimes he forgets what happened right before the episode starts too."

"Okay," Declan said as his mind began to work out what needed to happen. "Let me get the details from Zane and we'll go from there."

"I'm coming with you," Jagger said.

"Jagger-" Declan began to say.

"Please, Declan. I need to know."

Declan finally nodded and went to where Zane stood quietly near the storeroom entrance The officer that had been talking to Sutter as he was being treated by the paramedics nodded at Declan. He recognized him but couldn't remember his name.

"Officer…"

"Gerard, Detective."

"Officer Gerard, you get Sutter's statement?" he asked.

"He says this man" – the officer motioned to Zane – "assaulted him while he was talking to his boyfriend."

He felt Jagger stiffen behind him but was glad when Jagger kept quiet.

"The paramedics said his nose is broken and he'll probably need to be monitored for a head injury since he lost consciousness. He says he wants to press charges."

"Escort him to the hospital and stay on him. He violated the restraining order Mr. Talbot had on him. I'll take statements from everyone else and talk to the D.A. about charges."

"Yes sir," Gerard said and hurried off.

Declan turned his attention to Zane. "What happened?"

Zane glanced at Connor for a moment and then focused his attention on Declan. "I ran into your boy out front," he said. "We heard yelling and found Mr. Sutter had Mr. Talbot pinned against the shelves in there" – he pointed to the storeroom – "and was kissing and fondling him."

"It wasn't consensual?" Declan forced himself to ask even though he already knew the answer.

"No fucking way," Zane said. The fury caught Declan off guard but

Zane quickly brought himself under control again. "Mr. Talbot seemed confused by what was happening. He kept asking about a backpack. I pulled Mr. Sutter off of him while Ren checked on Mr. Talbot. It also sounded like someone struck someone else but neither of us witnessed it."

The red mark on Connor's face was proof enough of who'd struck who. "Okay, I need you to come down to the precinct and give me a formal statement. You good with that?"

Zane nodded. "I'll head down there now." He cast Connor one last look and turned to leave when Jagger suddenly stepped in front of him. Pride surged through Declan as Jagger stuck out his hand. Zane seemed reluctant to take it at first, but finally did.

"Thank you," Jagger said softly.

Zane gave him a curt nod and then left. Declan went back to where Ren was sitting with Connor. "Connor, I need you to come down to the precinct to give your statement so we can press charges against Jason."

Connor nodded and Jagger wrapped an arm around his shoulders as he climbed unsteadily to his feet. As they headed towards the entrance, Declan reached for Ren and dragged him into his arms. "Are you okay?" he asked.

"I'm good," Ren said.

"What were you doing here?"

"I came to ask Connor about Sutter. I was worried about the lawsuit and I wanted to find out what he knew about it."

Declan made himself release Ren and nodded in understanding. "We'll need to get your statement too."

Ren's eyes widened as he realized that meant he'd have to go to the precinct. "Will you be the one taking it?" Ren asked.

"No. We need to be able to show impartiality so Sutter can't claim I was biased. Another officer will have to do it."

Ren nodded. "Okay."

"You sure?" Declan asked.

"If it helps put that fucker behind bars, yeah, I'm sure."

"*D*on't think I've forgotten our deal," Jagger said as Declan snuggled back against him.

"What deal?" Ren asked. His head was resting on Declan's chest and his fingers were stroking up and down Declan's side.

"It's nothing," Declan murmured.

"Declan has some explaining to do about a few things."

He felt Declan sigh. It had been a long day between dealing with things at the bar and the fiasco at the station afterwards and Jagger had actually forgotten the promise he'd finagled out of Declan until he saw Mitchell sitting sullenly in his office as he stared daggers at Jagger as Jagger and Declan had waited for Ren's statement to be taken. By now Mitchell had to know he and Declan were lovers, but he hadn't used that or the fact that Jagger was once again involved in an assault on Sutter – albeit indirectly – to confront him. Whatever Declan had said to the man had clearly scared him.

"My grandfather was big in commercial development back in the 1950's. It made him a lot of money and a lot of friends. My father helped him run the business for a while before he and my mom decided it would be more fun to jet off to foreign countries and hang with the rich and famous. My father eventually became an ambassador and my mother kept busy throwing lavish parties and dinners."

"Wait, are you saying you're one of the Hales in Hale Development Services?" Jagger asked.

Declan nodded. "I don't have anything to do with the day to day operations but I still have a seat on the Board. My grandfather had always hoped I'd take over the business someday but after I told him I was gay, he never brought it up again."

"Shit, Declan, I'm sorry," Jagger whispered. He hadn't intended to bring up Declan's painful childhood.

"It's okay," Declan murmured. "It turned out to be a good thing. I can't imagine being anything other than a cop."

"So that's how you know all those people?" Ren asked.

"Some, but not all. My grandfather was very well connected politically and that ended up helping my career in law enforcement. One of his fishing buddies had been the Captain of the department I joined when I got out of the academy. He was the one who suggested I become a detective and he looked out for me once he became Chief and Mitchell took over as Captain." Declan hedged.

Jagger couldn't hide his surprise. "Was he protecting you from Mitchell?"

Declan nodded. "The first thing Mitchell did when he became Captain was get rid of any of the cops who wouldn't side with him. I knew he was garbage as soon as I met him and I made sure he knew it too. He's been trying to talk the Chief into getting rid of me for years."

"Fuck," Jagger murmured. "What about all the others? The mayor?"

"I met the mayor and his wife after I donated some money to a few hospitals in the area."

"A few?" Jagger asked. "Jesus, how much money do you have?"

"None beyond my detective's salary," Declan said.

"But if you own part of your grandfather's company-" Ren said.

"I give it all away." The bitterness in Declan's voice was clear and Jagger knew exactly what he wasn't saying – he didn't want a penny from the man who'd so cruelly dismissed him because Declan hadn't turned out to be the perfect version of the grandson the old man had wanted him to be.

"To charity?" Ren asked gently.

Declan nodded. "Sylvie and I each inherited a quarter of our grandfather's estate when he died. It came out to almost 6 million dollars for each of us. I wasn't interested in the money so I just pretended it didn't exist. When I found out Sylvie was sick again and that she wouldn't get better, I donated all of it to charities that helped kids with cancer. I realized I could do some good with the profits from my grandfather's company so I started donating that too. Homeless shelters, organizations that helped gay and transgender kids, hospitals...I tried to do it all anonymously but it got out what I was doing and people like the mayor started reaching out to me. Part of me wanted to tell them all to fuck off because I knew it was all just part of their game, but then I realized that I could use the connections to help others."

Declan's eyes shifted so they were staring at the ceiling. "Every time I'm around those people I feel like I'm still living my grandfather's lie. I hate it," he whispered.

Ren leaned over Declan and kissed him. "Then let it go, Declan. Put the lie in the past where it belongs."

Declan closed his eyes. "They won't accept us. They'll say what we have is unnatural and wrong."

Jagger spread his palm over Declan's face and waited until Declan opened his eyes. "Only the people that don't matter will say that. The people who really care about us will see that what we have is amazing and perfect. That it's what we've been searching for our whole lives."

"Soulmates," Ren said softly as he glanced at Jagger.

A smile spread across Jagger's lips as he remembered his and Ren's conversation about having more than one soulmate in life. He almost laughed as he remembered Ren's comment about not believing in soulmates.

"Soulmates," Jagger agreed.

CHAPTER 11

"*D*id you talk to him?" Jagger asked as he tucked the phone under his chin and began searching out his keys.

"Yeah. He said it's a good time to tell Ren. He suggested we do it at Ren's next session so he's there to give Ren some extra support if he needs it," Declan said.

"His next session's tomorrow, right?"

"Yeah."

"Fuck," Jagger muttered. "I'm nervous."

Declan was silent for a moment too and Jagger guessed he was thinking the same things as Jagger – that all the trust they'd been able to build up with Ren would be decimated. But their bigger concern had been making sure Ren was strong enough to deal with learning the truth about Rafe's childhood and they'd decided that approaching Ren's therapist to find out how best to break the news to Ren would be the wisest course of action.

"He'll understand," Declan said firmly. "He'll see that we were protecting him."

God, Jagger hoped like hell that Declan was right.

"How's Connor?" Declan asked.

"Struggling. He finally managed to talk Mags into letting him go home last night but I know he's frustrated with how things played out."

"At least he won't need to testify since Sutter was smart enough to take a plea."

"Thirty days in jail and two years probation? Fucker got off lucky," Jagger snapped.

"Yeah, but if he so much as even looks at Connor, he's back in for the full two years."

Jagger knew it was better than nothing. And at least the lawsuit had been dropped as soon as Zane threatened Lionel Sutter with a massive countersuit.

"Are you on your way home?" Jagger asked as he finally managed to get the door open.

"Yeah, be there in fifteen."

"Okay, see you in a bit. I'll make sure Ren looks real nice for you when you get here," Jagger added and he heard Declan let out a sharp breath.

"Be there in ten," Declan amended and then he hung up.

Jagger found Ren in the garage working on his car. He had music playing on the stereo so he hadn't heard Jagger come in. As much as Jagger would have liked to sneak in and place his body over Ren's where it was leaning over the engine, he wasn't willing to risk scaring Ren, so he called out his name instead. Ren's physical appearance had changed dramatically in the three months since he and Declan had found him at the cabin. His body had filled out as a result of good nutrition and using the weights Jagger kept in the homemade gym in his basement had given Ren's muscles some definition. His skin looked healthy and even had a touch of color from the sun and his hair had grown thick and lush. And while he still struggled with occasional nightmares, they were coming less often. Crowds continued to be his biggest challenge, so things like going down to the waterfront or the Market Place to walk around were still off limits. Loud sounds got his attention, but didn't set him off like they used to and he'd even managed to start watching some lighter action movies as long as they didn't have too much gunfire and bombs going off.

Since Ren hadn't heard him, Jagger went to the stereo and turned it off. Ren looked up from what he was doing and Jagger smiled at the sight of the grease on his hands and smeared across his forehead.

"Hey," Ren said with a smile.

Ren's smile was the biggest proof of his recovery. It was almost always present now and he wasn't content until he had the people around him smiling too. If Declan had a bad day at work, Ren used every ploy to drag a smile out of him. And if that didn't work, he unabashedly used his body which always did the trick. Ren had also started testing himself more by running errands like picking up groceries or gassing up their cars. The only thing he hadn't done yet was talk about when he was ready to see his brothers.

"What are you doing?" Jagger asked as Ren bent under the hood of the car once more, leaving his ass on perfect display for Jagger.

"Just checking a few things," Ren said as his ass shifted back and forth slightly. Jagger cursed - little fucker was playing with him. Jagger began unbuttoning his shirt as he moved closer to the car and he let his hands smooth over the denim covering Ren's ass.

"Was there something you needed?" Ren asked from under the hood as he pushed his ass back against Jagger's touch.

"Little shit," Jagger murmured as he yanked Ren free from the car and slammed the hood down. He pushed Ren down face first on the hood and leaned over him. His hands covered Ren's as he began rubbing his cock against Ren's ass. "I think there's something you need, isn't there?" Jagger asked as he leaned down and nipped Ren's ear.

"Yes," Ren moaned.

"Do you want me to fuck you up against your pretty little car, Ren?" He skimmed his lips down Ren's neck and then bit down gently.

"Yes, Jagger. Please!"

Jagger stood and yanked his shirt off. Ren made a move to stand but Jagger shoved him back down. Ren got the silent message and stayed where he was though his head was turned enough so he could see what Jagger was doing. Jagger nearly came when Ren licked his lips as Jagger freed his cock from his pants.

Jagger pushed Ren's pants down and then searched out his wallet and found the packet of lube he needed. He slathered some on his dick and put a little on Ren's hole. He leaned back over Ren and said, "I'm going to fuck you so hard that you're going to beg me to come but you won't, do you understand me?" He grabbed his dick and ran it up and down Ren's crease.

"Yes," Ren moaned.

"And when Declan gets here you're going to suck his cock for as long as he wants and then you're going to let him fuck you any way he wants."

"Jesus," Ren muttered. Jagger smiled as Ren's body shook beneath his.

Jagger pulled Ren's hips back so the angle was perfect and began pushing into him.

"God, yes," Ren snarled as he drove his hips backwards to meet Jagger's shallow thrusts. Once Jagger was fully seated, he pressed Ren back down on the hood of the car and began driving into him. He used his weight to hold Ren down and pinned his wrists when Ren tried to reach for him. Ren was begging for relief within minutes but Jagger kept up his brutal pace. But whenever Ren started to crest, Jagger slowed his pace dramatically. And then he started all over again.

By the time Declan got home, Ren's shirt was covered in sweat and sticking to his back and he was whimpering in need as Jagger slammed into him.

"Look who's home, baby," Jagger whispered against Ren's ear.

Ren managed to turn his head enough to see Declan but he was incapable of speech. Declan's eyes were heavy with lust and he was already peeling off his shirt.

"Remember what I said," Jagger said to Ren. Ren managed a nod and bit down on his lip. Jagger ruthlessly pounded into Ren over and over until his orgasm hit him and his come flooded Ren's channel. He stayed inside of Ren until the last aftershock eased and then slowly pulled his dick out. Declan came up next to him and they both watched as Jagger's semen began to trickle out of Ren's ass.

Declan dropped to his knees and licked his way up Ren's inner thigh before closing his mouth over Ren's hole and sucking gently. Ren moaned at the contact and tried to push back on Declan's face but Jagger placed his hand on Ren's back to keep him still. Declan kept eating Ren for several long seconds and then he stood and turned Ren over and kissed him. Jagger's breath nearly stopped at the sight of his come transferring from Declan's tongue to Ren's. The kiss turned hungry and impatient and Declan reared back and pushed his pants down. He grabbed Ren's legs and dragged him forward a bit before ramming into him. Ren screamed in pleasure at the harsh treatment and Jagger felt his own dick stirring as he heard the sound of his come squishing inside of Ren as Declan thrust into him over and over again.

"Please, I need to come!" Ren yelled.

Declan kept up his brutal pace and Jagger angled around Declan and Ren's body and closed his mouth over Ren's dick. As he sucked on Ren hard, he watched Declan's dick slide into Ren's body and couldn't hide the feeling of satisfaction that it was his own come that was glistening on Declan's dick and easing the way for Declan to torment Ren with thrust after vicious thrust.

Declan came first but Ren was only seconds behind and Jagger happily swallowed every bitter drop of release that shot down his throat. He released Ren with a pop and then Declan was tipping his head up for a kiss while Ren lay unmoving beneath them.

~

"I'll get it," Ren called over his shoulder when the doorbell rang.

He thought he'd been smart by claiming first dibs on the shower but he'd barely managed to get any of the grease off his hands before Jagger and Declan were joining him. But at least the grease had come off a lot faster with three pairs of hands instead of just one and he'd managed to sneak out while Declan and Jagger were focused on each other. He'd lost track of time as he'd been working on his car so he hadn't made the call to the restaurant to set up a dinner reservation like he'd planned before Jagger and Declan got home. His plan was to take them to dinner so he could finally tell them he was ready to see his brothers and that he wanted them there when he saw them. Ren had no doubt that his brothers would be confused to find him in a relationship with two men, but he was more concerned that they'd be upset with Declan and Jagger for keeping the truth from them for so long. Dom and Vin were the only family Declan had and Jagger needed the security of working for his brothers so he could finally put down roots in the city he'd spent so many years trying to stay away from.

Ren reached for the door and opened it. A man in his mid to late twenties with streaky blonde hair and blue eyes stood on the other side.

"Hi, can I help you?" Ren asked.

"Yeah, hi, I'm here to see Jagger. I've been trying to catch him at the office but I keep missing him and I didn't want to do this over the phone," the man said nervously.

"He's in the shower but he should be out in a second. You want to come in and wait?" Ren asked as he opened the door wider.

The man seemed to hesitate for a moment before he finally entered.

"Thanks," he said.

"How do you know Jagger?" Ren asked curiously.

"Um, he saved my life actually," the guy said. "That's why I'm here – to say thank you. Everything got crazy after the shooting and then the hospital…sorry, I'm babbling." The guy let out a self-deprecating laugh and extended his hand. "I'm Rafe Barretti."

Ren felt the bottom of his stomach drop out and he actually wrapped an arm around himself. "What?"

Rafe withdrew his hand nervously and looked around. "Are you okay?"

"Rafe?" Ren whispered. He covered his mouth with his hand and shook his head. "It can't be."

"It's him, Ren," Ren heard Jagger say and he looked up to see both his lovers standing half-dressed near the kitchen table.

"Ren?" Rafe said in wonder. "Ren!" he repeated and then suddenly he was throwing himself into Ren's arms.

Sobs wracked Ren as he wrapped his arms around his brother. He could feel Rafe shuddering against him and the tears against his shoulder were proof the Rafe had lost it too. Ren finally managed to push Rafe back a bit so he could study him.

"You're so big," Ren said with a laugh. "We're the same size now."

Rafe laughed. "Yeah, no more sitting on me until I do what you tell me."

Ren dragged Rafe into his arms again and stroked his hands up and down his back. He could feel the uneven texture of the skin through Rafe's shirt and he froze because he knew instantly what he was feeling. Rafe drew back from him and said, "Long story."

Ren forced back the emotion in his throat as he realized whatever story Rafe would be telling him about his past probably wasn't going to be a good one.

"Come on, let me introduce you to..." Ren started to say as he grabbed Rafe's hand and began leading him farther into the house but then his brain began to catch up and he stuttered to a halt. Rafe had come here to see Jagger. They knew each other. A chill went down Ren's spine as he looked up and found Jagger's eyes. Jagger knew Rafe had been found and he hadn't told him.

"It's a mistake," Ren whispered. "It's some kind of mistake." His eyes went from Jagger's to Declan's and he saw the same exact thing – regret. *They both knew.*

"Oh God," Ren said as he took several steps back.

"Ren," Jagger said. He saw Jagger take a step towards him but he threw his hand up.

"No! Don't!"

"Ren, what's going on?" Rafe asked.

Bile rose in Ren's throat and he tried to swallow it back down as tears stung his eyes. But his stomach wouldn't cooperate and he leaned over and vomited all over the floor. A glass of water was pressed into his hand and he quickly drank it down but it just came back up again. He scrambled back when he felt the familiar hands rubbing his back.

"Don't touch me!"

"Ren, talk to me," Rafe said desperately. "What's happening?"

"Can you get me out of here?" he whispered.

Rafe looked between him and Declan and Jagger who only stood a few feet away. Both men looked like they were in agony but Ren didn't care. He needed to escape.

"Please, Rafe."

"Okay, let's go," Rafe said.

"Ren, please just hear us out," Declan said.

Ren shook his head violently. His skin was crawling and he felt like he was going to throw up again. "Now, Rafe," Ren said.

Ren felt Rafe grab his arm and then he was being led down the steps toward the sidewalk. He couldn't hear anything besides a roaring sound in his ears. He jammed his hands over his ears but the sound wouldn't stop. He could see Rafe talking to him but the noise was too loud for him to hear what he was saying. He let Rafe lead him to a car and then he was being buckled in. The seatbelt felt too tight as he rocked back and forth against it.

A hand closed around his and he started to yank free of it until he realized it wasn't either of the ones he'd thought it would be. He followed the arm up to Rafe's face and saw him talking but since he still couldn't hear him, Ren closed his eyes. And then he felt the darkness settle around him and he shifted against the dirt and angled his body around the sharp rocks. He could hear the earth come alive beneath his ear as he laid his head down and he smiled as he finally realized he was back in the place where things like love and trust and hope didn't matter. Nothing mattered. The dream was over and he was back where he belonged.

∼

"Yeah, he's here. He's safe."

Ren winced at the sound of the deep, unfamiliar voice. It wasn't that the voice was loud – it just wasn't the right one...or ones rather. There should be two voices.

"Ren?"

Another voice, but still not quite right.

"Ren, you're scaring me. I need you to wake up."

Ren tried to say he was too tired but his mouth felt dry.

"Cade-" the voice said anxiously.

"He'll be okay, baby. He just needs a little bit of time."

"Did Jagger tell you what was going on?"

"Yeah, he did. We need to call Vin and Dom."

"No," Ren whispered though he had no idea if the words cleared his throat.

"Ren?"

He realized it was Rafe's voice and he burned it into his mind so he'd never forget it again. His baby brother was home.

"Water?" Ren asked. Hands helped him to sit up and a glass was instantly pressed against his lips. He took just a few swallows. A hand stroked his hair and then his brother's voice told him to drink a little more.

"You're not supposed to tell me what to do," Ren managed to say. "You're the baby, remember?"

Rafe chuckled and it was then that Ren realized he was leaning against his brother. He forced his eyes open and took his time letting them adjust.

"Where are we?" he asked as his eyes focused on a white leather sofa across from them.

"Our apartment. Cade's and mine."

Ren forced himself to sit up so he could take in the entire apartment. It was an open floor plan with mostly hardwood floors and contrasting dark walls. The living room had three couches in a U shape and there was a huge flat screen TV on the opposite wall.

"Cade?" Ren asked stupidly.

"My boyfriend," Rafe said and Ren finally realized there was a man sitting next to Rafe on the couch. He was tall and had black hair and dark green eyes.

"Cade Gamble," the guy said as he stuck out his hand. But then he glanced lovingly down at Rafe and said. "Soon to be Cade Barretti."

Ren shook his hand and watched Cade lean down and brush a kiss over Rafe's lips. "I'll let you guys talk for a bit."

Rafe nodded and watched him go. So not only was his baby brother gay, he was in love. Pain went through Ren as a feeling of loss settled into his gut. He'd thought the same thing – that he was in love. But people who loved you didn't lie to you.

Ren had no idea how he'd gotten here. The last thing he remembered was throwing up on Jagger's pretty hardwood floor. "Did I hurt anyone?" he asked.

"No," Rafe said. "You were out of it in the car but you were able to follow me up here," Rafe said. "Talk to me, Ren. Tell me what happened."

Jesus, where the hell did he even start? "Did Dom and Vin tell you what I did to Mia after Vin brought me home?"

Rafe nodded. "They told me about the shooting too. You saved her life."

Ren shook his head. "I was stalking her," he said bitterly

"You saved her life," Rafe repeated. "You saved Vinny's too."

That caught Ren off guard and he turned to look at his brother.

"I've seen the way he looks at her, Ren. He's completely in love with her. If he'd lost her that day…I'm not sure he would have gotten over that."

Ren fell silent.

"Is she the reason you left?" Rafe asked.

"Part of it," Ren said. "I was so full of rage and hate. I was worried about hurting someone I loved."

"Where did you go?"

Ren gave Rafe the details about Declan's offer to stay in the cabin and Declan and Jagger's arrival and plan to help him put his life back together.

"How could they do this?" he whispered. "They said I could trust them. I did trust them." Tears began to spill down his cheeks and he felt Rafe put his arm around his shoulder. "I told them things I never told anyone else."

"Were you with them, Ren?" Rafe asked gently. Ren understood what Rafe was asking and nodded.

"I thought I loved them," Ren said. "I thought they loved me."

"You don't think they love you anymore?"

"I don't know," Ren whispered. "I don't know anything anymore."

"What all did they lie about?" Rafe asked as he gently pushed Ren upright so they were facing each other.

"You."

"That's it?"

"That I know of," Ren said bitterly. But then his thoughts drifted to all the things Declan and Jagger had shared with him. Their painful pasts, the things that made them feel weak and vulnerable.

He dropped his eyes and studied his hands. At some point Rafe had managed to push a tissue into it and he used it to wipe at his eyes. "I think it was just you," he finally said. "How long have you been back?"

"Almost three months," Rafe said.

Ren shook his head. They'd been lying to him from almost the beginning.

"Ren, I know why they lied about me but it's not going to be easy for you to hear."

Ren steeled himself because he'd guessed as much.

"I began hacking Dom and Vin's computer servers earlier this year. I was looking for information to use against them."

"I don't understand. For what?"

"To hurt them," Rafe said. "To destroy their reputations, ruin their business. I was even planning on taking down their loved ones."

"Why?"

"Because I wanted revenge. I blamed Vin and Dom for what happened to me after Gary took me away."

Ren had been too young to understand what was happening twenty years ago when a man claiming to be Rafe's real father had shown up and demanded that Rafe belonged to him. He remembered Vin and Dom promising Rafe that he wasn't going anywhere and then one day they'd come home and said Rafe had to go with the man. He hadn't understood when they explained that a judge had said Rafe couldn't live with them anymore and he remembered yelling at his brothers not to let anyone take Rafe away.

"What happened after Gary took you?" Ren asked as he tried to mentally prepare himself for the answer.

Rafe hesitated. "I'm okay now, that's what matters."

Ren shook his head as fresh tears blurred his vision. "He hurt you?"

He felt Rafe grab his hand. "Ren, look at me. I'm okay."

Ren managed a nod. "Tell me," he said. "I need to hear it."

"Ren…"

"Please, Rafe" Ren asked.

"He sold me to other men," Rafe said softly. He was surprised at how strong Rafe sounded.

"Oh God, Rafe, I'm so sorry." He felt Rafe drag him into his arms once more and felt him whisper that he was okay over and over against Ren's head.

Minutes passed before Rafe softly said, "Ren, would you have been strong enough to hear this three months ago?"

Ren realized that he wouldn't have and he shook his head.

"One month ago?"

One month ago he'd just started the process of therapy. No way in hell would he have been able to deal with such devastating news and stay on track with his recovery. What if Jagger and Declan had just been waiting until he was strong enough to tell him the truth?

But it didn't matter because there was a new reality he just couldn't get past. "I don't trust them anymore," Ren said as he felt his heart break into pieces.

~

"*A*re you going into work today?" Jagger asked as he reached across Declan and turned the alarm clock off.

Declan shook his head but didn't speak. It had been the same routine for nearly a week since they'd watched Ren walk out of their lives. They hadn't tried to stop him since they'd known nothing they could say or do would take away the agony he'd felt at their betrayal. The only consolation they had had was knowing Ren was safe with Cade and Rafe and Cade was kind enough to call them with daily updates. He and Declan had both been relieved to hear that Ren was keeping up with his therapy sessions and that he'd held up well upon learning the truth about Rafe's past. But apparently he still wasn't ready to see his brothers.

"Declan, we should try to keep things as normal as possible so that when he comes back-"

"He's not coming back, Jagger," Declan mumbled. "He'll never trust us again."

Jagger rolled Declan onto his back and settled on top of him. "He will. He'll see that we were just trying to protect him."

"Even if he sees that, it doesn't mean he'll trust us."

"Then we'll earn his trust back. We'll beg, we'll promise – fuck, I don't care if we have to kidnap him and fuck his brains out for a week – we're going to get him back."

Declan's fingers brushed over his scarred cheek. "And if he doesn't, is what we have enough for you?"

Jagger leaned down and brushed his lips over Declan's. "It's never been all or nothing for me. I love you. Period. Whether he's with us or he isn't, I love you. Will a piece of us always be missing if he doesn't come back? Yes. But I'm not going to give up a life with you. He may have been the reason we came together but he isn't going to be the reason we stay together."

"I love you, Jagger."

Jagger smiled and leaned down to kiss him.

"Would you come somewhere with me tonight?" Declan asked.

"Yes, anywhere," Jagger whispered just before claiming Declan's mouth again.

❧

"You didn't say anything about having to wear a monkey suit," Jagger snapped as he tugged at the bow tie around his neck.

"I think a tux is considered a penguin suit," Declan said as he got out of the car and handed the keys to the Valet. He went around the front of the car to where Jagger waited on the sidewalk. The man looked unbelievably hot all decked out and Declan couldn't help but imagine Ren standing next to him looking equally stunning.

Declan reached for Jagger's hand and murmured, "I am so regretting not getting a limo for the night…the things I could have done to you in the backseat."

"Fuck," Jagger snarled just before he kissed Declan. It didn't seem to matter to Jagger at all that fancily dressed people were walking past them as they made their way into the hotel or even that there were a few flashes going off from the cameras belonging to the society pages reporters.

Declan hadn't planned to make an appearance at the benefit tonight, but Jagger's words had stuck with him. As much as they loved Ren and he belonged with them, he wasn't the glue holding them together. If it had been Jagger who had walked away, Declan wouldn't have been able to leave Ren and he definitely wouldn't have wanted Jagger and Ren to let go of one another if Declan couldn't remain in the relationship.

Declan took Jagger's hand in his.

"You sure you want to do this?" Jagger asked.

"Absolutely."

❧

*J*agger had lost count of how many hands he'd shaken or how many looks of surprise he and Declan had received each time Declan introduced him as his boyfriend. And Declan hadn't stopped there. After introducing Jagger, he informed the other party that his other boyfriend hadn't been able to attend but hopefully they'd get to meet him next time. They'd gotten their fair share of disgusted looks but most people had been polite and some had actually seemed interested. For Declan, the biggest hurdle had been the Chief of Police, but the distinguished, older man had simply smiled and greeted Jagger as he would have any other person. Even the mention of Ren hadn't deterred the man or his wife who promptly invited the three of them to dinner. The most interesting part had been when the Chief asked Declan why he hadn't taken the Lieutenant's exam. He'd then pulled Declan aside for a brief, private discussion while Jagger had chatted with the Chief's wife.

"Declan, Jagger!"

Jagger froze at the sound of Vin's voice and he felt Declan's hand tighten in his.

They both turned and saw Vin and Dom winding through the crowd with their significant others in tow. It wasn't until both men noticed that he and Declan were holding hands that they fell silent.

"Are you..." Dom lifted his eyes from their joined hands. "Are you two together?"

"Yeah, we are," Declan said.

Dom and Vin exchanged glances. "Declan, I'm sorry, I never knew..."

"Nobody did, Dom. I made sure of it."

Dom seemed at a loss for words and it was Logan who broke the tension. He dragged Declan into a bear hug. "Congratulations you two," he said as he reached for Jagger. After that there were more hugs and questions about how they'd met but Jagger could feel the tension running through Declan and he knew the stress of lying to the two men he considered family was taking its toll. For whatever reason,

Ren still hadn't reached out to his brothers to tell them he was back and it wasn't their place to do so either.

"Declan, you mind if we cut out early?" Jagger asked. "My head's starting to hurt a bit."

"Yeah, sure," Declan said and Jagger could feel the relief go through him.

They said their goodbyes and began walking towards the front entrance but Jagger was caught off guard when Declan dragged him into a secluded alcove and wrapped his arms around him.

"I miss him so much," Declan whispered.

He held Declan tight against him. "I do too. He would have loved watching you do this tonight," Jagger murmured.

"Thanks for getting us out of there."

"Let's go home, Declan."

Declan nodded against his neck. Jagger took the keys from the Valet when the car was brought around. Once they were on the road he asked, "What did you and the Chief talk about?"

"He wants me to take the Lieutenant's exam."

"Why?"

"He didn't say it directly but I got the impression he wants me to be Captain at some point. You have to be a Lieutenant for at least a year before you can become Captain."

"You think he wants Mitchell out?" Jagger asked.

"I think so. He kept saying it was time for the department to catch up to the times."

"You going to do it?"

Declan was silent for a moment. "I don't know. What do you think?"

"I think you'd be fucking incredible at it," Jagger said. "Haven't you ever thought about it?"

"Once or twice but it's such a high profile job that I was always worried it would be harder to hide my secret."

Jagger grinned at him. "Well, you took care of that in a big way tonight."

Declan smiled. "Yeah. God, that felt good."

They both fell silent as Jagger drove but Declan soon said, "Where are you going? You missed the turn."

Jagger steered the car into a deserted parking lot and got out. He waited until Declan came around to his side of the car but cut off the tirade he was on about what they were doing there with a kiss. He yanked open the back door of the car and pushed Declan inside. He climbed in after him and closed the door and used the key fob to lock the car.

"Jagger, what the hell-"

Jagger kissed him again and then began reaching for the bow tie around his neck. "Now what is it that you were saying you wanted to do to me in the back seat of the limo you neglected to rent?"

Declan smiled broadly and then reached for the button on Jagger's pants.

CHAPTER 12

*R*en watched his brother kiss Cade goodbye. It was strange to see his baby brother all grown up and in a relationship with someone, but it offered him a measure of comfort to know that Rafe had finally found the happiness he deserved.

"You want some more coffee?" Rafe asked.

Ren shook his head. Rafe filled his own cup and returned to sit on the couch next to him.

"You don't need to stay and babysit me, you know. You can go back to work."

"Is it babysitting if I'm not getting paid?" Rafe joked.

Ren smiled but then sobered. "How are Dom and Vin?"

"They're good," Rafe said. "I think they're still struggling with everything that's happened but we're taking it really slow."

"They're blaming themselves for what happened with Gary?"

Rafe nodded. "It doesn't help that I blamed them for so long. If I'd been a smarter hacker, I would have thought to check their files for information about me."

"What do you mean?"

"I always thought they hadn't looked for me. If I'd done a search on myself, I would have seen all the files and notes they had on the searches they did for me, the PIs they'd hired."

"Would you have come back here if you'd known?" Ren asked.

Rafe fell silent at that. "No," he finally said. "I was too hung up on the belief that being around them would make me think of Gary and everything that had happened."

"It doesn't?"

Rafe shook his head. "New memories are replacing the old ones. Like watching Dom and Vin bicker over the stupidest things like when we were kids. Or family dinner."

"Family dinner?"

Rafe nodded. "I guess it's something Logan's side of the family started but now it includes Dom and Vin and Mia. Cade and I started going a couple weeks ago – it's gotten so big that they had to move it to Vin's house."

Ren's heart sank as he realized that even if he got to a point where he was a part of family celebrations, not all of his family would be there.

"Sorry," Rafe whispered.

Ren shook his head. "I guess it would have been hard to explain to Vin and Dom why I'd need two extra chairs at the dinner table instead of just one."

"You know that wouldn't matter to them."

Ren fell silent as pain bloomed in his chest. "I miss them so much," he whispered. "You know, I actually started to believe I could have a normal life. That I'd been forgiven for what I did to my team...for what I did to Brandon."

"You can still have that," Rafe said softly.

Ren shook his head. "All those men died because I was a fool. Because I made the wrong choice-"

"Jesus, Ren, didn't anyone tell you?"

"Tell me what?"

"Fuck," Rafe said as he suddenly stood. He quickly disappeared down the hallway leading to the bedrooms but was back a moment later with a sheaf of papers in his hand. "I thought the military would have told you when they debriefed you."

"Tell me what?" Ren repeated in frustration.

"Geraldine Holt got your team's exact location from one of your teammates, not you."

"What?"

"Shit, let me start at the beginning. When I started hacking Dom and Vin's servers for information to steal, I discovered emails that described the ambush on your unit and your imprisonment. I didn't even know you were missing until then. I decided to do some investigating and found some emails on the DOD's servers that a guy named Phillip Benton had deleted."

"You hacked the Department of Defense?"

Rafe brushed him off and continued. "The emails mentioned a villager who knew where you were being held hostage and I was able to anonymously send the coordinates to Vin."

Ren couldn't believe what he was hearing. Rafe was the reason he'd been found?

"I didn't look at all the emails and it wasn't until someone came after me in L.A. that we figured out the rest – that Geri and Benton had been working together to sell the weapons your team was escorting. Benton's the guy Jagger shot when he came after me a couple months ago. After Cade got out of the hospital, I went back and started looking through more and more of the emails. I found an email between Geri and Benton where Geri was saying the cowboy had finally given her what she needed. It didn't make any sense to me until I saw another email where she was talking about a stallion that wasn't biting."

"I don't understand-"

"What was the name of your high school football team?"

Ren froze. "The stallions," he whispered.

"You know a guy named Danning?"

Ren nodded. "He was on my team. Holt Danning."

"Danning went to Oklahoma State University. Their football team is the-"

"Cowboys," Ren said in amazement.

"I hacked Danning's email and texts. I found pictures of him and Geri together – pictures he'd sent his folks. He told them that he and Geri were engaged."

Ren's head began to pound as pieces clicked into place. He'd never had a clear idea of exactly how Geri had determined their exact route – he'd only told her the general vicinity.

"Danning used his government email to send the pictures to his parents. We figured someone must have made the connection at the DOD. We assumed they would have told you during your debriefing in Germany. Vin said you didn't say much about it."

"Jesus," Ren said as he stood on shaky legs. "It wasn't my fault?" he whispered.

"It wasn't your fault," Rafe responded as he also stood. Ren couldn't move or speak as he felt Rafe's arms wrap around him. He just stood there as his brother held him and tried to make sense of it all.

~

*D*eclan stepped off the elevator and nodded at Dom's secretary. "Hi Cecile."

"Good afternoon, Detective Hale," she said with a smile. "You can go on in. Mr. Barretti will be in shortly."

"Thanks," Declan said as he went into the conference room on the other side of Cecile's desk. His gut tightened as he saw the blinds were drawn on the glass wall. When he opened the door, his stomach fell when he saw Jagger pacing back and forth in front of the windows that overlooked the city.

"Fuck, this can't be good," Jagger murmured as he came around the table and gave Declan a quick kiss.

"Do you know what this is about?" Declan asked.

Jagger shook his head. "Dom's secretary called me and said there was a staff meeting."

"Hey guys," Dom said as he walked into the room, a bright smile on his face. Vin was right behind him.

Declan reached his hand down to clasp Jagger's. He'd been preparing for this moment since the day he'd told Ren he would keep his secret but he still wasn't ready to say goodbye to the only two men that had been a part of his life longer than anyone else.

"So what's up?" Vin asked as he dropped down into one of the fancy, high backed leather chairs that surrounded the huge table.

Declan glanced at Jagger in confusion and then at Dom. "Didn't you call this meeting?"

"No, we thought you did," Dom said as he glanced at Vin.

"I called it." All four men turned to see Cade stride into the room. Rafe was right behind him. Anticipation went through Declan as he saw Rafe glance behind him and then Ren was walking into the room, his eyes instantly seeking him and Jagger out.

"Oh God," Declan heard Dom whisper and then Ren was in Dom's arms. Vin's arms wrapped around both of his brothers and then somehow Rafe was being dragged into the mix. Declan felt tears sting his eyes and he turned into Jagger's embrace.

As happy as he was for the brothers to finally be reunited, Declan had seen the look in Ren's eyes when their gazes had briefly connected. There'd been no joy at seeing them – just pain. And in that instant Declan had known that Ren wasn't coming home.

The group hug went on for several minutes and Declan could hear Ren's soft murmurs as he spoke to his brothers. Dom and Vin finally released them and sat down.

"Would you sit, please?" Ren asked as he glanced first at Jagger and then at Declan. The scene was surreal as Vin and Dom sat on one side of the table and Declan and Jagger on the other. Ren sat at the head of the table while Rafe and Cade stood off to the side.

Ren turned his attention on Dom and Vin. "I need you to let me say what I need to say before you start asking questions, okay?"

Dom and Vin both nodded.

"I'm sorry for disappearing like I did after the shooting. I was scared..." Ren said. He glanced at Declan and Jagger for a moment before turning his attention back to Vin and Dom. "I was scared that I was going to end up hurting one of you or one of the people that you loved. But I knew you wouldn't just let me go if I asked you to. After Declan told me there wouldn't be any charges against me, I tried to leave. He told me I should wait to talk to you but when he saw that I was going to leave anyway, he made me a deal."

Declan shuddered as he felt Ren's eyes shift to him again and hold his gaze as he spoke. "He offered me the use of a cabin he owned in the mountains and gave me some money. I told him the only way I would agree is if he promised he would stay away."

"You knew where he was?" Vin said angrily.

"Vinny," Ren said softly and Vin fell silent when his eyes returned to his brother. Ren's eyes drifted down to where his hand was idly rubbing against the tabletop. "But I didn't go straight to the cabin."

Ren was silent for so long that Dom finally asked, "Where'd you go, Ren?"

"I went to buy a gun."

～

*R*en heard Dom suck in his breath at his response. God, what he wouldn't give to be sitting between Declan and Jagger right now. To be able to draw from their strength. He forced his eyes up and looked at Dom and Vin. He could tell they had a million questions but they were doing their best to respect his request to not ask them.

"It took me 3 days to find someone who would sell me a gun. Once I had it, I went to the cabin. It was still light out when I got there but as it got darker I started hearing things. I thought...I thought they were coming to get me to take me back to my hole," he said softly as he dropped his eyes back to the table.

"Part of me was actually kind of glad because at least in my hole I knew what to expect. I had already accepted that I would die down there so it was okay. But another part of me had decided I wasn't going to go out in that shithole and that I would take as many of them out as I could…I just had to remember to save one bullet."

"Jesus," he heard someone mutter – one of his brothers presumably since he knew Jagger and Declan's voices by heart.

"I don't remember everything after the first shot," he admitted. "I guess some big asshole knocked the door down to save my ass and I took a shot at him," he said with a small smile and he glanced up in time to see Jagger smiling at him. He forced himself to turn his attention back to his brothers. "Declan and Jagger saved my life that night. And every night after that," he added.

Vin and Dom both cast glances at Declan and Jagger but quickly turned their focus back on him. "They knew it wasn't safe for me to be alone or around other people so they made a deal with me. They would keep me safe so I could focus on getting better. My condition was that they not tell you where I was."

He didn't miss the hurt in either of his brother's eyes but he pressed on. "I need you both to be okay with them lying to you so they could keep their promise to me. They knew I needed professional help but that I couldn't be forced into it so they gave me the time I needed to figure that out. You're Declan's family and I don't want him to lose that. And you guys gave Jagger a place he can finally call home. Please don't punish them for choosing to save me over their loyalty to you."

Dom shook his head. "We won't, Ren." He looked straight at Declan and Jagger. "We won't," he repeated.

"Ren," Vin said softly. "Is there more between the three of you than them just watching over you?"

Ren smiled slightly. "I found what you guys did," he said as he glanced at each of his brothers. "My soulmate." He looked over at Declan and Jagger and felt his heart swell. "Except it turns out I have two," he softly.

Ren got up and went to where Declan and Jagger sat. "I love you," he whispered to Declan before brushing a kiss over his lips.

He leaned across Declan and kissed Jagger before murmuring, "I love you" to him. Both men had said it back to him and looked at him expectantly. He drew up a chair and closed his hands over each of theirs. "I know now why you didn't tell me about Rafe. But it made me realize that I can't be an equal partner in this relationship if you have to keep things from me because I'm not strong enough to deal with them."

"Ren, it doesn't matter," Jagger started to say.

"It matters to me. I can get there if you give me time."

He could tell both men were disappointed but they nodded. He'd had no doubt that they would give him exactly what he needed – that was what they'd been doing from day one. They both got to their feet when he did and he went into their arms willingly. Jagger told him to stay safe while Declan told him to come home soon. As he forced himself to walk away, he cast one last look at them and saw they were hugging each other and in that moment he promised himself that he would become everything they needed him to be and more so that they'd never have to be apart again.

CHAPTER 13

"How's Connor doing?" Declan asked as he handed Jagger the coffee the cashier had placed on the counter.

"Good," Jagger said. "Says Sutter hasn't contacted him even once since he was released."

"Fucker got off easy with 30 days," Declan said.

They managed to find a seat outside at one of the small metal tables. The coffee shop had turned out to be an ideal meeting spot since it was within walking distance from the precinct and the building where Barretti Security Group was housed.

"You have to work late tonight?" Jagger asked.

"Nope. Told Captain Fuckwad I was taking the rest of the day off."

Jagger chuckled. "He figured out yet that Lieutenant Hale will be Captain Hale by this time next year?"

Declan smiled. "Yeah, he's scrambling. Rumor has it he's got an offer from some dive town in Texas."

"He does. It's in Greenley, Texas."

Declan shook his head. "Shit, Jagger...your mom?"

"She called me this morning to tell me. He's offered to get her set up in a house, give her a monthly allowance."

"Fuck. I'm sorry, Jagger. I didn't even think about that when I took the Lieutenant's exam. I'll talk to the Chief and tell him I've changed my mind-"

Jagger's lips cut him off. "God, I fucking love you," Jagger whispered before he drew back. "My mother told him to have a nice trip."

"What?" Declan asked in surprise.

Jagger smiled. "She told him she had a son to look after. She mentioned something about grandkids too but I chose to tune that part out."

"You think she'll give in?"

"I hope not. She says she hasn't seen him in almost a month and I believe her."

Declan closed his hand over Jagger's. As well as things had been going lately, they'd been struggling to get through each day without word from Ren. Neither of them had been expecting Ren to go to bat for them with his brothers but the move had worked. Dom and Vin had expressed their gratitude for their intervention and hadn't even balked at the idea of their baby brother in a relationship with the two of them. Although Ren hadn't contacted them directly, Dom had provided enough information that Ren was making good progress with his therapy. Declan had feared that something would happen to make Ren rethink their relationship but Jagger's faith was unwavering and Declan drew from that during his weak moments.

Jagger's phone beeped and he glanced at it. He stared at the screen for several long seconds. "It's from Vin. The meeting this afternoon with Fordam Industries has been canceled." He turned the screen so Declan could look at it. "Did I get it right?" Jagger asked.

Declan smiled and nodded. He couldn't help the surge of pride that went through him. Jagger had been nervous about trying to tackle his dyslexia after it had caused him so much pain growing up. But he'd found a good tutor who'd given him the tools he needed and his plan was to eventually get his GED. Not that it mattered to Declan and Declan knew Ren didn't care either, but it had been important to Jagger.

"So if your meeting got canceled and I'm off the rest of the day,"

Declan said suggestively. He laughed when Jagger grabbed his hand and began dragging him towards his office.

"My car's at the precinct."

"Mine's closer. We'll get yours later," Jagger muttered.

Declan heard a faint buzzing sound and yanked Jagger to a stop.

"What the fuck?" Jagger asked.

Declan searched his pockets desperately until he found his phone. His heart was in his throat as he turned it over.

"What is it?" he heard Jagger ask. "Everything okay?"

Everything was fucking perfect. He turned his phone so Jagger could see. "Someone just disabled the security system at the cabin."

$\sim$

*R*en smiled as he heard the sound of tires churning over gravel. Jagger definitely had to be the one driving since Declan wouldn't dare take the turn at the base of the roadway leading to the cabin so tight. He glanced at his watch and saw that his men had made record time and he had to wonder if Declan had used his police siren for part of the long journey to the mountains. He had his answer when he saw Jagger's car tearing up the road. So just crazy ass speeding.

He stood and began walking towards the car. It came to a screeching stop just inches from him and then Declan was out and pulling him into his arms. Ren wrapped his arms around Declan's shoulders and when he felt Jagger reach them, he lifted one arm and dragged Jagger down into their embrace. No one spoke as they clung to each other. It was Jagger who finally pulled back and put his hands on Ren's face as if to hold him still while he looked him up and down. And then Jagger's mouth was moving over his and tears flooded Ren's eyes at the familiarity.

"Love you," Jagger murmured against his mouth before Declan took his place. Declan's kiss wasn't as long, but he dragged Ren into another bone crushing hug and Ren could feel the dampness against his neck as Declan wept. He'd always guessed their separation would be just a little harder on Declan since he'd had so many people turn their backs on him and never return when he was a child. It had made his decision to walk away all the more difficult, but he'd realized that if he never found the strength to stand on his own two feet, he'd never be able to stand up for his men when they needed him. He knew that no amount of therapy would make him the Ren Barretti he'd once been, but he could be the Ren that Declan and Jagger needed him to be…the Ren they had sacrificed so much for.

"Are you back?" Declan asked.

"I'm back," Ren said. "I'm exactly where I'm supposed to be."

"Thank fuck," Declan murmured and then he gave Ren the kiss he'd been waiting for.

"Who's this?" he heard Jagger ask.

Declan released Ren so he could drop down and pet the dog sitting quietly at his feet. "My service dog," Ren said. "She alerts me to when I'm starting to get anxious and helps calm me down."

"She's beautiful," Declan said as he knelt down and began petting the Golden Retriever.

"What's her name?" Jagger asked. Ren couldn't stop the smile that spread across his lips.

"Mick."

"What?" Jagger said as Declan began howling with laughter.

"Her name is Mick."

"Are you fucking kidding me?" Jagger croaked. "Declan, shut the fuck up!"

"You named her Mick?" Declan said as he tried to stifle his laughter.

"She came with the name."

"So you're telling me that when you introduce us, it will be Mick, Jagger and Declan?" Declan said.

Ren started to laugh and looked up at Jagger apologetically. Jagger dragged him up and pulled him flush against his body but his eyes were on Declan when he said, "At least I'm next in line after the dog" just before he covered Ren's mouth with his own.

～

"*O*kay?" Jagger whispered against Ren's neck. He forced himself to keep still as Ren's body clutched him within his depths.

Ren nodded and turned his head for a kiss. Jagger put all of his emotions into that one kiss and he could tell Ren felt every one because Ren's eyes locked with his and gave him the tiniest of nods.

"Show us how much you missed us," Jagger said. He groaned as Ren slid his hips forward.

"Fuck, yes," Declan groaned as Ren's forward motion caused him to push into Declan to the hilt. A slide back had Ren's body sucking Jagger's cock into him as he nearly pulled free of Declan. Jagger didn't move as Ren continued to work himself back and forth between him and Declan but he couldn't stop his fingers from pressing into Ren's hips. Jagger let his eyes drift down so he could watch Ren's glistening cock slide smoothly in and out of Declan. It was a heady experience to watch Ren work them both in tandem. Ren was in complete control and he knew it and he was reveling in it because every move was orchestrated to bring all three of them maximum pleasure. Jagger watched Ren lift one arm and then he was leaning back against Jagger's chest and wrapping it around Jagger's neck.

Jagger let his teeth nip over the corded muscles of Ren's throat as he stroked his hands down Ren's sides. Ren's body had filled out perfectly and from the muscles that rippled beneath his palms, Jagger could tell that Ren had been hitting the gym. Jagger let his fingers trail down to where Declan's ass was pulled up against Ren's thighs and the backs of his legs were pressed against Ren's chest. The angle seemed to be working perfectly for Declan because he was moaning with every twist of Ren's hips and his fists were clenched in the bed sheets. Jagger skimmed his hand over Declan's ass as he writhed against Ren and then he dipped a finger into Declan on Ren's next surge forward. Declan let out a gasp at the added pressure and Ren's eyes glittered with lust as he watched his cock and Jagger's finger disappear together inside of Declan.

"Hold him tight," Jagger whispered as he added another finger. He used his free hand to grasp Ren's hip and began thrusting up into Ren which sent him deeper into Declan. Ren's arm disappeared from around his neck and wrapped around Declan's legs to hold him in place as Jagger hammered into them both. Ren's cock pulsed against his fingers while Declan's smooth walls gripped him.

"Oh God, harder," Declan said harshly.

Jagger increased his thrusts as he sought out Ren's lips. He let his tongue explore Ren's mouth slowly even as his hips moved faster and faster. He managed to glance down and saw that Declan was furiously stroking himself as Ren's body and Jagger's fingers breached him over and over.

"Watch how fucking beautiful he is when he comes," Jagger murmured to Ren.

"Jagger!" Declan screamed.

"Show him, baby. Show him how much you missed him," Jagger said.

"Love you Ren!" Declan cried out as he slammed his body down on both of them. Spurts of come hit his chest and abdomen as wave after wave of pleasure rolled through him. Ren let out a rough curse as his whole body seized and Jagger felt liquid fire drench his fingers as Ren continued to fuck in and out of Declan. Jagger gave up fighting his own release and bit down on Ren's shoulder as he came. The blissful agony seemed to go on forever but when all three of their bodies began to loosen as the aftermath overtook them, Ren released Declan's legs so Jagger could push him forward onto Declan's chest. He pulled his fingers free of Declan's body and put them up to Declan's mouth. Declan immediately sucked them in and licked them clean. When he released Jagger's fingers, Ren's tongue took their place and Jagger let them kiss for a while before he dragged Ren's mouth to his so he could get a taste too.

∾

"You understand why I had to stay away, right?" Declan heard Ren whisper against his chest. Jagger was at Declan's back but from his even breathing, Declan could tell he was asleep.

"I do," he said as he ran his fingers through Ren's now thick hair. He could still feel the scars along his scalp. "You had to fix the scars Jagger and I couldn't reach."

Ren lifted his face so their lips were just inches apart. "Do you still see any part of the Ren you first fell in love with?"

Declan smiled and nodded. "I didn't think it was possible but I love this Ren even more."

"You and Jagger saved me, Declan."

Declan trailed his fingers over Ren's cheek and whispered, "No, Ren, we saved each other."

EPILOGUE

*R*en couldn't get over the sheer volume of people seated around Vin's dining room table. With Jagger's mom, the number came out to an even 16. And he hadn't even counted Gabe and Riley's baby who was asleep in the crook of her father's arm at the moment. He wondered how the hell Vin was going to manage the seating once more and more babies started joining the growing group. As if on cue, Vin stood up and the whole table quieted.

"As everyone can see, our family dinners are starting to get a little bigger," he said as looked around the table. "And I for one could not be happier about that," he said softly.

"Hear, hear," several people said.

"Growing up, Dom, Ren, Rafe and I were taught that family were the people who shared your blood. But I think my brothers will agree with me when I say family is so much more than that. It's about the people who will be there when you come home. Or will look for you when you're lost. They'll bring light to your darkness" – Vin glanced down at Mia who was watching him with damp eyes – "and comfort you in your sorrow." He paused for a long moment before saying, "I look around this table and can't think of a better family for Mia and I to welcome our babies into in six months."

Everybody was quiet for a moment as Vin's words sank in and then there were shouts of joy as the whole table started talking at once.

"Oh, and you're all invited to the wedding," Vin added. "It's next weekend!" he said with a grin.

Ren smiled as everyone around him got up and began to make their way to the head of the table to give their congratulations to the soon to be parents. If it hadn't been for Declan and Jagger, he would have missed out on this. He would have missed out on a lot of things.

Being apart from Jagger and Declan had been one of the hardest things Ren had ever done, but he'd used the time to find out who he was outside of their relationship and beyond the shroud of PTSD. He'd spent time with each of his brothers and their loved ones and had realized that, like Declan and Jagger, they saw him as more than broken or damaged. They'd laughed over forgotten memories and shared new ones. There'd been no judgement about his involvement with two men instead of one and no discussion about his seemingly sudden change in sexuality. And when he'd finally been ready to open up about the details of the ambush and his imprisonment, every one of his brothers had cried with him for the brothers-in-arms he'd lost and they'd thanked him for staying strong long enough so that they could bring him home.

Each time he shared a memory with a family member or with his therapy group, he found the good parts and stored them away in his mind and accepted and forgave himself for the not so good parts. His biggest struggle continued to be in finding the forgiveness within himself for Brandon, but he knew in his heart he'd get there someday. It was what Brandon would have wanted for him.

A pair of hands came around his neck and slid down his chest as a kiss was brushed over his cheek.

"Damn, twins. Did you know?" Jagger asked.

"She told me yesterday," Ren admitted. Making amends to Mia had been difficult for him. Her fear-stricken voice had haunted him in the months after he'd attacked her and he hadn't expected or deserved her forgiveness. But she'd given it to him anyway and had welcomed him with open arms the second he'd stepped into Vin's home for the first time since that terrible night. And right after forgiving him, she'd invited him to stay with them for a while.

"So you're going to be an uncle," Declan said as he sat back down in his chair next to Ren and rested his hand on Ren's thigh.

"We're going to be uncles," Ren corrected as he laced his fingers with Declan's and lifted his head up for a quick kiss from Jagger. "And godfathers," he added.

"I don't think three is allowed," Jagger said.

"I think three is the perfect number," Ren responded cheekily and he got another kiss for his trouble.

"You nervous about tomorrow?" Declan asked.

Ren nodded. He was glad when Declan and Jagger had readily agreed to fly to Indiana with him to deliver Brandon's last words to his parents and fiancée. He wouldn't share the entire truth of what had happened to Brandon, but he would tell them how brave he'd been because that was one hundred percent true.

"You think they're watching over us, Declan?"

"Who?"

"Brandon and Sylvie."

"Yeah, baby, I do."

"Yeah," Ren said with a sigh as he tightened his hand around Declan's and closed his other hand over the forearm Jagger had draped across his chest. "Me too."

The End

ABOUT THE AUTHOR

Dear Reader,

As an independent author, I am always grateful for feedback so if you have the time and desire, please leave a review, good or bad, so I can continue to find out what my readers like and don't like. You can also send me feedback via email at sloane@sloanekennedy.com

Join my Facebook Fan Group: Sloane's Secret Sinners

Connect with me:
www.sloanekennedy.com
sloane@sloanekennedy.com

ALSO BY SLOANE KENNEDY

(Note: Not all titles will be available on all retail sites)

The Escort Series
Gabriel's Rule (M/F)
Shane's Fall (M/F)
Logan's Need (M/M)

Barretti Security Series
Loving Vin (M/F)
Redeeming Rafe (M/M)
Saving Ren (M/M/M)
Freeing Zane (M/M)

Finding Series
Finding Home (M/M/M)
Finding Trust (M/M)
Finding Peace (M/M)
Finding Forgiveness (M/M)
Finding Hope (M/M/M)

The Protectors
Absolution (M/M/M)
Salvation (M/M)
Retribution (M/M)
Forsaken (M/M)
Vengeance (M/M/M)

A Protectors Family Christmas

Atonement (M/M)

Revelation (M/M)

Redemption (M/M)

Non-Series

Letting Go (M/F)

Printed in Great Britain
by Amazon